Feel:DEAL:Heal

by
Jayne Collett

Feel Deal Heal
Copyright © 2024 Jayne Collett

First Edition

Paperback ISBN: 9780958072892
Hardback ISBN: 9781763540606
eBook ISBN: 9780958072885

Cover and interior design by Jayne Collett
Back cover photo by Lauren Saliu

Buy a paperback, hardback or eBook from Amazon

The moral right of the author has been asserted

Author's Note

There is a transgender character in this story. Please read the following for context.

This story is set in 2005. The LGBTQIA+ community went by only the first four letters. There were two classifications for people - male or female. Non-binary and gender-fluid didn't exist. The words to describe males who had female leanings were transgender, transsexual, transvestite, crossdresser. In 2005, men who wanted to become women more often than not dealt with it privately, rather than publicly. Gender and transgender weren't the controversial, contentious, or emotion-charged issues they are today. Please read the relevant parts through this filter and allow for character development. Thank you.

Social media was in its infancy. Facebook was one. X (formerly Twitter) was still a year away and Instagram was five years away. Touch screen phones for the mass market wouldn't be available until 2007. iPods were four. Angelina Jolie and Brad Pitt had only recently started their relationship.

I wrote this book in 2005, hence why it is set in that year. Because the themes are still as relevant today as they were then, I decided to leave it as is.

The counselling methods described in this book are based on Re-evaluation Counselling (RC) aka Co-counselling. The processes and theories were developed in the 1950s by Harvey Jackins. There is a lot of information available online.

I have used artistic license when naming or explaining some of the processes as this is a work of fiction and is not intended to be a full and complete representation of Re-evaluation Counselling.

For my sister Susan,
my number 1 fan!
who has read everything I've ever
written (at least she says she has lol)

Thank you for your support,
encouragement, wisdom, and
exceptional counselling skills.

Thank you for your belief in me
and your love.

Love you.

Monday 25th April, 2005
10.30 pm

His name is Di. He, sorry she, probably began life as an Adam or a David. He cried into his lace hanky.

"If only I had the courage to do this outside of this room. I wish I could live as a woman all the time."

You can. Become over-tired, under-appreciated and give up a third of your wage. It's not that hard. And what's with the skirts that show half your arse and the 38 double Ds? You're like some grotesque caricature. Look around you, Di. Except for you, there's not another single painted talon, stiletto or fishnet in this room. It's all tracky daks, jeans and uggies. Do a bit more homework.

I'm thinking Di is short for Diabolical.

Then Tina started. Ears, prepare to bleed.

Victim! That's what I wanted to yell at her. You're nothing but a victim with your boo hoo and poor me crap. If your husband's such a pig, divorce him. If you hate your job, quit. If you mother ignores you, don't visit her. If your brother comes freeloading, tell him you're not a bank. Get a backbone! And stop taking up all the space. You're not the only one who hurts. Your issues and dramas aren't worthy of more air time than anyone else's.

I understand why the Phoenix spontaneously combusts.

This is what Louise expects me to put up with twice a week for my growth and evolvement.

How did I get roped into this? How????

Tuesday 26th
2.24 am

Di. Tina. Tina. Di. I can't stop thinking about them!

If Louise hadn't suckered me into this Feel:Deal:Heal thing four weeks ago, I'd have a head devoid of thoughts and I'd be blissfully asleep.

She said, "I want you to do a healing course with me."

"Why? I don't want to be a healer."

She laughed. "No. It's a course that will heal us."

I was confused. "We're not sick."

"Not physically. Emotionally. Jodie, you're sad all the time. In the last two years, you've barely left the house. You sleep a lot. You do nothing for days on end. You spend too much time alone. Your life wants you back."

If we weren't housemates, I could have denied it and lied about my life. But she sees me every day. She knows how I live.

Even though I knew she was right, that little place inside me that always says, 'What's the point?' answered for me. "Nah, I'm not interested."

Lou is used to me saying no to most things so she ignored it. "I worry about you. It'll be good for you. And me."

I shrugged.

Then she brought out her sad, sweet smile. "Don't let the rest of your life be like this."

That hit a tender spot, and that other little place inside that whispers to me in the night, 'Jodie, you have got to get your shit together', managed to help me form the words, "Fine. I'll give it a try."

She looked excited, and relieved. "Excellent. I'll call Bernadette. She's the one who runs the course. Classes start next week, on the 4th. We go Mondays and Wednesdays, 7 – 10. There'll be us and ten other women." Then she handed me, you. "It's a journal."

Louise bought you for me because she knew I wouldn't make the effort to buy you for myself. She even personalised you. She covered you with a picture of a snowy wilderness and, using blue lettering, embossed the words, 'Healing Dialogue Journal, by Jodie Winters' on the front and down the spine. You look really good. Like a proper hardback novel.

On the back, she wrote … 'This journal documents the healing journey of Jodie during her 20 weeks at 'Feel:Deal:Heal'. In it, she shares her deepest thoughts and feelings so she can heal herself and start living again'.

It's not a great blurb but all is forgiven because Lou is a graphic designer, not a writer. When I read the blurb, I laughed. She was obviously confident I'd say yes! Or maybe, Journal, you were her bargaining chip if I flatly refused. She knows I wouldn't be able to resist a book with my name on it.

She even bought me the blue gel pen I'm writing with. I love this pen. It glides across the page and makes me want to write neatly. And in cursive.

Four weeks later and, in all that time, all I've done is stare at you. I've managed to quash every urge to pick you up and actually share any of the stuff the blurb promises. You looked so nice and pristine and I just couldn't bring myself to trash you with my mean thoughts and untidy chicken scrawl. No matter how hard I try to be neat, it always gets messy.

But last night nearly did me in. For the last three weeks, I have ever so politely endured Di and Tina. It's been easy because I've been like a ghostly presence at Feel:Deal:Heal and I've observed everything from afar, something like how I imagine an out-of-body experience would be.

Anyway, something happened. I don't know why, but I suddenly crash-landed back in my body and I felt irritated beyond measure.

Di's tears flowed and out came the familiar, impossibly white, lace hanky. Who uses hankies nowadays? And where on earth does she buy them? Church fetes?

As usual, Bernadette swooped in and did her Bernadette nurturing thing. I watched Bernadette hold and soothe Di and I suddenly felt something. At first I didn't recognise what it was but then I realised I felt jealous and resentful that Di was getting attention and that Bernadette was caring about her.

Di eventually settled down into minor eye dabbing and the occasional sniff. Then Tina started. Those two are like a tag team! My jaw clenched. I looked at Louise, rolled my eyes and tried to discreetly mime that my ears were bleeding. Lou looked confused. In the car on the way home she said it looked like I was grooming something bushy that was growing out the side of my head! This is why we don't play charades.

As Tina bawled, Bernadette cradled her in her arms. "Tell me all about it," she said. "Tell me all about it. I'm listening. I'm interested."

Bernadette looked at us. "Tina needed this kind of attention when she was a child."

Didn't we all. My jealousy and resentment were off the charts!

"The power of good attention should not be underestimated."

When Tina finally calmed down, Bernadette asked her to choose someone to snuggle close with.

She looked at me. Eyes glistening. Vulnerable.

I can't believe she picked me. Couldn't she feel my daggers? Any other night I would have happily put a stiff arm around her and pretended to care.

Mask time. I smiled warmly and fantasised about strangling her as I supported her grief.

As we were leaving, Bernadette gave me an extra long, extra warm hug and whispered, "Welcome to your feelings. I look forward to meeting them."

Is that right? Yeah, well. Good luck with that!

Ok. Now I've gotten all that off my chest, you and I, Journal, can go back to living separate lives. Nice to chat but sayonara, adios, catch ya on the flip.

2.19 pm

Yes, I know what I said about separate lives but Louise left her notes explaining the fundamentals of Feel:Deal:Heal by the kettle this morning. She must have been reading them when she was making her breakfast.

Bernadette handed them out during our very first class and told us to read them every day to remind ourselves of why we were there. Without even bothering to read mine at all, I ditched them in the recycling the moment we got home. I should have known Lou would keep hers, and that she'd do the 'right' thing and read them regularly.

When Bernadette went through the notes in class, I didn't hear a word because my brain and I were busy having a private chat about Di. We were wondering why she would wear high-heels and tight clothing to an informal gathering. We concluded that maybe the clothes are actually a fetish? Like those men who wear nappies and pretend they're babies. Or people who have a weird thing for feet.

As I was ruminating about Di, she was staring at Bernadette, concentrating intensely on every word she uttered. Her painted face not moving. Her long-lashed eyes barely blinking. I was mesmerised by her flawlessness and how focused she was. Maybe she wasn't listening either and was having her own internal conversation wondering why we were all dressed so casually and so … comfortably.

As the weeks have gone on, Di no longer bothers with the false lashes. They proved to be an inconvenience when mopping up floods of tears.

Anyway, the notes … I read them and to practise my cursive with this lovely pen, I thought I'd jot them down. (Ok, I confess. I'm bored and feeling a tad guilty. By filling you with notes it looks like I'm a good friend who appreciates Lou's gift. Let's see how long it takes before my nicely formed letters become illegible blobs of blue ink.)

"FDH is a form of counselling that's designed around the theory that we are all born happy, intelligent, creative and co-operative and all the behaviours we exhibit contrary to those are just the result of being hurt. From experiencing shock or grief or trauma. From feeling unloved, or being rejected, ignored, bullied, intimidated, ostracised, abused, blamed, unsupported. The list is endless.

"It's not so much the hurts that are at fault, it's the fact we're stopped from expressing any of them. The feelings erupt forth for a reason yet we're denied the right to flow with them. As children, we're told not to cry or have a tantrum. We're shushed quickly and distracted from expressing. If we persist, we're called sissies and sooks, hard to handle, unreasonable and difficult. We're shamed into stuffing down our feelings. And we're never asked why we feel how we feel. We're just told not to feel.

"It's the worst thing that can happen because the feelings don't get processed properly and they're misfiled in our brain where, for the rest of our lives, they take every chance they can get to be properly expressed. Which, of course, we refuse to allow because of our conditioning.

"Over the years, we add layer upon layer until eventually we only ever act from a place of unexpressed feelings. We're irrational, fearful, angry, depressed, needy. We can't cope. We indulge in addictions and destructive behaviours. We pop pills. We lose our ability to live a full life.

"If we were allowed to express our feelings in the moment we had them, we'd be free of them instantly. We'd think clearly, rationally and intelligently all the time and we'd be joyful and in the moment. Things like depression, anger, anxiety, and addiction wouldn't exist."

As Bernadette handed us our take-home copy, the movement snapped me out of my zoned-out reverie so I did hear her say, "There's more to it than that, which you'll discover as we go, but the basic premise is that human beings need to be able to express their feelings and be given encouragement and good attention while they do it. And all the methods and techniques you'll be learning and practising are designed to encourage you to express the unexpressed and return you to a state of balance and function and empowerment."

I want to be cynical and say what a crock but Bernadette is hard to resist. She's 65 and wrinkly, and hers is the softest skin I have ever felt. When she presses her crinkled, silken cheek against mine, for that brief moment I feel like a safe, loved child. I imagine her baking me biscuits and tucking me into bed. I imagine her being proud of me.

I reckon Tina and Di cry so much just for the hugs. They probably feel that way too.

(Side note: Seven minutes until the cursive became a sad mix of print, scribble and blob. But I do like my doodles of pointy shoes and pointy cats. Just like Dad's. We used to tease him about his pointy drawings but I've since learned his 'art' style is called whimsical! Who knew?)

Wednesday 27th
11.15 pm

Yes, it's me again! I know what you're thinking, Journal. 'Look who's back! Look who suddenly needs me after ignoring me for weeks'.

I can't sleep. And I had a weird experience in class.

Louise and I arrived first tonight. That's never happened before. We sank into the burnt-orange two-seater and waited for the others. With the counselling room devoid of crying women, I had a good chance to really take it in. Bernadette told us it was added to the house 10 years ago when she renovated. It's so beautiful, it's impossible not to love it. The colours are warm, like those of a sunset at the end of a perfect summer's day. The sofas and chairs are plush and inviting, perfectly shaped for weary bodies to sink down deep into their cocooning, nurturing softness. Big, brightly-coloured cushions in soothing velvet and satin fabrics are strewn around the floor, ready to offer comfort and support if you feel like lying down.

Magical, ethereal images of the Moon and Nature and the Elements – Fire, Earth, Air, Water – adorn the walls. Most of them a celebration of the feminine. And it always smells so wonderful – sandalwood, lavender, orange, patchouli, rose. Each time we go, we're met by a new fragrance.

The whole room has the peaceful feel of a temple and tonight it lulled me into a false sense of security, as if I was there for meditation and not to rage out unexpressed hurts. But one by one the women arrived and reality bit. By seven, everyone was there.

We started with our usual opening round of 'something good', where we each have to share a piece of positive news. I said, "I bought myself an iPod and I was trying to set up my library and download some songs but I couldn't figure it out because I'm not techno savvy and my other housemate, Dan, came along and did it for me." I should have left it there, but then I added, "I didn't even ask him. He noticed I was having trouble and he just took charge and got it sorted. So that was nice." I realise now, I should have kept my mouth shut. We're always wiser after the event!

Anyway, round over, Bernadette launched into Feel:Deal:Heal theory about the difficulty so many of us face when it comes to admitting we have feelings and then, if we allow ourselves to admit them, the mammoth challenge of expressing them.

She said, "We don't say, 'I think depressed. I think sad. I think hurt. We say, 'I feel depressed. I feel sad. I feel hurt'. Yet people will talk endlessly about their problems, going through them logically and coldly, without ever once collapsing into the emotion. By all means, use words to get you started but understand that they'll only get you so far because feelings can't be expressed in words. Only thoughts can. Feelings are expressed via laughter, tears, sweat, nausea, shaking. We allow ourselves laughter and controlled, restrained crying, but that's about it. We've become too shy and self-conscious to allow anything else. But we can return to that state where feelings feel natural and normal."

She stood up and moved to the centre of the room. "Jodie, can you come and stand with me."

Shit. Why me? I dragged myself from the hug of the sofa and stood facing her. She took my hands.

"I want you to say, 'I need your help. Please notice that I need your help'."

What? I can't say that. It's ridiculous.

Bernadette moved in closer. She is so non-threatening yet I felt like a cornered animal. And I didn't like everyone looking at me. It was uncomfortable. The words were stuck in my throat. Just say it so you can sit down, my head begged. I took a deep breath and repeated the words.

"Jodie," Bernadette cooed softly, "can you say it again. This time, with feeling."

I thought I had done it with feeling. An impatient sigh followed by a slit-eyed stare. That's feelings, Mum style.

Hello, my mother's popped in!

Bernie worked her doe eyes and loving look overtime but no amount of encouragement could get me to say it again. I would not budge. I could not budge. If only I could resist chocolate that well.

Bernadette addressed the group. "When someone has difficulty expressing themselves, it sometimes helps if you express for them."

Then she started yelling.

"I need your help. How the hell can't you see that? I'll tell you how, because everything is always about you, you disapproving, self-centred, self-interested, sanctimonious cow. You're the one who should be taking responsibility, not me. You're the one who should be supporting me. You're the one who should be strong. I'm the child, remember. You're the parent. Fucking act like it."

The words spun around my brain and I felt a bit confused. I didn't know whether I wanted to laugh or cry so I did neither. Just stood there like a statue.

Bernie kept it up until I suddenly laughed. There. I'd expressed a feeling. Even if it was only embarrassment. When she let go of my hands, I noticed one of us had excessively sweaty palms. I think it was me because my pits were flowing faster than Niagara. Interesting.

I self-consciously moved back to my seat. Louise nodded encouragingly and smiled in that half happy, half sad way that only a good actor can pull off.

She will pay. Dearly.

"Inside our bodies are years of hurt, and unexpressed feelings," Bernadette said. "They can't be dealt with chronologically. Whatever needs your attention first will make itself known. Pay attention to your thoughts and words. They'll lead you to the feelings – and the reasons for them."

Thursday 28th
11.06 am

I didn't sleep well and for some reason I woke up thinking about how orangutans are having their habitats destroyed so stupid, greedy people can plant palm oil trees. What the fuck for? Oh, that's right. There's only a thousand cooking oils in the world and we need a thousand and one!

And when the displaced, distressed orangutans try to go home, even though they have no home left, they're often killed for their trouble. Why? Why? It doesn't make sense. And how is shit like this allowed to happen in the first place? Why doesn't someone in power say, 'Fuck off and leave them alone', and make it illegal to cut even so much as a blade of grass?

Because people suck, that's why. We're cruel, hateful bullies and we've completely fucked up the planet. We take, take, take. We leave a trail of death and destruction in our wake and when a swarm of locusts eat our crops we get up in arms and all affronted, as much as to say, 'How dare they. How dare they leave us with nothing to eat'. HELLO. What do we do every day. EVERY DAY!!!! How many food sources have we destroyed? How many homes have we decimated? How many habitats have we destroyed? How much water and earth have we poisoned? And then a tsunami wreaks havoc and people are on about how cruel nature can be. Really!!! Stop. Think. Open your eyes. Take a bloody good look around. A wave or an earthquake or a shark attack is nothing, NOTHING, compared to the hellish things we do every second of every day. We cut things down; smother the earth with cement and bitumen; crowd-out and over-populate every piece of land we can. We kill and maim and torture all the beautiful creatures. We take advantage of their gentle, trusting natures. We swat and shoot and spray and starve and poison. We haven't got a clue. Not a fucking clue. Nature was doing just fine before we came along and stuffed everything up. Nature used to work in perfect harmony; able to balance itself; regenerate itself. Not anymore though. Oh no. We don't deserve the patience that nature shows us. We don't deserve this beautiful home. We don't deserve to live.

Friday 29th
9.53 pm

I talked to Lou earlier and told her I can't do this feelings stuff. "I started off ok but as the weeks have gone on, I'm finding it harder to stay detached. I like detached. It's easy. Now I feel stirred up all the time. It's confusing. My emotions clearly don't want to be disturbed. They were overworked when I was younger so they took an early retirement. Who am I to tell them they need to get back to work?"

Lou smiled. "I know. It's tough at first but it's worth it in the end. Detached is easy but it's no way to live because you miss out on happiness and joy as well. You just exist on a flat line. It's not how we're supposed to live. Life should be more … intense than that. Life should feel rich and full."

"Is there value in recalling those things that have caused pain? How can dredging up memories change me for the better?"

"Remember what Bernadette said, 'It's not recalling the memories that changes you. It's the new way in which you deal with them that changes you'."

"Well, I'm screwed because I don't know how to deal with them."

"You're dealing with them now."

"How?"

"Well, you haven't locked yourself in your room and pretended nothing's wrong. You've admitted you feel agitated and now you're talking to me about it. So what's going on in your head?"

"I'm worried about the orangutans. I'm worried that no one's protecting them."

"Anything else?"

"I keep thinking about those poor bears who spend their whole lives chained up and trapped in tiny cages, being tortured for their bile, and the gorillas who have their hands hacked off so people can make souvenir ashtrays out of them and the elephants who are still being slaughtered for their ivory and the sharks who, after having their fins butchered off, are tossed back into the ocean to drown and … it's too much."

I could feel the anguish on my face and my jaw hurt but I held myself together. So stubborn. So determined not to let the feelings flow.

Then Louise hugged me. "I'm sorry you're hurting for all the animals. Just knowing that you care about them would mean so much to them."

And then I burst into tears. "So much beauty, carelessly destroyed. I just wish people were kinder."

"I know you do. Me too."

She held me until I stopped sobbing then she sat me down, opened a bottle of white, and whipped us up a creamy chicken and mushroom pasta thing for dinner. As she cooked, she told me about a new guy at work who she fancies. His name's Liam, he's a printer, and he's been there for a month. She's been flirting with him like mad for the last week and he's been all charming and funny. She really wants him to ask her out. She won't ask him because she hasn't got the courage and she couldn't bear it if he said no. Fair enough. Rejection's tough.

Then I reminded her that life is supposed to be intense and rich and full.

Then she threw a sprig of parsley at me!

Saturday 30th
3.07 pm

I slept a lot better and I feel ok today. Less anxious.

I'm so lucky Louise was there for me. We're both 40 but sometimes it feels as if she's older than me – and wiser. She's always looked out for me and sometimes I think she makes a lot more effort for me, than I make for her.

Louise is good with people though. She's got a lot of friends and she likes to spend time with them. She's social and she enjoys company. By comparison, I'm a loner. I struggle to connect.

This is why sharing a room with ten strangers is no big deal for her. Having said that though, I do notice that Lou can be quite guarded. She gives the impression of being relaxed and fully participating in the process but she only shares to a point. She's there, but she's not.

She carefully chooses what she talks about and keeps things fairly superficial. She won't admit to anything too deep or too distressing. She did a whole healing thing after her divorce, yet her divorce is often her go-to 'hurt'. That ship sailed years ago! I know of worse distresses she could be mentioning. It's as if she's keeping herself safe. It will be interesting to see what Bernadette drags out of her as the weeks go on.

Sunday 1st May
12.54 pm

I got up 'early' today - 11.30 - and wandered into the kitchen for my start-me-up cuppa and, lo and behold, Louise had left her 'Healing Dialogue' journal on the kitchen table. She's covered hers with an amazing picture of an old growth forest and used green for the lettering. Her pen is green, too. She didn't bother with a blurb.

Green cover. Green embossing. Green pen. Lou is drawn to green. I think it's because of her eyes. They're a deep green, like that of the dark, glossy leaves you find in a rainforest. And they shine with health and life. I envy them because mine are boring blue, and dull.

I did the right thing and walked away from it, but then I couldn't help myself. I took a sneaky peek.

'Di wore a gorgeous scarf on Monday. Silk, I think.

Heidi had a hole in her t-shirt.

Arrabella did a really nice thing with her hair.

Finn's eyebrows are definitely tattooed on'.

I quickly scanned all the entries and yep, there's three weeks of the same.

Unbelievable! She's the one who pitched the journal idea to Bernadette and the others in the first place. She'd kept a journal as part of the post-divorce healing course and couldn't gush about it enough. I vaguely remember the half hour spiel.

"…healing journey … get in touch with your soul … inner world … deepest feelings … learn so much … capture memories … express without censorship … blah, blah, blah."

Maybe this is Louise's attempt at healing all those fatal fashion errors she made during the '80s? All those pointy shoes!!

I knew from week one about Finn's eyebrows. Wonder how long it'll be before Louise twigs to the collagen lips?

Monday 2nd
10.50 pm

Di shouldn't have worn orange.

Meredith had new slippers. Must be pension week.

Bernadette had a beetroot stain on her cuff.

Cathartic? Well, pumpkin coloured clothing, velour footwear, and soiled fabric does evoke a mild concern within me, so I guess it is.

I love that Meredith rocks up to someone's home in her slippers. Shows she's pretty relaxed, considering.

People do get comfortable with each other quite quickly, really. Even when thrown together for our own personal reasons, we form bonds.

I was looking around the room tonight and found myself wondering how an odd assortment of women from varying backgrounds came to be together in the same place, at the same time, for the same reason. Fate? Random chance?

Our ages range from 67, being Meredith, down to Arrabella and Finn at 23. Yet, to see them chatting and sharing their memories, you wouldn't know there was such an age gap. Well, Meredith and Finn chatter away.

Arrabella hardly says a word.

Eva and Nicole are chalk and cheese. Eva, 36, is abrasive and Nicole, 38, is apologetic. Marion, 48, is funny and Tina, 35, is worried. Di, 32, is glamorous and Gretel, 54, is frumpy. And Heidi, 24, is off with the fairies. There's barely anything in common amongst us. Only our feelings. Feelings that Feel:Deal:Heal purposely sets out to trigger.

Each class, Bernadette first gives us counselling theory then throws up questions. We have to see where our memories take us. And it's so interesting how there is never one specific event that always comes up. Each question triggers a different memory. The question she likes to ask a lot is about early memories – 'What's your earliest memory around …', and we each talk about whatever pops in - 'I remember when I was five …' 'I remember when I was 24 …' 'I remember when I was at this wedding …' 'I remember hearing my father sing …' 'Once, when I was at school …' and if someone is particularly emotional about what's come up, Bernadette gives them a chance to look at it in depth and go through all the feelings; to deal with what was never dealt with.

Writing about it makes it seem like a bizarre process. Self-indulgent, even. But there's no harm in trying to make sense of things. There comes a day when we have to start doing things differently, otherwise nothing changes. And we're all there because we're desperate for change.

Lou asked everyone to bring their journals on Wednesday just to see how we're all going with them. She was in a brilliant mood tonight because Liam asked her out. Yay!

They're going to dinner tomorrow. Boo, that means beans on toast for me.

Tuesday 3rd
11.36 pm

I'm snuggled up in my bed. I love my bed. It's soft and cosy and it doesn't expect me to express my feelings. Cool's fast asleep against my legs. Every now and then she twitches and makes weird leg and face movements and strange whimpers. It makes me think she's having a dream about chasing mice. I wonder if cats do dream?

Louise got home about 20 minutes ago. She saw my light on and came in for a chat. She was beaming. The date went brilliantly and Liam is funny and polite and gentlemanly and sweet and hot and… etc. I hope he was as happy about Lou!

She had a night of bests. Best seafood ever. Best steak ever. Best crème brulee ever. Best coffee ever. Best kiss ever.

Not to be outdone, I got my own in. "I had the best risotto ever."

"Risotto? I thought you were having beans."

"Dan took pity and saved me from the beans. He cooked."

"At least we won't have a struggle to think of our 'something good' tomorrow night," she said.

"That we won't," I said. That we won't.

Wednesday 4th
10.55 pm

Louise was still on a date high at Feel:Deal:Heal so she was a touch hyper, a touch obnoxious, and a touch holier-than-thou. She gets like that when her endorphins are over-producing.

Bernadette sat back and let Lou take the floor for the first half hour of the class. She was a bit (a lot!) put out by our obvious lack of interest in the journals because five of us hadn't written a single word, two of us had only started them yesterday, "This is week four, people," one of us had 'misplaced' hers (Heidi), and the rest of us weren't writing enough. I swear I remember her using the word voluntary? Louise felt we should have filled at least twenty pages by now. Yeah, just like you Louise!

"Maybe if you personalise them, you might use them. Show them yours, Jodie."

I dutifully held you up, Journal, and there were oohs and aahs. The ladies thought you were very attractive. Di said she might cover hers with a picture of a leopard or a wolf. Nice.

Before the others had a chance to say what image they'd choose, Lou pushed on. "Do I need to remind anybody about why I suggested journals; why I consider them to be so very important?"

No need to remind us, thanks all the same.

"These journals allow us to say, 'This is what I think, and I approve'."

Then, "Shouldn't we be writing about our feelings, not our thoughts?"

The collective intake of breath was audible. Had Eva just challenged Louise? Everybody hoped so. There's nothing quite like vicarious confrontation. Noticed Nicole's eyes were especially shiny.

Louise took a deep Zen breath and probably thought about butterfly wings and one hand clapping.

"Eva, you can write about anything you want. Thoughts, feelings, hopes, dreams …"

"Fashion," I piped in.

"I could write about fashion," Di baritoned.

Suuure.

"The point is," Louise continued, "so many of us have been shut-down; silenced; ignored. This is your chance to start getting comfortable with expressing yourself so hopefully you'll get confident enough to express yourself out loud."

I can just hear Louise now, "Eva, you're defensive but your earrings are lovely."

"Now, is there anybody here who would like to 'make their voice heard'? Obviously not you Heidi."

A black hole of silence threatened to consume us.

Then we were saved. Marion volunteered. She opened her journal to the one and only line of writing.

"If he tries to fuck me up the arse one more time, I'm gonna take a knife to his ball bag."

Bernadette clapped.

Thursday 5th
10.09 pm

I met Mick and Donna at the pub for our annual. Cheers, Dad.

It's been 28 years since he died and we still miss him. Some things just leave a crater in your soul.

I love that we started this ritual 16 years ago. It was Mick's idea. Actually it was his girlfriend's idea. She was big on celebrating important days like birthdays and anniversaries. She said such things honoured life. How I wish Mick had married her instead of Liz.

It's so rare that only the three of us get together. I love seeing the two of them by themselves, without Liz and Craig. They're more relaxed and more open. We always have a laugh and we 'get' each other because we share a history, and DNA. When you're raised in the same household, you know each other's stories. No one else will ever know you on that level. If the world was fair, family would be your safety net; ready to catch you when the rest of the world pushes you.

Without fail, year after year, when we say goodnight, I always find myself wishing they were going home to better people. People who appreciated them more. People who supported their strengths instead of exploiting their weaknesses. People who saw only the best of who they are.

I look at them and see how the things they went through growing up created the people they are today. It's becoming clear to me that we are the sum of our history. It goes where we go. We carry the past with us every day. It can't help but become the present.

Friday 6th
1.45 pm

I feel flat today. I've been thinking about people. Considering we're at the top of the food chain, we're not that strong. We're really quite fragile and easily broken. Certain events and certain moments can damage us so badly, we're never the same again.

And it's always other people causing the damage to begin with. I sit in a room with 11 other women who talk about the pain someone else has caused them and how that pain then shaped their lives; how they became afraid and unhappy and angry and how they then compromised themselves and their own lives and never reached their full potential because of it. If the microcosm is the macrocosm, there's a lot of unhappy, dysfunctional people out there.

I wonder how many people I've put into therapy?

Why aren't we stronger? Why do the things people say or do affect us so deeply? Why can't everything we experience be just that, an experience, where it leaves no marks or scars? Why do we take everything to heart?

Human beings are the walking wounded and thinking about the enormous scale of the problem makes me feel exhausted. How can everything that's wrong in the world be fixed? How can we stop hurting each other and everything around us? How can we embrace this thing we call life, instead of thinking it's a waste of time and an experience not worth having?

Sigh. Maybe we just over-think everything which then over-complicates everything? Probably. But how do we stop thinking?

Saturday 7th
4.20pm

Dragged myself out of bed at 12 today and I had such a lead head. I've got to try and sleep less. 10 hours is too much. Actually, it was more like 11. I'll try from Monday to get up earlier.

I think my head weighed a ton because Lou tried to get me up at around nine. I wasn't tired and I could have easily gotten up but I was toasty and it was cold outside so I refused to move. I lay there for awhile feeling a bit guilty that I didn't go for a walk with her but the guilt soon gave way to sleep. It was that extra, unneeded, sleep that made me feel like crap.

When I finally emerged, Lou was in the kitchen working her culinary magic. She was cooking some exotic lamb thing and three vegetable dishes for the dinner party tonight. It's our turn to host so I tidied up and set the table.

The delicious aromas brought Dan floating into the kitchen. I was surprised to see him home. He's usually out all weekend. He mooched around the pots and looked in the oven. Louise scooped a spoonful of vegetable something from one of the pots and offered it to him to taste. His face looked enraptured.

"That's amazing. Can I put some of that on a sandwich?" he asked.

"Course you can."

He made his sandwich and as he ate it, we caught up on the news of the week.

Lou told him about Liam. I told him I put a few more songs on my iPod (yep, a busy, exciting week for me!) and he told us he was a single man again. Seems Psycho Chick could no longer put up with him using shampoo bought from a supermarket, or his insistence on wearing t-shirts he'd bought at concerts, which were clearly meant to mock her. Even Dan didn't know what she meant by that one. Maybe she's tone-deaf or something? I'll miss her - so disturbing, yet so entertaining.

The shampoo comment, although bizarre, was obviously reasonable in her mind because she's a hairdresser who firmly believes salon shampoo is made from pixie dust, and other such magical things, by fairy hair experts somewhere in a fantastical land of unicorns and sleeping princesses.

Loopy as she is, she's a brilliant hairdresser if Dan's hair is anything to go by. She fixed his mop to suit his face and hair type. His hair reminds me of Matt Dillon's in the movie 'The Outsiders', but a bit longer. It's the same colour, too. Gorgeous.

Lou served Dan a spoonful of each of the other veg dishes. "If you've got nothing on, come to the dinner party."

"Cool. Thanks. Do we get to meet Liam tonight?"

Lou shook her head. "His parents are celebrating their 50th Wedding Anniversary so there's a big party. And it's Mother's Day tomorrow so he's gonna hang at their place for the weekend. I probably would have gone if we didn't have the dinner. But I'm kinda glad it's worked out this way. Meeting the entire family in one go like that is too scary."

It's a pity Liam won't be coming. I was looking forward to meeting him.

Sunday 8th
Mother's Day
2.15 am

The dinner party's over and I'm sitting here in bed wondering if expressing my feelings the moment I have them is actually a good thing. Bernadette would say yes, but I think my expression of said feelings needs work. Allow me to elaborate, dear Journal.

With the occasional variation in numbers and participants, and the odd cancellation here and there, every month, for the last eight years, ten people have sat around a table, all talking over the top of each other trying to get in a month's worth of news whilst shovelling food down their throats and guzzling booze by the gallon. Ten different personalities trying to find common ground so the night is a success and we all look forward to doing it again in four weeks. Old friends who take a few hours out of their busy lives to keep in contact because there just doesn't seem to be any other time to do it.

It's nice, if you don't count Lennie.

Lennie's what I like to call a 'copybiter'. He latches onto lines and ideas from movies and TV shows and rips them off the celluloid into real life, where they really don't belong. On-screen, things work within context of the story being told to reveal character or plot. Off-screen, they're just out of place and have no bearing on reality. He gets these lines and ideas between his teeth and does not let them go. And we have to endure them long, long, long after their use-by date. Seriously, GET SOME NEW MATERIAL LENNIE.

The subject got around to sex. As it always does. Lennie can't help himself. He thinks talking about sex makes him cool and hip and appear as if he's getting plenty. All it really does is make him look creepy and inappropriate.

As usual, Lennie loudly informed everyone that Katrina hasn't gone down on him in years. Guffaw. Guffaw.

We know Lennie. We've heard this a thousand times before, ever since you stole it from a movie way back in 1999, in fact.

Normally he just pauses a moment before delivering the punch-line but my, now, ever-present emotions had an urge to speak. So I let them.

"Why is that, Lennie?"

"She kisses my kids with that mouth."

So I said, "Are you saying then, Lennie, that your penis is filthy?"

In half a heartbeat it went quieter than a Nun's bedroom.

Lennie stared very hard at me. He seemed confused. I took this as an indication he hadn't quite understood the question. So I rephrased.

"Are you saying there is something quite foul about it? Is it toxic in some way that would be detrimental to your children? Should we be concerned?"

Louise was cringing so much, she looked like a detoxing contortionist. Dan looked amused.

Lennie was stunned. Never before has anyone ever bothered to comment. It gets let go with half-hearted laughs and eye rolling. He really didn't know what to do. There were no lines from any movies that he could use to save himself.

With nothing else for it, he fake guffawed and said, "Jodes, ya dag. You know it's just a joke."

No Lennie, this is a joke: A grasshopper walks into a bar and orders a beer. The bartender says, "Hey, we've got a cocktail named after you." And the grasshopper says, "What? Marvin!"

I tried to look innocent. "A joke? Oh, I'm sorry. My mistake."

I popped some veggies into my gob and threw out the question, "Did anyone see that bit on the news about the dog that saved that baby?"

There was a chorus of "Oh yeah," and conversation resumed as if nothing had happened.

I think everyone was secretly glad I had a dig at Lennie. Even Katrina. He was pretty quiet after that and I don't reckon he'll ever say those fateful words again. Yay! One issue down. A thousand to go!

On reflection, maybe expressing in the moment does have merit.

Ok, better get some sleep. I need to be well-rested to face the Mother's Day lunch.

11.15 am

Because Nan isn't going to be at lunch, I did my duty and visited her this morning. First words out of her mouth, "Don't get old, Jodie. It's not worth it. No one cares about you and you're nothing but a burden."

Thanks Nan, I'll try to remember that.

I tried to be all Bernadette-like and pay her good attention while she launched into her usual whinge about the home, the staff, the bad food, the other residents who, according to her, are just too old. (Well, it is an old folks' home! Stands to reason. And you're no spring chicken at 92.) There's the lousy view from her window, the lack of anything good on TV, the lumpy chair in her room which isn't even hers and which she doesn't even want but no one will take it away. Too hot. Too cold. Too dull. Too bright. Too everything! The woman is completely draining. I reckon I managed a solid five minutes of attention. Well done me. That's a record.

I usually stay for an obligatory half hour, which goes excruciatingly slow because I can never think of anything to talk about and neither can Nan. Neither of us ever go anywhere, so we've never got any news. It's a struggle.

What makes it even harder for me is the smell. The whole place stinks like diarrhoea that's had disinfectant poured on it. The stench gets in my mouth and I can taste it for hours after.

For all her complaints, Nan's got cause to whinge about the staff though. They are a condescending, patronizing lot. Quite a few of them are bullies too. They're engaged in some kind of power play – with old people! Who does that?

That place depresses me. It's just wall-to-wall mothers and fathers. Lonely. Isolated. Ignored.

Maybe they were bad parents?

The old lady who reaches out a feeble hand to a stranger may have used that hand to strike her children, or push them away.

The old man who can't walk may have chased his son, belt in hand, and then beaten him.

The old lady who can't talk may have abused and criticised.

The old man who can't hear may have never wanted to listen.

We can't know. But I'm willing to bet we do, in fact, reap what we sow.

Please don't let me end up like Nan. Miserable. Friendless. Abandoned. Full of fluid.

5.30 pm

Just got back from Donna's. She was good enough to do lunch this year. I could not get away fast enough. I can see how a person can become a recluse. Dealing with people is hard. All the feelings they stir up. It's challenging.

I found myself staring at these people who are my family and instead of feeling uplifted and delighted, I felt sad and angry and hopeless.

Mick. My wonderful brother. My shoulder whenever I've needed one. My friendly rival who taught me to be a gracious loser because he beat me at everything. Two years younger than me, but so much older and wiser. And such a good guy. Easy-going. Funny. Kind. Great dad.

And on the flip-side – over-responsible, over-protective, over-burdened, subservient, running around after Emily and Sarah 'cause Liz, 'he's lucky to have me', "isn't taking responsibility for them today."

So what else is new?

"He wanted them. He can look after them. It's Mother's Day. My day off." You're a mother alright. And you take every day off, Liz. If you hadn't had to turn up for the births, you wouldn't have. Have another Prozac. What the hell. Take them all.

God she makes me feel so hostile. Bernadette says people like that are gifts because they show us the areas we need to work on. Say, 'thank you, Liz'.

Say, 'divorce her Mick'.

Donna. My baby sister by nearly four years. My go-to person when I need to remind myself that there is good in the world. Beautiful and sensitive. Clever. Creative. Intuitive.

Qualities that are all too often over-shadowed by her neediness and insecurity. 'Tell me what to think Craig because I don't know'. 'Don't I always Don? Have I let you down yet?' 'No Craig. You're wonderful. Isn't he wonderful, everybody?'

Would it kill you to laugh or smile once in awhile Craig? Would it kill you to join in? Would it kill you not to be such a smarmy prick?

He doesn't make me feel as murderous as Liz, but there've been times when he's come close.

Mum. At 66 she's a year older than Bernadette, but she's got barely a line on her face. She's stunning. Always has been. Intelligent. Adventurous. Disciplined. The story goes – Nan wanted to name her Beatrice but Grandad hated it and for the only time in his life, he put his foot down. He named her Laura, after his favourite Aunt.

To me, she always 'feels' lonely. It's just something she exudes. She puts on appearances and to the untrained observer she'd appear fine. But I know her better than that. I also know she's cold, controlled, and neurotic. But these traits are rarely observed by others. She's artful, and I think she mostly saves them for me anyway.

Yet she'll happily show the world her obedience. The Fuhrer says 'Jump', she says, 'How high?' 'Beg, sit, catch, fetch'. 'Yes dear, right away'. She thinks it says, 'I am a dutiful, respectful wife'. Doesn't she know it really says, 'My husband is an abusive arsehole'.

The Fuhrer. Face like a police identikit photo. Bully. Martyr. 'Laura, remind them again why I'm doing you all a favour by taking on a widow with three young children'.

Feel free to fuck the hell off, Rob. Exits are located here, here and here. But wait. Where would you go? No one else would put up with you. You'd never even had a girlfriend until Mum tripped over your wallet. Let me remind you, Rob, we've got nothing to be grateful for. You're the lucky one.

Him, I could happily throw into a wood chipper, while he's alive and fully conscious. It's best I stay away from him. He's bad for my ability to stay above the law.

Monday 9th
3.19 am

I can't sleep. I'm still thinking about lunch.

It's so hard to know if Mum cares about anything. Her expression never changes. Maybe she thinks she's Cher? We all pitched in and bought her a pile of Jurlique stuff. She opened the box, nodded, then resumed her drink and conversation with the Fuhrer.

It made me remember when I was six and I wrote her that story about Roger the hamster. I drew pictures and put it together like a proper book, with a cover. I was so proud and excited when I gave it to her and she just flicked through it, not reading a single word. Then she cast it aside. No acknowledgement. Nothing. And Dad picked it up and sat in his chair and turned every page slowly and laughed and oohed and aahed and pointed. But it was for her. So it wasn't the same.

I can hear Bernadette's voice, *"What did you want from her in that moment?"*

Please approve of me.

11.28 pm

Just before we trotted off to 'Feel:Deal:Heal', Louise told me I didn't have to go anymore if I didn't want to.

"I know you never really wanted to go anyway and you think I over-analyse everything and focus too much on the past and that I should just move on and why should you have to suffer just because I want to do it but you know I dragged you along to this healing and personal development thing because you're my best friend and I believe in your potential but you don't have to do it if it's too much. I'm only saying, because of the Lennie thing."

She didn't even take a breath. Impressive.

"Lou, have I ever spoken out before, the way I did?"

"No."

"Well then, it's working. I'm starting to express myself, right? Starting to feel my feelings and find my personal power. Starting to come back to life."

Like a proud parent, Louise beamed at me. I wondered how she even knew how to convey that particular look. She's never been on the receiving end of it.

I told Bernadette about Saturday night. She was thrilled I'd chosen to speak up. Then she asked Louise if she'd done the same.

Absolutely not! She'd been nice to Lennie.

Anyway, she's not angry like me. She needs to heal some sadness, that's all.

Yeah. Try telling that to all the road users you abused on the way home.

"You fucking idiot. Jesus Christ, would you look at that moron. Use your indicator, idiot. Move it, you stupid fuck. It's a 60 zone not a snooze zone you stupid old fart. Why are you braking? The light's orange, not red! Can't anybody drive? Am I the only good driver left? Absolute dickheads. Who gives these people licences? Other dickheads, that's who."

And she expressed it all without even knowing she was doing it.

Lou, Bernadette's not the only one who's got your number. I've got it too. Your nicey, nicey act can't go on much longer. I know what lies beneath those crunched abs of yours - a liver over-flowing with anger. God help the transplant recipient who scores that lump of pâté.

Tuesday 10th
3.33 pm

Well, would you look at us, Journal. Seeing each other every day like this. Anyone'd think we were going steady!

At least I'm writing again. Now when people ask if I've written anything lately, I can say yes. Makes a nice change from lying. They used to follow up the writing question with the publisher question but I don't think they can bear to hear me use the word 'rejected' anymore. It's thoughtful of them, I guess. Or else they really don't give a toss.

Bernadette was so kind to me last night. She made such a fuss about how I'd dealt with Lennie. She was proud of me and hoped that I could recognise and acknowledge the significance of it.

I played it cool and casual, but I felt secretly chuffed that she made a big thing of it. However, the aftermath in my head over a simple kind word is not worth it. 'Bernadette's only being nice because she has to. She's not actually proud of you. I don't even think she likes you. Why would she? You're fat and stupid'. On and on and on it goes. Just leave me alone.

An echo of Bernadette's voice has just popped in. *"Pay attention to your thoughts and words. They'll lead you to the feelings – and the reasons for them."*

Whatever!

Yay, a distraction - my phone's just beeped. Better check to see who's messaging me …

It was an SMS from Mum. She's going to Bali with the Fuhrer next week. It's a spur of the moment thing. She said she'd bring me back a t-shirt. In that case, I hope they sell ones that say, 'I bought my daughter this t-shirt when all she really wanted was a hug'.

Whatever!

Wednesday 11th
10.25 pm

Let me tell you, Journal - looks can be so deceiving. I had 'frumpy' Gretel, she of the owl glasses and sensible shoes, pegged as a bit of a blanket-crocheting homebody who wouldn't say boo but, man, was I wrong.

She started off innocently enough by talking about her regrets over not becoming a mother. This is familiar territory because she's mentioned it a few times. What was different tonight though is that she quickly dumped that old chestnut and got stuck into her, "God-bothering, country-bumpkin, uptight, fanatical, hypocritical, abusive" family.

She ran the entire gamut of emotions from angry to zealous. It was a beautiful thing. Everyone featured. Mother, father, brother, sister, aunty, uncle, dog, cat, goat - Barnaby - he was a delicious, but tragic, substitute in a Moroccan Lamb recipe. She was also holding onto some grief from an episode with a chicken, a goose and an electric fence.

After she'd shed a tear for the animals and run out of swear words for the relatives, she said, "I realise one of my biggest regrets is that I never told my mother and father that I have orgies."

Say what? Did we hear that right?

Apparently yes. Orgies, dear Journal. Orgies. Turns out she's a swinger! I didn't think that was actually a real thing, but it is.

Well, she had our attention then. We learnt many new things this evening and interesting fetishes, kinky sex, group sex, and kinky group sex have a way of widening eyes and leaving mouths agape, that's for sure. I don't think any of us will ever look at smoked cod or rubber gloves in the same way again!

And when she started down that road, Gretel was in her element. She was being deliberately naughty and I think she wanted to see if she could shock us because, for the most part, we're a polite bunch who keep our topics above the waist. But she wasn't sleazy, like how Lennie can be. She was funny and cheeky and earthy.

We ended up having such a laugh. It reminded me of a hen's night. All we needed was a stripper. Di was practically jumping out of her seat with girlish glee and she tried to look coy when Gretel described her favourite vibrator. It wasn't a convincing look. I'm tipping Di owns the entire Fist-O-Rama range.

It was a really good night. I haven't laughed like that in years.

And it was such a welcome move away from heavy feelings and being overly nice. Gretel broke down a barrier. She made things feel 'real'.

Thursday 12th
6.52 pm

I've just remembered the riddle I was trying to think of last night:

What's the difference between erotic and perverted?

Erotic is when you use a feather. Perverted is when you use the whole chicken!

Just before Louise headed out to meet Liam, she asked if I wanna double date on Saturday with a friend of his. "His name's Stuart. Apparently he's good-looking and a nice guy. It could be fun."

Straight away my head said 'no', but I'm trying to get out of the habit of refusing everything. I couldn't quite get myself to say yes so I told her I'd think about it.

"It was Liam's idea. He said, 'The more the merrier'."

I burst out laughing.

"What?"

"Does Liam know Gretel by any chance?"

Lou's eye twitched all the way to the door.

Friday 13th
10.25 pm

After fighting with my head for ages – no, yes, no, yes – I finally told Lou I'd go tomorrow night. I have no intention of doing hair removal though.

I'm praying to Vishnu et al. that this blind date doesn't suck. I don't know that I fully trust the concept after the 'Boy with a Thousand Hands' debacle. I was 15. I could have been scarred for life. Wait a minute …

I can't remember his name. I do, however, remember the dirty blonde hair, patchy whiskers, oily skin, and raging boner pressed into my thigh all night.

And drool. The guy was the spawn of Pavlov's dog. He may as well have handed me a cup of saliva and told me to drink up. It would have been less disgusting. Wonder what he's doing now? Hopefully swallowing!

Saturday 14th
6.20 pm

Bird's nest coiffure, puffy eyes, thighs that could pin down Schwarzenegger, body hair an ape would envy, dressed in stuff an op shop would reject. The Phantom of the Opera is better looking. Seriously. It's true. I'm not exaggerating.

"To break the pattern of the put-down, say something nice about yourself. It may feel uncomfortable at first. If it does, notice why it's uncomfortable. Notice any feelings it brings up."

Alright Bernadette, here goes. I appreciate that … I'm colour co-ordinated.

(No purple with red here.) I appreciate that I don't look 40. (Early 30s, or so I've been told.) My elbows are moist. (Thanks body butter.)

That'll do. Don't wanna get a big head.

I wonder if I could get an emergency fluidectomy on my engorged eyelids? Correction - my 'wonderfully hydrated' eyelids!!

Louise has just given me a yell so I'm off for my big date. He'd better not slobber.

Sunday 15th
10.27 am

Stuart was alright (nicely controlled saliva), but his whole look, manner, and blandness reminded me of Fox Mulder from the 'X-Files'. And for some reason, it put me off. I don't know if he's naturally that way, or if Fox was his hero and he's never moved on. I wouldn't be too surprised, though, if he's got one of those 'I Want To Believe' poster's on the back of his toilet door and a room full of 'X-Files' stuff and alien autopsy videos.

I could have gotten past the Mulder thing, but he really lost me when he ordered food with lashings of garlic. Way to repulse me Stewie. Especially after I'd gone to great pains with the waitress to order food with none because I hate it.

Liam's really nice. Friendly. Relaxed. He's got nice eyes. They're happy looking. Nice hair, too. Dark brown and straight. Both him and Stuart are 43, but Liam looks younger and … fresher.

Liam kept the conversation going and made things feel easy. Stu and I didn't talk to each other much. We tried, but nothing was flowing. Our difficulty was made more glaring because of Lou and Liam.

It's clear they really like each other. And they proved just how much when we got home. Over and over. For hours. I guess it's to be expected because it was their first time. And second. And third … They're still in bed. Mercifully asleep. That girl can really project her voice. She could be on the stage. I'm thinking musical theatre.

Stewie would have liked a bit of the old rumpy-pumpy as well.

Brazen as you like, he said, "You wanna have sex?"

Gee Stu, just give me a minute to soak up the compliments and the romance and I'll be ready to get right down to it. Oh no. Gosh darn it all.

Can't. Just remembered, "I've got my period," I lied.

"OK. See ya."

I see. I'm good enough to stick your dick into but I'm not good enough to spend quality, getting-to-know-you, time with. I'll remember that Stu.

Anyway Stewie, I can achieve a much more satisfying orgasm all on my own thanks. Without all the mess. And the brutalising of my breasts. So, catch ya on the flip.

Monday 16th
12.47 pm

Why can I instantly say 'no' to everything anyone ever asks me to do, except if it's my mother doing the asking? Somehow she renders me incapable of saying the word.

She rang me last night and said, "I need you to take us to the airport tomorrow."

I'm fine thanks, how are you?

"Mick and Donna are working and I don't like to ask our friends. Rob said you'd likely be doing nothing ..."

Oh did he. Fuck him. If anything was going to compel me to say 'no', it was that. Still, I couldn't. Catch a taxi or take the bus, I wanted to tell her, but I don't know how to say such things to my mother.

Against my desire to do so, I said, "Sure. What time?"

"Pick us up at nine. See you then."

Nine. That's the crack of dawn!

I literally dragged myself up at eight and arrived at her door on the dot. First words: "You look tired." Second words: "Is that the only jumper you own? I always see you in it. And it's got cat fur on it." Tut.

In the car, Mum asked me, "What are you doing for the rest of the day?"

The Fuhrer answered, "Going back to bed, probably."

"I might buy a wood chipper," I said.

"What on earth for?" Mum asked.

"You never know when you might need one." I shot a serial killer look at the Fuhrer through the rear view mirror. But his head was up his arse so he missed it.

So as my mother jets off to Bali full of life and joy, I sit here writing empty words on a page. There is something desperately wrong with this picture.

11.15 pm

Tonight's class was so relevant to my airport dilemma, it's eerie. I swear Bernadette is psychic.

She said, "Everyone's full of solutions to your problems. Everyone knows exactly what you should do. If only they were in your shoes, they'd have your life working like a well-oiled machine in a matter of minutes. But the fact is, the only authority on you, is you.

"Pair up and take it in turns to talk about an issue, and see if you can work out your own solution. The one listening just has to give good attention. That's all. Don't fix anything. Don't offer advice. Trust they can work it out."

Sounds easy. Right?

Wrong. It's bloody hard.

I worked with Nicole. For god's sake woman, lick your lips, they're drier than Marion's wit. I found myself over-licking my lips in the hope she'd copy me. She didn't.

Once her crinkly lips got to flapping, all I wanted to do was fix everything, and I knew exactly how. I could see all the solutions: Don't be intimidated. Tell him to get stuffed. You're not his slave. Ungrateful, lazy-arsed turd. You deserve better. Tell him NO.

In my head, I was so full of bravado and sass, you'd think this morning had never happened. I spent a few fanciful minutes working out where she could dispose of the body. I've noticed I'm quite inclined to murderous thoughts!

Her issue - "My husband expects a 3-course dinner every night. Starter, main, dessert. All the food has to be fresh and prepared from scratch. He won't eat processed or pre-packaged food. Not only that, he invites people over on the weekend, and sometimes during the week, and I have to cook great feasts for them too. Every day, I get up a five o'clock and it's non-stop. I get myself ready, then I get Geoff and the boys up, do their breakfast and lunch and then organise anything else they need for their day. I'm at work by 7.30 and most days I don't get home until six. My job is demanding so I'm tired when I get home. And then I have to start cooking. It's a push to get here twice a week."

I felt exhausted for her. And furious. So very, very furious. Seriously, who signs up for that shit? I doubt her vows included, 'I, Nicole, promise to put up with crap, work like a dog, have my needs overlooked, give every ounce of myself to everyone else, do all the child-rearing, forego a life of my own, and quietly endure my husband's selfishness'.

After 15 minutes of talking around in circles and nervously trying to work out how best to address the issue, what she decided was that now, after a hard day at work, she'll only cook a two-course meal every night, instead of a three.

I didn't exactly feel like pumping my fist in the air and saying, "You go girl!" but at least she arrived at a solution that she felt she was capable of implementing.

I told my airport story and I could see that, inside her head, Nicole was full of bravado for me. I reckon she was working out where to dispose of the bodies as well! Her lips moved a few times as if she was about to speak, but she managed to hold her tongue. It is really frustrating to witness someone else's weakness.

Making my attempt to be brave for myself, I decided that next time Mum has an expectation of me, I'd tell her that I'd appreciate it if she'd ask me rather than assume. I'm pretty sure I can do that.

It was an interesting exercise and it seems everyone wanted to give advice and fix, fix, fix. Eva couldn't contain herself. She actually screamed with the frustration of having to hold her tongue.

Bernie's been down this road a thousand times. "We all have the capacity and the intelligence to figure out for ourselves what we need to do. Grab a good listener, and duct tape for their mouth, talk through the problem, allow yourself to express any feelings that arise and the clear thinking will naturally follow. It might not happen right in the moment, but your answers will come. It's empowering to be responsible for your choices. Don't leave your life to others."

Tuesday 17th
6.04 pm

I've been so tired today. Cool woke me three times last night, purring in my ear and putting her whiskers up my nose. She sleeps all day and walks on my head all night.

Louise is all, "It's your own fault for giving in to her all the time. Don't let her sleep on your bed. Let her know who's boss."

"I don't want to be the boss of her."

"You're supposed to be. You own her."

"No I don't. She's not a dinner set! She's a living, breathing entity. We can't own anything that has life."

"People own pets. That's just the way it goes."

"Just because it's an accepted turn of phrase, doesn't make it right. I choose to give her care and love. She chooses to give me companionship."

"As if she makes choices! Cats are dumb."

I scoffed. "They're smarter than people. No alarm clocks. No rushing off to jobs they hate. No sitting in peak-hour traffic. No money stresses. No dramas. Pleasing themselves every day. They don't end up at self-help groups."

"That's it. I'm coming back as a cat. You can be my ... 'possession challenged life-sharer'. And so you know – I love smoked salmon."

"Deal. As long as you don't breathe cat food breath on me."

Speaking of cat food breath, Meredith said something interesting last night.

She said, "If I had my life to live over, I'd forget that the rest of the world existed and I'd concentrate only on my own existence."

That's easy for her to say because she's past her prime. At 67 you can declare yourself a sheep shagging Fascist with necrophilic leanings and, really, no one gives a toss. How nice. Old people don't become eccentric, they become free.

Just like we're full of bravado for everyone else, we're also full of bravado after the event. Meredith's forgotten what it feels like to be caught up in the thick of life; how you live as if you're the centre of the universe; as if everyone is focusing on what you're doing and how you're behaving.

If she could do it again, she'd do it the same. Maybe not intentionally. I figure that even if you don't face the world head on, it's always going to be in your peripheral.

Meredith, I like your sentiment and I reckon everyone would probably love to live a totally free, unselfconscious, uninhibited life. So, what stops us?

Wednesday 18th
11.40 pm
End of week six

Eva looked like she hasn't brushed her hair in days.

Heidi smelt like curry.

Arrabella sniffed incessantly.

Meredith picked and picked and picked at her chin hair.

Louise will probably write – 'There was a nice bohemian feel to the group tonight'.

I asked Bernadette what stops everybody from living free lives. "Why are we all so worried about appearances; about what other people think?"

"Say, 'I', 'me', 'my'. Speak only for yourself. Nobody needs you to speak for them. If they've got something to say, let them say it."

"But Bernie, there's safety in numbers."

"There's power in self-declaration."

Fine!

"I worry about appearances; that everything I do is being constantly scrutinised, dissected, judged. Then I wait to be criticised."

"How many people do you know?"

"I don't know. Maybe a hundred, give or take."

"Can you tell me what each of them is doing right now?"

"No."

"There are nearly seven billion people on this planet. Can you tell me what each of them is doing?"

I tutted. "No. That's ridiculous."

"Think of someone you're really close to – other than Louise. Would they know what you're doing right now?"

"No."

"How about the seven billion you don't know?"

"Alright. I get it." (Wrestler name for Bernadette: The Sledgehammer!)

She then spoke to the group. "Logically, Jodie can see that it's not possible for everyone to be concerning themselves with what she's doing. Unfortunately, feelings aren't logical. Jodie's feelings of being closely watched are real and they had to come from somewhere."

She turned back to me. "Do you have any early memories of feeling as if you were under a microscope?"

Before I even had a chance to think, a memory was there. 19 years old. 48 kilos. Underfed and over-exercised. My thin, haunted face contorted with anxiety and guilt as I hid in my room and stuffed a packet of biscuits down my throat, safe from the scrutinising eyes of the Fuhrer. His years of bullying, which started when I was 13, having forced me into that pathetic state. And there were his words, still fresh in my head.

"You're fat. You're an embarrassment to your mother and me. You need to lose weight so I'm going to be checking what you eat. If I think it's ok, you can have it. If not, then you can't. I'll be watching you so don't try and sneak food, because I'll know. And I'll be asking your friends what you've been eating. You can't hide from me.

"I'm doing you a favour because you can't afford those extra kilos on your frame. You're too short and thick-set. If you were taller like Donna, then maybe. But you're not, so bad luck for you.

"Nobody likes fat people. Everyone thinks they're disgusting and lazy. And because we know that, we know that when people look at you, they're thinking, 'Jodie's fat and ugly and stupid and lazy'. You'll have enough trouble finding love as it is. Be thin. It might help."

Every day. Every fucking day. For years.

But no matter how many deep breaths I took, I couldn't tell Bernadette. Speak, I begged myself. Speak. Cry. Scream. Anything. But nothing happened. I looked at the floor.

Bernadette took my hot face in her hands, tilted it upwards and smiled so lovingly at me I don't know how I didn't cry. "It's OK. When you're ready."

Soon, I hope. My chest feels heavy and my jaw aches from holding back the tears.

Thursday 19th
1.00 pm

I feel like absolute crap today. I had a horrible dream where I was being mauled by a big, black dog, which shocked me awake, and then I never really went back to sleep. Cool's purrs and whiskers were a nice comfort, for a change.

I stormed around the house yelling about dust ball tumbleweeds and fungus of mass destruction in the shower. I didn't do anything about either, just yelled and blamed my housemates for not sticking to the cleaning roster, which was ignored the moment the ink on the page dried.

Dan asked when was the last time I did any housework?

As if that should matter!

But I knew what he was thinking. That he and Lou worked and I was home all day contemplating my navel or "writing" or whatever it was I claimed to be doing to justify not having to get a 'real' job.

"So how's the book coming along?" he asked.

Ha! I knew it. "Fine."

"When will it be finished?"

"Soon…ish. And why aren't you at work?"

"Flexi."

Released from his bondage for one day only to have to work extra long days to accumulate enough hours to get another day off in a fortnight. Wow. What an awesome set up human beings have. Work the best part of the day for the best part of your life and get paid just enough to sustain you from one week to the next so you've got no choice but to keep turning up. And we call it living. I call it barely existing.

I couldn't stand his job. I'd rather die than spend my time trapped in an office somewhere handling papers all day that no one will ever see again, or even remember exist. All those trees sacrificing their lives for triplicate copies of 500 page reports on the impact of deforestation.

I can see it now, the Brazilian Rainforest will become nothing more than one big storage area for forgotten filing cabinets brimming with the bleached pulp of old growth trees.

No wonder the XX wax is called a Brazilian because your bits resemble the Amazon – hardly any bush left. It's bloody cruel. The tree thing and the waxing thing!

I realise the profits from the sale of my ex-marital home won't last forever so I'll have to rejoin the rat race in order to survive, but I'm gonna hold out as long as I can. And pray for a best-seller in between time. If only I'd thought of Harry Potter. Mind you if I had, it would probably still be a thought.

Gotta actually write the thoughts down, Jodie!!

Friday 20th
5.47 pm

I met Donna for lunch. She was really sad. "I'm desperate for a baby, but I can't get pregnant."

I wanted to say, "Pretend you're 16, get pissed and have a really bad shag in the back of a car. It's a guarantee of success." But I didn't. She needed some loving support. And I doubted Craig was giving her any. Puffed up arsehole.

I told her about Feel:Deal:Heal. Even though I'm hardly a great advertisement for it. But she didn't need to know that.

She seemed really interested then her face fell. "Craig thinks stuff like that is for losers. He doesn't think you need to worry about feelings or what happened in the past. Just think differently and everything will be OK. Move on, build a bridge, and all that."

That's great Don, but what do you think? I'm so sick of hearing you quote your husband ad nauseam. Don't you have a single thought or opinion of your own? Craig said this. Craig said that. In case you've never noticed, I avoid talking with your husband for this very reason. I don't give a shit what he thinks.

If I wasn't so full of hostility towards Craig I might be able to feel empathy for him and say he's only doing to Donna what was done to him. He was lectured mercilessly by his father; never allowed to express a single independent thought; never allowed to have an opinion. Donna was a perfect choice for him – he could sense her insecurity and self-doubt and he saw his chance to take a piece of power for the first time in his life. The oppressed becomes the oppressor.

Don't tell me, Craig, that your past doesn't impact on you every day. You're a living, breathing example that it does.

"Well," I said, "If you think it's something you might be interested in, Bernadette is running another group when ours finishes. I'll let you know when, if you like."

She looked almost frightened. "Thanks. I'll think about it."

Sometimes Donna really breaks my heart.

I spent the rest of the afternoon thinking about Donna's obsession with having a baby. I get the impression she thinks her life will suddenly be perfect and that all will be well in her world. I wonder if she thinks a baby will fill an empty space inside her? Doesn't she know that having a baby brings up all the stuff you've spent years stuffing down. I have a theory that post-natal depression occurs because you take one look at your baby and your own childhood suddenly erupts to the surface.

I applied a Feel:Deal:Heal technique and asked myself why I never wanted kids. My non-maternal feelings had to come from somewhere.

It's funny what thoughts your brain suddenly produces. Seems I was too frightened to become a mother in case I screwed up. A baby is a human being, not a toy; not something you can afford to grow bored with or suddenly find a gross inconvenience. And what if you don't like your child? They'd know. Right there you've set them up for a life of dysfunction – confusion, self-blame, self-loathing, neediness. Then one day they have to go and make their way in the world; figure out how to survive. What if they find it too hard? What if the things they want elude them? What if they don't know where they fit? Is it fair to set an unsuspecting human being up for that?

I don't know how Mick manages to be a good dad. I used to lie awake worrying that he'd either die or he'd forget his kids were alive. Not a good feeling.

Bloody hell, my stuff could keep a team of Bernadette's busy for the next millennium. I want to feel good. I want to function properly in the world. I want to appreciate life. I promise I'll try and let her in.

Saturday 21st
9.45 pm

Louise and Liam were whispering conspiratorially when I walked into the kitchen this morning. They denied it, of course. Said they were just speaking quietly so as not to wake me or Dan. As if! Those two are never quiet. Dan and I know everything we never wanted to know about their sex life. Lou was bedraggled but beaming. She fully looked as if she'd been tossed around in a hurricane all night. Good for her.

I was going to visit Nan today but I didn't feel like having my energy stolen by a bunch of old people who are fading and drying up. I need to surround myself with vital, alive people. People I can steal energy from. Maybe I should join Lou's Yoga class. They're supposed to be full of good energy and all the joys of the Universe.

I need talk about the old folks' fading and drying up. For a relatively young woman, I'm an old lady. Here I sit on a Saturday night, all alone, writing in you, dear Journal. Don't get me wrong, I appreciate I've got you but, really, this sucks.

I should have taken Dan up on his offer and gone to the pub. But nursing an orange juice half the night so I can keep myself in check does not for a fun evening make. I need to let my hair down and have a good time. So what if I'm overly-friendly when I've had a few? So what if all my inhibitions disappear? There are worse things to be than friendly and flirty.

Sometimes I long for the good old days of carefree abandonment; those wild and crazy moments that took me away from my real life. Smoking and drinking and dancing the night away. Staggering home in the early hours, happy to feel alive. I loved those snatches of time when everything felt funny and fun. What happened? Where did the party girl go?

She became self-conscious, that's what happened. She became embarrassed by her behaviour. She became controlled and constrained.

She became her mother.

Now I've depressed myself. I'm going to bed.

Sunday 22nd
4.59 pm

Dan had one of those 'never again' looks going when I told him I'd go to the pub next time. Fortunately his resolve to start living a quiet life more suitable to his 41 years won't last. Come next Saturday, he'll be raring to go again.

Even though he sounded rough as, I noticed that he looked really good. He'd just staggered out of bed but his hair was sexily mussed and his skin looked firm and peachy. There's barely a line on his face. Bastard! I don't know how he does it. If I'd had a big night, I'd look like a bag-lady for at least the next month.

Lou fessed up and told me her and Liam were whispering about how to get me to go out with Stewie again. Apparently he's up for it. They're willing to double date, if I want.

Do I want to go out with him? I don't know. But what have I got to lose? I could get all glamorous and be all flirty. Maybe I should. Make me feel like that spunky young woman I miss.

I think I'll go. But on our own.

Monday 23rd
10.50 pm

Nicole was a no-show. Probably at home cooking soufflés for 30.

Eva was bloody bitchy tonight. And she needs a shower. You could cook a roast in her hair. Every time someone opened their mouth, she was on them like a seagull on a chip. She's got an attitude at the best of times, but she was especially nasty and aggressive. Her gall bladder is definitely under a lot of pressure. It's not going to last the distance. Not unless she drops dead next week. Bernadette offered her the chance to 'get it out' but Eva just stormed out instead.

Bernadette said it was a pity Eva had gone because having the chance to talk about your stuff when it's right there on the surface like that is the perfect moment. Eva would have had lots of good attention, understanding and support. Out in the open, the issue loses its power and its emotional hold.

I've noticed that after Gretel really opened up a week or so ago, everyone is a lot more relaxed and trusting; more inclined to share their stories. You take a big risk exposing your hurts. These are the places we are weakest and most vulnerable. These are the places we need the most love to flow. And we're relying on veritable strangers to supply that love. That's huge!

Maybe there are a few good people in the world.

Tuesday 24th
12.25 pm

Lou pulled a sickie today. She dragged me out of bed at 8.30 and made me go on an hour long walk up every hill she could find! She's insane. Says she wants to lose a few kilos. I don't know from where. She looks fantastic. She's obviously going through the usual new relationship 'got to be perfect' stuff.

I can't say anything because I can totally relate. Rocked up for my own wedding severely undernourished and didn't eat properly for the next four years. A teenage problem that never, ever fades.

I remember Mum being thrilled that I was bordering on size six. How could my new husband not love me now?

I always wonder what it would be like going through life with an effortlessly gorgeous body. A body worn with confidence and pride. One that's easy to dress and look after. And a brain that gives absolutely no mind to it because it's too busy with other more important stuff. How nice. Maybe in my next life? If there are other lives, at the very minimum I'm gonna demand nice legs and nice hair. And boobs.

As we power-walked our way to skeletal proportions, Lou and I gossiped about the women in the group. We're not supposed to. For trust and safety reasons everything that goes on at group, stays at group. No one is ever allowed to mention your stuff to you or anyone else. We couldn't help ourselves though. We've been best friends since we were 11 so we figured the rules didn't apply to us in the same way.

"What's going on with Eva? She really looks like shit." Lou said.

"I know. Her hair is gross."

"She hates Di, I reckon."

"I swear, if Di mentions the challenges of being a woman one more time I'm going to rip her penis off."

"Speaking of penises - Heidi's a virgin! She said she's risen above the energy of her three lower chakras and doesn't need anything as primal as sex. She's all about love and spiritual connection."

"No wonder she doesn't care about how she smells."

"Gretel was mortified and offered to take her to the next swingers meeting."

"No! What did she say?"

"She got snooty and reminded Gretel about the listening without judgement rule."

"How do you know all this?" I asked.

"When we were paired up doing the 'early sexual memories' thing, I could hear them."

"Where was I?"

"Helping Tina find a box of tissues."

"Really, nothing beats a good bonk."

"Does that mean you're gonna do it with Stewart this time?"

"I don't know. Depends. I might knock back a few vinos to help make him more attractive."

"He's nice looking."

"Yeah, but he's not sexy. He's probably a one minute missionary man and I can't be bothered taking my knickers off for that."

"Didn't stop you when you were 17!"

"Or you!"

"Oh yeah. Those were the days ..."

Wednesday 25th
11.35 pm

Eva was back, looking worse than ever. She appeared to have her emotions in check and refused Bernadette's invitation to talk about what was going on.

Finn must have done some thinking about getting stuff out in the open because twenty minutes in she suddenly leapt out of her chair and declared in a loud, nervous voice, "I'm a lesbian and anyone who doesn't like it can get fucked."

It should have been a defining moment for Finn; her big chance to stand in her power; to release the shame and the guilt that has dogged her since she was 10 so she could finally live her truth.

Except ...

In what she obviously felt was a show of solidarity, Di shot up out of her chair and said, "I'm a lesbian too."

If looks could kill ...

Everyone looked gobsmacked, even Bernadette.

Eva's fat bull-neck throbbed. Emotions in check had just checked out. She turned viciously on Di. "Get a grip. You can't be a fucking lesbian. You're a bloke."

I have never seen pain like I saw move in slow motion across Di's face. It looked like her guts had been ripped out. I don't know how I didn't cry.

Everyone stopped breathing. Di stood stock still.

Bernadette was torn between supporting Finn, acknowledging Di, and asking Eva who she was really angry at.

But Eva didn't give Berns a chance to do anything because she hadn't finished.

"Look at you. You don't look anything like a real woman. Your tits are huge. You've got no hips. You trowel on the make-up. You wear clingy, trashy clothes. Your nails are claws. You look like a fucking drag queen."

Di wailed.

Bernadette abandoned Finn and rushed to Eva. She embraced her and said ever so lovingly, "Don't direct your anger at Di."

"She's a … he's a …"

"Eva, what's going on? You've got our attention and we're very interested to hear whatever you've got to say."

And for the first time ever, Eva burst into tears. Sobs racked her body for ages. I thought she'd never stop. Heat was coming off her in waves and sweat poured out of every pore. I have never seen anyone cry like that. Her grief was so raw. This normally big, angry woman looked so small; like a child.

Exhaustion finally took over and she calmed down enough to splutter that her hubby had left her a week ago for a woman who looked like Di.

"He said I was … I was …" A fresh wave of tears.

"You're doing well," Bernadette soothed. "Keep expressing."

"He said I was … a slob. That he was em … embarrassed to be seen with me."

Every heart in that room broke.

"He said a woman should keep herself nice if she expects a man to stay interested. And my anger is … ugly."

Bernadette directed Eva to the couch. I sat Di down and continued to hold her hand. Arrabella supported Finn.

Eva said a bit more but mostly she just cried while Bernadette loved her and encouraged and welcomed her feelings.

When Eva was calm enough, Bernie turned her attention to Finn.

"Finn, I'm sorry the attention was taken away from you just when you needed it most but now's a perfect time to express any feelings about what happened."

Finn couldn't meet anyone's eyes and she struggled to find anything to say. Bernadette went and gave her a hug, pulling her in close. Finn's tears flowed.

"This always happens to me. Whenever I finally get the courage to speak up someone always comes along and ruins it. I don't know why I bother." Finn's body sagged in Bernadette's arms.

"Finn, don't give up and don't turn the feelings inwards. Get them out. Come on. Be indignant. Say – 'How dare you. How dare you take away my proudest moment. It took a lot of courage for me to tell you I'm a lesbian. I deserve to be excited and I deserve to be congratulated'."

Finn cried harder.

"Come on, look at me and say it."

Finn looked at her and yelled. "It was my moment and I was cheated out of it. It's not fair. It was my moment."

Then Di got her chance. With great control she squeaked a semi-apology to Finn then she told Eva her words were hurtful but she understood why she was so upset.

"Di," Bernadette said, "don't be so polite. I want you to break your pattern of being 'nice' and 'understanding'. Let the fury and the hurt speak."

But Di had switched off from her feelings and we all knew it. "I promise I will next time. For now, I don't want to go there."

Everyone looked completely spent by the end of the night. I think Eva, in particular, has tapped into a very deep well that's had the lid on for a long time. I hope she's got the strength to let the feelings flow.

What a night.

Thursday 26th
10.52 am

I woke up in the night thinking about Eva's hubby and his comment that women should never wear clothes with elasticised waists. Fuck him. What does he know about small waists and 'child-bearing hips' and the living hell of trying to get clothes that fit properly. Most women suffer from poor body image and dysfunctional eating habits as it is without stupid comments like those adding to our self-loathing.

Eva is overweight and she's no glamour but it doesn't give her hubby the right to abuse her. Did he ever think to sit down with her and ask what was wrong; why she was putting on weight? If he'd cared about her for even a moment, he would have reached out to her and she might have realised she was worth caring about. It's sad that no one asks if there's a problem. There's just a lot of finger-pointing and judgement. Or ignoring.

I have to agree though, her anger is ugly. Her face twists and contorts as she spits venom and blame. She's loud and abusive and she gets all self-righteous and victim-y. She's quite frightening really.

I hope my anger doesn't look like that.

It probably does. Shit!

Lou noticed that when Eva laid into Di, I moved straight to Di and supported her with real compassion. I hadn't realised, so it was nice of Lou to point out a positive change in my ability to connect.

Maybe there's hope for me yet?

Friday 27th
11.38 am

I snuck another look in Lou's journal to catch up on the latest fashion news but she's moved from a clothing theme to a wedding theme because there's lots of love hearts and Liam's name all over the pages and she's signed Mrs. Louise Morrison in a dozen different ways. Anyone'd think she was in high school!

I shouldn't bag her. It's nice to be in love. When Di next wears a halter top or Arrabella rocks up in a tie-dyed hemp dress, I'm sure she'll see fit to comment.

Arrabella is so quiet. She starts to speak and then her voice just trails off. Could be because, half the time, she's stoned. I don't know how she manages to drive. Both times I got stoned, all I was capable of was lying on the floor and laughing so much I thought I would die. And contrary to popular myth, I didn't have a single creative thought. That's the main reason I got stoned in the first place. Most disappointing.

Olli wrote two crap songs that had more hums than actual words and we ate three bags of corn chips. That was the extent of our great foray into the psychedelic world of 'drug taking for brilliant creations which lead immediately to fame and profit'. Still, it was fun and it was one of the few things we did together and I was glad when he was home with me. At least then it was me he was loving.

Olli's my ex-husband, Journal. I don't feel like talking about him right now, so I'll just add him to my list of things to be dealt with another day.

Saturday 28th
6.00 pm

Well, I've made an effort. I'm defuzzed, exfoliated, moisturised, made-up and sleekly coiffed. I have no clothes, and I wore my only 'going out' outfit last time, so I borrowed a dress from Lou. It's a bit tight around the waist, but it looks good. It hides my chunky bits really well and coupled with my push-up, padded, moulded-cup bra it looks like I've got boobs. It may be false advertising … but too bad! I'm glad it's cold so I can wear my boots. They make my legs look longer.

Stu will be here in about an hour. I'm sipping a red to try and get relaxed. For some reason I feel a bit nervous. This will be the first time I've been on a one-on-one since my divorce.

I wonder what Olli is doing tonight? Changing nappies, probably. Unless he's already cheating on Jill, in which case he'll be using his 'need some me time' excuse as he packs his hiking boots and pretends to spend a couple of days walking some obscure trail.

Anyway, enough of that. Today is a new day and Stu will not have to pay for the sins of my ex.

As Lou and Liam walked out the door, Liam winked at me and told me I looked good. He was just being friendly but Lou looked like she'd been punched in the guts.

I know that look. In a nanosecond she'd regressed to when we were 16 and we both loved Gregory Tranndore and he preferred me. Tonight, Liam is going to witness the ugly face of insecurity.

Sunday 29th
3.45 pm

I was going to try and write a positive entry about last night. Really I was. But I can't do it. I gotta express so that means I gotta bitch.

When Stu picked me up, the first 10 seconds were good. Then he tried for a tonguey and a grope. Gross!

He was trying to be all sexy and suggestive, telling me I looked hot but it just came across as creepy.

At dinner he talked about himself incessantly. Incessantly!! His ex-wife. His kids. His job. His ex-wife. Where he's been. Where he wants to go. His acupuncture for some lumpy rash. (Nice one, that's gonna get me into bed!) His ex-wife. His ex-wife. His ex-wife. God!!

All I could do was stare at him and wonder wistfully what it must be like to be Angelina staring across the table at Brad.

After many long, boring hours, during which I either fell asleep, blacked out, or lapsed into a coma, we got back here. He finally turned his attention to me.

"Wanna have sex?"

There was a mad moment several hours before he picked me up when I'd decided I'd say yes just for the hell of it. That moment took its own life somewhere around the entree.

"Can't. Got my period."

"Again?"

"Still. Early menopause."

For a moment he looked confused, then he smiled. "I get it. Treat 'em mean, keep 'em keen."

Wake up and smell the KY Stu, I'm just not that into you. (Hallmark, here I come.)

"You know," he said, "I'm a bit surprised you're not leaping at the chance for sex. You're not getting any younger. You're divorced. You should take your opportunities where you can get them. You don't want to end up a lonely old cat lady, do you?"

One cat does not a cat lady make!

As I stood in stony, sober silence, he stared at me and I could almost see his little brain ticking over. "Are you a lesbian?"

Well I must be because, clearly, you're irresistible.

I've got to give him points for persistence because then he said, "Look, even if we can't do, you know, you can still use your mouth can't you?"

"Sure can Stu. Read my lips. Fuck off."

If this was a few years ago I would have bent over backwards (and forwards) to please Stu. Yet for all his efforts to tap into my insecurity, I couldn't be manipulated. A part of me wanted to thank him for looking my way, and to show my gratitude, but not a big enough part.

Really, I don't feel any less insecure so I don't know why I didn't cave?

What Stu has made me realise is that I'm ready to get back on the horse. I want to desire and be desired. I'm tired of being alone.

It was only 10.30 when I walked in but I knew Lou was in bed because her door was closed. And I knew she was sleeping alone because it was eerily quiet in her room.

She emerged briefly this afternoon to go to the toilet and get a drink. I greeted her and got a grunt in return. I don't need a clairvoyant to know she's blaming me for whatever's happened. This is a road already travelled.

Monday 30th
5.30pm

Sometimes Lou shits me to tears. She's always the victim and I'm always the bitch who's done her wrong. She waltzed in from work all hostile and said she wasn't going to group.

"Under the circumstances, don't you think going is the perfect thing to do? You're full of feelings that desperately need expressing. It's the best and only place you should be."

"You're not the boss of me and I'm not full of feelings. I'm fine."

Think loving thoughts. Be patient. She's just hurting. Deep breath.

"You wanted to go in the first place. Isn't this what it's about - Feel your hurts. Deal with them. Heal and move on."

"You never even wanted to go and now you think you know everything about it. Typical. Look at Jodie. She's so perfect and everybody loves her."

Breathe. Breathe.

"I'm telling you now, I am going to drag your sorry arse there and you can deal with your shit."

"Up yours."

I'll get her there and I hope Bernadette can help her see I've done nothing wrong.

11.30pm

After a failed attempt to keep Lou strapped in the passenger seat, Dan helped put her in the back and I literally sat on her while he drove us to group. We were 10 minutes late and everyone could tell we were off with each other, probably because I was dragging her through the door and she was telling me to piss off.

With a scene nicely made and no need for a cheery façade, I flung her into the centre of the room, looked at Bernadette and hissed, "She's pissed off because her boyfriend told me I looked nice. Fucking fix her before I kill her."

Louise was already heading for the door. "Fuck you."

Bernadette blocked her exit. "Is this true?"

"She wishes! As if she ever looks nice."

Even though I know it's only her hurt feelings talking, it's really hard to keep detached from that shit. I swear a part of her really means it.

"So why are you angry with her?"

"I'm not. She just decided I was. She's the one with the problem. Not me."

Bernadette actually sighed. She even looked irritated for a moment. Then she composed herself. Really, Bernie would have to get a bit sick and tired of the never-ending dramas she deals with. I know she does it for a living but there would be times when she probably wants to kill everyone herself. She just sees an endless stream of fucked up people. I wonder if she ever wishes she'd become something good like a travel writer instead of a counsellor. See the world for free. Mix with happy people on holiday. Why choose the same four walls day after day, experiencing only drama and angst? I might ask her about that.

Bernadette didn't say another word. She embraced Louise in a hug and just held her. Louise stood as stiff as a board, unsure about what to do with her arms.

After about a minute, Lou relaxed enough to put her arms around Bernadette. This was Bernie's cue.

"Did Liam upset you?"

Louise pulled away and pointed at me. "No, she did. She was wearing my dress, which is too tight for her anyway because she's too fat so she really shouldn't have worn it, and she was all posing and pouting and flirting with my boyfriend. In my dress."

"I wasn't posing, pouting or flirting. Jesus Christ you make up some shit."

"She does this all the time."

"All the time! Once, when were we 16, we both fancied the same guy. And just because he preferred me and asked me out you think I somehow manipulated him because no one would ever choose me over you. You're prettier and thinner and nicer."

My jaw was clenched so tight I don't know how I didn't break all my teeth.

"I should have been wearing the dress. Not her. Then he would have told me I look ..."

And thankfully the tears fell. Just to shut her up!

Bernadette addressed the others, who were completely enthralled by the show. "Emotions are illogical and they can tell such lies." Then she turned Lou's face to hers. "Louise, what did Liam do?"

"She ..."

"Louise, we're talking about Liam. What did he do? Not what you think he did, but what he actually did."

Louise scanned her brain for the truth. "He winked at her and told her she looked good."

"And what did Jodie do?"

Louise shrugged and looked unsure.

"Jodie did nothing," I piped in. "Because Jodie knew that Liam meant nothing by it. But I'm sure he deeply regrets it now because of the hell you would have put him through."

"What happened with Liam?" Bernadette asked.

Between the tears and the snot and the surety that Liam now hates her, Lou managed to splutter that after she gave him the silent treatment for the first hour and shunned all his advances, she then launched into a tirade of abuse about his personality, clothes, and iPod song list, followed by accusations of his fidelity, and she finished off with uncontrollable wailing and incoherent ramblings that if he preferred me, maybe he should just piss off now and put them both out of their misery. I was going to steal him anyway, so why waste anymore time.

Poor Liam. He would have been so confused.

Bernadette imparted her wisdom. "What happened to you when Liam told Jodie she looked good is very common. You stopped being in the present moment and your mind and emotions took you back to another time and place. In your case, to when you were 16. A boy you liked hurt you and made you feel insecure and unworthy. But rather than face the truth that he preferred Jodie, because that hurts too much to admit, you convinced yourself that Jodie stole him away from you.

"I want you to know that men cannot be stolen. Men are capable of thinking for themselves and making their own decisions. When Angelina Jolie was accused of stealing Brad Pitt, I just shuddered. It is a form of oppression to make the woman the vixenish villain and the man a bemused victim. I'm pretty sure Brad went willingly and it doesn't look like he's being held prisoner. And I don't remember Jennifer Aniston calling the cops to report the theft. For all we know, she may have been glad to see the back of him!

"Oppression is a huge topic so we'll talk more about it next time. One more thing - Louise, your insecurity and irrational feelings began long before you were 16. Think about where your feelings of rejection come from."

Louise was quiet on the drive home and she looked exhausted. I'm glad Dan was in the car. His presence neutralised the weird energy.

Tuesday 31st
1.08 pm

Lou pulled another sickie. That's the second Tuesday in a row. I'm glad she did. She was drained and there's no way she could have functioned at work. Sometimes you just need a mental health day. She's staying in her room though. And she's still not talking to me. I hope she takes the opportunity to write something meaningful in her journal.

Eva was a no show last night. Bernadette said it's not unusual for someone who's had a 'feeling' breakthrough to do a runner. It's so foreign that our brains can barely cope with the release. The intensity of the feelings get too overwhelming and we get frightened by it all. And embarrassed.

Pity she wasn't there to see Di wearing jeans and a very conservative blouse. Minimal make-up, short nails, hair in a simple ponytail. She looked really good. Even with the whisker shadow and Adam's apple. Mind you, I've seen actual chromosomally correct women with more facial hair than Di.

Di was so lovely to me last night. She sat me down next to her and held my hand all night, squeezing it every now and then to remind me of the connection. I bet she'd make a really good Mum. Nurturing and warm and caring. Guess she'll have to settle for being a lovely dad instead. A dad who cries a lot and wears lacy frocks, but a lovely dad nevertheless. A child could do much worse, let me tell ya!

How ridiculous that the things we cover our bodies in can be used against us; to judge us. Why can't a man wear any colour and fabric and style he wants? Who made up these rules? And even worse, why do we stick to them?

I had an SMS from Mum. She's home. I forgot it was today. Thank goodness she arranged for Donna to pick her up otherwise she'd still be at the airport!

Wednesday 1st June
5.45 pm

So, I caught up with Mum and there's really not enough ink in this pen to express all that I need to. Seems Donna told her I was going to Feel: Deal:Heal and instead of asking about it, or even asking why I would need to go to such a thing, she shook her head and said, "You've got too much time on your hands and you know how your imagination runs away with you when you're bored. Get a job and a boyfriend and you'll be too busy to worry about petty things."

I don't know why I was surprised, I really don't. This is how every conversation goes but I always live with a glimmer of hope that one day she'll look at me with love and empathy and say, 'Tell me about your pain'. All I managed to splutter was that I've got a couple (why did I not say a lot??) of childhood issues I'm hoping to heal.

"Childhood issues! You always were dramatic. Honestly, I don't know where you get it from. Except for losing your father, which we all dealt with at the time, you had a good childhood. Mick and Donna had the same childhood as you, and they're fine."

At least she had the good grace to cast her eyes down when she said the last sentence. She knows they're not fine, but denial helps get her through the day.

I didn't feel like getting into hostilities in the middle of a coffee shop so I asked her about Bali. And because she loves talking about herself, she happily rambled for the next hour. Just before we left, she gave me my souvenir - not a crappy t-shirt, but a collection of crystals. A surprisingly thoughtful gift!

But we couldn't leave our get-together on a high. Oh no. As we were walking back to our cars, she suddenly said, "You've been on your own for nearly four years now. It's too long and it's not natural. Women need men. Don't leave it too much longer. Age is a factor, you know."

She must have mistaken my look of disdain for something else because she then said, "Are you a lesbian? It's ok if you are."

That's the second time I've been asked that this week! Just to irritate her, because I know she wouldn't be ok with it at all, I said, "I'm considering it. I just have to decide if I'm going to be the butch one or the feminine one. Can't make up my mind."

Her nostrils stayed flared as she drove away.

11.30 pm

Group was so interesting tonight. Eva was back because Bernie had rung her and convinced her to return. She looked pretty good. Fresher and calmer.

She started things off by apologising to Di for abusing her. "I was in a bad place and it was a case of bad timing. I'm sorry I said all that stuff."

I guess it counts as an apology because the word 'sorry' was used. They attempted an awkward hug and Di thanked her, even though it was obvious there was still a 'thing' between them and Eva really could have offered up something better than 'bad timing'.

Di then looked at Finn. "I'm so sorry, Finn. I want you to know that I'm full of remorse over what happened. I respect your bravery and your honesty. I hope my actions won't stop you from expressing yourself in future. And I promise I won't interrupt you again. I hope you can forgive me for being so insensitive."

Now that's an apology.

Finn stood up and gave Di the warmest hug ever. "Thank you."

Di's eyes filled with tears. "I just wanted to fit in. I've never fit anywhere because I'm neither a man nor a woman. I live a half life full of lies and secrecy. And I really thought it was only me who faced struggles. But I see now that it's not. What bothers me most is that my wife can go out wearing a pair of Y-fronts and look, for all the world to see, like a man and no one cares. But I can't go out in a skirt without facing threats of violence, verbal abuse, or being ridiculed and shamed. Why is it bad to be a woman?"

Bernadette - "It's oppression; a way to keep us feeling less than. And it's a bastard of a thing. In some cultures, females are a disappointment from the start. Imagine living with that knowledge – that you weren't really wanted, and then watching the males be adored and treated like prizes. Don't get me wrong - males have their own set of oppressions, but we'll talk about those another time.

"Females put up with a lot of abuse their whole lives. If it's not name calling, it's shame mongering. TV and movies continually portray us as gold-diggers, neurotic bitches, nagging control-freaks, prostitutes.

"If homosexuals and people of colour were blatantly abused the way women are, under the guise of 'entertainment', there would be an uproar. On TV, or in a movie, no one would dare call someone a nigger or a poofta or a kike or a gook, yet we're casually labelled sluts, whores and skanks. That's actually just as abusive and just as demeaning, and people don't even bat an eyelid over the whole 'bros before hos' thing. In fact, it gets a laugh.

"The intent of these words is to oppress a woman's right to have and enjoy sex – which is a natural part of life. They suggest that women who have sex are somehow dirty. They are designed to engender guilt and shame. The questions that need to be posed are:

- Why is sex considered to be degrading for women?
- Why is it suggested that women who have casual sex suffer from low-self-esteem, implying that sex is an act of self-abuse?

"Nearly everything we do and everything we are attracts a negative label of some sort. And it's not enough that we cop it from the males, we abuse ourselves and each other as well. We fell for the propaganda and we've been brainwashed – 'women are jealous bitches; women dress for other women; women set out to steal other women's men; to keep a man – talk less, pole-dance more'. I'm sure you can all think of more examples.

"The oppression is so internalised, we don't even see it. We just accept that 'this is the way things are' so we perpetuate it, generation after generation. It's very damaging.

"We try to conform and be good and behave how 'society' says we should. We deny our urges and our needs. And we apologise if we fail. In the end, we keep ourselves 'in our place'. We no longer need external forces to keep us down because we do a good enough job on our own.

"We laugh along with, or even say ourselves: 'you big girl', 'you hit like a girl', you scream/cry/act like a girl'. It's an actual insult because, apparently, it's shit to be a girl.

"Women don't know how to support each other because they can barely support themselves. In much of nature, the male still has to fight for the right to mate with the female but humans have turned that on its head and now the woman has to preen and present herself and put up the competition. It's not natural, but we do it because it's what we've been trained into.

"Females need to embrace all the things that make us female. We should be proud of everything we are – in all our shades and all our colours. And we shouldn't have to apologise for being 'such a girl'. And female leaders need to lead like a woman, not a faux man. Because what's the point in having a female leader at all if she's not going to bring her uniqueness and her femaleness to the table? Women who rule like men are making a big mistake.

"We are all so different but, at the core of it, we are all the same. I love women. They are the great unsung. That's why I run these groups. So women everywhere can return to who they really are, walk proud, be true to themselves and afford other women the same. We are all worthy."

Thursday 2nd
5.25 am

Just woke up from a weird dream about Dad. I haven't dreamt about him in years. I was standing at the gate of our old house and he was riding his pushy towards me and then he suddenly disappeared down a hole in the road. He looked how he did in the last Christmas photo we had taken.

I suppose he's popped into my consciousness because Mum mentioned him the other day. I remember when he died. It was a Thursday. Mick, Donna and I suddenly heard Mum screaming hysterically. We ran in from the garden and saw two police officers looking down at her. Mum was slumped on the floor, white as a sheet, clutching her chest and sobbing uncontrollably. I stopped dead and just stared at her, but Donna and Mick ran straight over, crying and begging to know what was wrong. I can't remember who spoke but all I heard was father and killed.

I felt so sick and I couldn't breathe. I stared at the three of them, clutching and wailing, and I felt like a complete stranger to them and to myself.

I vomited on my shoes.

I ran back into the garden and curled myself around Lucky and sobbed into her fur. And that big, old beautiful dog just lay there and let me.

8.30 pm

Memory is an amazing thing. There are some memories I have where I can recall smells and minute details and there are others that are so vague – just snippets of events on the periphery of my brain. Stored somewhere in my brain must be every word I've ever heard and spoken, every image I've ever seen, and every feeling I've ever had. The brain is quite a stew. And some of the ingredients are off!

I told Lou and Dan about my dad dream. She didn't say much, but she's getting chattier than she was. Dan's been talking more than usual this past week to try and fill the unusual silence. He told us his dad was gay and that his mum found out when she questioned him about some gay porn she found in his wardrobe. He died from an AIDS related illness in 1985. Seems everyone's got a story of heart-wrenching loss.

Friday 3rd
6.32 pm

Lou's speaking to me full-time again. She and Liam are finally back to normal so that's probably helped her become reasonable again. In a way, we're in a strange situation. We're both 40, both childless, and still house-sharing as if we were 20. A lot of the time it feels as if we've never really grown up. The dynamics of our relationship hasn't matured. After Olli and I split, moving in with Lou seemed the perfect thing to do. She'd been on her own for six months and was struggling to meet the mortgage. I didn't want to live on my own, so it was a win-win. And getting Dan in really helped the finances. Three divorced people who finally had a bit of money to spend on themselves.

Dan's ex re-married and moved interstate so he didn't have to do the usual weekend dad thing either. He web chats. It seems to be enough for him.

I can feel that things are going to change though. Lou and Liam seem quite serious and they'll make the next step soon. They'll probably want to live on their own. Which is the way it should be. This just means I need to get my shit together and decide what I'm going to do. I could put a deposit on a townhouse but then I'd have to get a job to pay the mortgage. And that idea doesn't thrill me. But I can't wander around homeless for the rest of my life. Bloody money. Why does it get to determine the quality of my life?

Saturday 4th
3.15 pm

I went to Mick's and got there just in time to hear Liz calling Emily an idiot and hear Sarah crying. Straight away I felt so angry and my murderous thoughts kicked in. It's funny – I will scoop up a bug from the house and pop it back in the garden because I can't bear the thought of killing it, and I've saved many a mouse from Cool, yet I'd happily hack Liz limb from limb so Mick and the girls could live in peace and happiness.

One of these days I will actually confront her about her shit behaviour and the vile way she speaks to Mick and her kids.

I walked in and we fake smiled at each other and did our obligatory air kiss. The girls ran over to me and we had the best hug. Mick was cleaning up Sarah's ex-fruit smoothie.

I purposely visit on a Saturday morning because Liz is always at her beauty spa, but apparently it went bust a few days ago. Pity those places don't make you beautiful on the inside. With malicious intent, thinly disguised as an innocent question, she said, "Do you know any good beauty … oh no, you probably wouldn't." She waved the question away. "Forget I asked."

I know I'm supposed to support the sisterhood. I know I'm supposed to understand that Liz was badly bullied and oppressed and that her behaviour is a result of her having been hurt. I know I'm supposed to see her as being intrinsically good. But you know what, I don't care. I don't care if she was a slave to her arsehole, misogynist father and a whipping boy to her weak, flaky, alcoholic mother. The fact is, she's a bitch. Sometimes you have to call a spade a spade.

If she hated their behaviour so much, then why does she just emulate it?

With our two requisite minutes of small talk out the way, Liz rushed out the door to who knows where. Good riddance.

I took the girls to the park and Mick rocked up half an hour later. Emily's nearly 12 and when I was watching her it struck me that she's nearly as old as I was when Dad died. Mick was the same age as Sarah. I can't imagine my nieces dealing with death.

And poor Mick, just shy of being ten, being told that he was now the man of the house; that he had to be responsible. There's a male oppression right there. He was just a child. What a terrible burden to lay on him. And he was told to toughen up. Boys don't cry. Another male oppression. Boys do cry because I saw it and I heard it, night after night for more than a month.

God, how did we cope? And we had absolutely no support. We just had to figure it out as we went. I remember at the funeral, everyone milled around Mum as if she was the only one who'd lost someone. We didn't get a look in because we were just the kids.

As I was leaving, I grabbed Mick in a big hug, kissed his cheek and told him that he was an awesome man, a brilliant father and that I loved him very much. He was a bit surprised but he smiled so proudly and he said, "Ditto … oh, except for the man/father thing. Substitute woman/aunty."

I love that guy. He makes my heart swell.

Sunday 5th
11.35 am

I've got so much going on in my head at the moment. Just a few short weeks ago, I could go for days and barely think about anything meaningful, but Bernadette has opened up my brain. She talks about things I was sort of aware of, but never really knew how to articulate.

Every moment of our life involves a feeling of some sort. There have been times when I've only heard something, or only seen something, or only touched something, but in every single moment, there has been a feeling present as well. Even a blind, deaf, mute person has feelings. Feelings are non-negotiable. They are ever-present. Our emotional selves cannot be ignored or discounted. We try, of course. We drink, smoke, gamble, over-eat, shop – all in an attempt to not feel anything. But trying to stuff down feelings only creates a whole new set. It's a vicious cycle. Eventually we're so full of feelings we can't function. This is why half the population is on anti-depressants.

Berns told us that if we just figure out how to understand the feelings -understand when, where and why they began; understand why they continue to make their presence known; understand why they impact upon us and what they're trying to tell us about ourselves, we can heal what we need to and live happier, true-to-ourselves lives. Once the hurt feelings dissipate, instead of being reactive all the time and being dragged into the past, we'll be in the present moment and able to make intelligent, well-considered choices and decisions.

Lou told me she was sorry about the Liam thing. She realised her reaction was unfounded and that her insecurity stemmed from her mother leaving. She said she'd work on it in group.

I need to work on what Mum said – that we all dealt with Dad's death at the time and that I had a good childhood. It keeps playing on a loop in my head and I feel pissed off by it.

Monday 6th
10.25 pm

As usual, group started with Bernie asking us to share something positive we've done. She went first and said she'd bought herself a mobile and taught herself how to text.

Heidi discovered an awesome vegan chocolate at the market.

Di told a guy at work he had an oppressive attitude.

Arrabella rescued a dog and a cat from the shelter.

Finn got her navel pierced. (Ouch!)

Meredith started volunteering at Meals on Wheels.

Nicole hung up on a pushy telemarketer.

Marion hired movies she wanted to watch, for a change.

Eva changed the locks.

Gretel tried Yoga.

Louise patched it up with Liam.

I perused the employment section of the paper.

And Tina, well Tina – the big-time crier; the victim to end all victims – she must have gone grave robbing because she got herself a backbone! In front of staff and customers, as loudly as she could, she quit her job and called her supervisor, who had been bullying her, a cunt. She then drove round to her parents and told them she wouldn't be visiting anymore because she was sick of being ignored and treated like a mistake. She rang her brother and told him he was allowed to visit only when he didn't want something and then she told her hubby that if he didn't start respecting her and their home, he'd soon find himself with neither!

OMG! I can't even give Liz a dirty look and Tina did all those empowered, life-changing things in one day. How did she do that? How?

Bernadette went to Tina, hugged her and asked her if she was ok?

Without shedding a single tear, she said, "I've never felt better."

Bernadette looked worried, as if Tina wasn't fully aware of what she'd actually done. This was a woman who'd spent her whole life being walked all over and after a few weeks of Feel:Deal:Heal she was doing the stomping.

Bernadette studied Tina's face. "Has what you've done really sunk in?"

"I was aware of what I was doing, if that's what you're asking? I woke up this morning and I just felt different inside myself; calm and unafraid. I'm here in the first place because I knew I had to change. Does it matter that it only took me a short amount of time? I would have got to this point eventually – so isn't it better for me to get here sooner? Why are you worrying about the time-frame? Do you think I've done something wrong?"

Bernadette didn't know what to say for a moment. She started speaking as a counsellor, "In my experience, I've found that …" Her voice trailed off. She stared at Tina's worried expression. "Actually, I feel nervous. That's what I'm feeling but it's got nothing to do with you or what you've done. What you did is brilliant, amazing, brave. It's … I remember the first time I stood up for myself. I felt sick for days and then I regretted it. I ended up back-tracking and apologising just so things would go back to normal. It was a stupid thing to do and I'm scared you'll do the same."

"I won't. This is the first day of my life when I haven't felt sick. And you'll all help me if I need it."

Yes we will Tina, my Goddess heroine. Yes we will.

Tuesday 7th
8.45 pm

Lou can't stop talking about Tina. She wonders what clicked inside her that caused such a huge shift.

"She's been crying and expressing for nine weeks solid," I said, "and she's been getting a lot of good attention. I'd be worried if she didn't change! We should both do one empowered thing this week and see how it feels."

"Ok. You tell Liz to shut up and I'll tell … umm …"

"At the dinner party, when one of them upsets you – and you know they will – I want you to tell them."

Lou looked nervous. In my stomach, butterflies hatched in the thousands. But we agreed.

I rang Mick and organised to take the girls to the movies after school on Friday. I figured that Liz would be home by the time I dropped them off.

If I practise ahead of time what to say, then I won't stuff it up on the day. I'd love to say, "Shut the fuck up, you nasty, spiteful, bullying bitch. I am so sick of hearing the abusive shit that comes out of your fucking mouth. Just leave them the fuck alone, you humourless, angry, fucked up fucker." Seems I love the word 'fuck'!

What I'll say instead is, "Liz, please don't speak to my brother and my nieces like that. It's abusive, there's no need for it and I don't appreciate it. Perhaps you should get some counselling for your anger."

That seems fair. It's reasonable and it addresses the issue in a polite way.

Wednesday 8th
10.50 pm

Marion was funny tonight. She was telling us how every Friday night is fish, chips and sex night – has been for 15 years. Come rain, hail, sleet, snow, or needy offspring – they eat their greasy fare, watch some TV, then get down to it.

In the early days, they also enjoyed pasta and sex Monday, stir-fry and sex Wednesday and the once a fortnight 'spontaneity' of apricot chicken Saturday! They died off after the kids arrived.

Marion's witty and she's good at telling a story and I sometimes wonder why she's doing Feel:Deal:Heal because she comes across as being reasonably sane. And I swear she's never cried. Most of the others do nothing but! But it's twice now she's bought up sex – the first time was her famous ball-bag line from her journal, and now this. If she's got some kind of issue, she's keeping it low-key. She does use humour a lot to deflect though. She's one to watch.

Heidi was in a weird mood. She babbled about some guy in her meditation group who'd invited her out to dinner but she couldn't go because her lower chakras would get disturbed. When Bernadette asked her what she was feeling, she said, "I can't believe I gave up an Enjo party for this. I really, really need a shower mitt."

Just another night at the nut house!

Thursday 9th
10.50 pm

Told Lou I've been practising my Liz speech. She's prepped a generic line of her own for Saturday night.

"At every dinner party, someone always says something oppressive – Bernadette would be proud of me – about women. So I'm gonna say, 'Excuse me, but that's very oppressive. Nelson Mandela would tear you a new one if he heard you say that. Women are allowed to do whatever they want, without being judged for it or told they can't. Next time you say something about a woman, make sure it's something positive."

I didn't have the heart to tell her that Mandela rallied predominantly against black oppression. Hopefully the others will get her point.

Friday 10th
8.39 pm

When I dropped the girls home after the movie, Liz's car was in the driveway so I knew she was home. My stomach lurched, but I was ready to say my lines.

Liz greeted the girls quite nicely.

"Did you enjoy the movie?"

"It was really good and --"

"-- We had ice-cream and lollies."

And in a nano-second, the nice was gone. "You know you're not allowed to have that kind of stuff. Why did you have it? Are you stupid? Did you somehow forget?"

Then she turned to me. "You know I don't let them eat sugar. Did you forget?"

Then she turned to Mick. "Fuck, Mick, I told you to remind your sister not to buy them any lollies and crap. I should have known you wouldn't say anything. You never fucking do."

Back to me. "So you know for next time – don't give my girls any sugar-filled shit. I don't want them to get fat and giving them lollies won't score you any points with them. It won't make them love you."

And just like that, we were done. Liz shunted the girls off to have a bath before their tasteless tofu dinner and Mick and I stood awkward and silent.

I turned to leave. "I'm sorry about that," Mick said. "She's a bit stressed at work."

"It's ok. My bad. I'm sorry I got you and the girls into trouble."

"No trouble. I can handle her." Even he didn't look convinced.

When Lou got home, I was just finishing a whole block of chocolate.

"Bad day?"

"I'm pathetic. Liz shat all over me, and I let her."

I told Lou what had happened.

"I feel so shitty with myself."

"You'll do it next time," she said. "Rome wasn't built in a day."

Clever ploy, Ms. Peterson. Now I can't be mad at you if you don't speak up for yourself tomorrow night.

Saturday 11th
10.30 am

I'm lying here feeling crappy. Liz threw me for a six and I find my head is bringing up stuff from when I was a teenager - all my body issues and how Mick, Donna and I just stood limp and useless at every diatribe that came our way.

Mostly I find I'm thinking about how no one ever stood up for us.

There's banging and clanging coming from the kitchen. It's probably Lou baking the cheesecake and the chocolate thingy for tonight. Thank goodness she's a wiz in the kitchen. I can barely boil water!

Yep, it's her because her loud singing has escaped and it's sneaking into my room. She's even managed to wake Cool who looks most unimpressed! She's so tuneless, but it sounds like she's having fun.

Ok, Jodes, stop feeling sorry for yourself. You need to smile. Drag your sorry arse out of bed, get in there and join her. She is AB. Together you are ABBA. Singing makes you happy. Go be happy.

5.00 pm

The mini-concert from this morning made me feel happy so I'm in a good space now.

We're at Alice and Rusty's tonight. Hope they lock up their dog. Crotch-sniffing brute.

Their house is always in a shambles. I know they've got teenagers who slob and sloth all over the house but it bothers me that they don't tidy up for guests. And it always smells of wet dog. Louise never seems to notice it and she says I'm picky and anal.

Now I think about it, I'm really just a trained monkey. To sum up an endless barrage – "It's all about appearances, Jodie. What will other people think?"

We've been friends with Alice since high school. We all smoked on the oval and wagged it together and we gave her hell because she played the flute. They gave me hell because I loved Barbra Streisand!

While the rest of us were on a continual man-hunt, she didn't have to look very far for Rusty because he was her brother's best friend. Her and Rusty and Heath and Penny are the only original couples left.

Liam's got a buck's night so he's not coming. It would have been Lou's chance to finally introduce him to everyone. Next time.

Lou asked if I was going to behave tonight; no repeat performances of last month. Of course I'll behave. Even smiled angelically to prove it.

Dabbed a bit of lavender behind my ears for that extra calming effect.

Sunday 12th
12.20 pm

I think the bush my lavender oil came from may have been cross-bred with a Triffid. I say this because I felt murderously calm. Is that possible? I don't know.

When Lou and I arrived, the first sound to greet us was Lennie's guffaw. Should have turned around and gone home then. What the hell Katrina sees in him, I'll never know.

We walked in to find the girls and guys had already divided up. Katrina, Alice, Penny, and Emma were organising food. Brenton was mixing drinks. Heath and Rusty were feeding dip to the dog. Lennie was hovering.

With greetings out the way, I made a bee-line for Brenton and got a large glass of red.

The evening progressed civilly. Everyone was chatty and the food was delicious. Emma made the main this time – some beef thing – and it was truly delicious.

Brenton re-filled my glass. "You got a boyfriend yet Jode?"

I don't know how anyone else heard him because there were three other conversations going on and he said it in a lowish tone, but the next thing I hear is Alice's foghorn voice. "Just to get out of having sex, Jodie told Stewart she had her period – twice!" How the hell did Alice know? I shot Louise a foul look.

Then Lennie weighed in. "Never trust anyone who bleeds for five days and doesn't die." Guffaw. Guffaw.

I did a Louise Zen breath. I smelt lavender and remembered to be calm. But calm was pissed off too.

"You're a dickhead Lennie."

Oh no. Here we go again, they all thought. 18 eyes looked directly at me. 17 if you minus Heath's lazy one.

"You owe your life to that blood. It nurtured you when you were in the womb. Then it nurtured your children. That blood is something to be revered, not reviled."

A beat of silence was broken by Louise gushing, "That's so true. Jodie's right. She's right." Yeah, you'd better kiss my arse because I'm gonna be kicking yours later you big-mouth!

I resumed my dinner. New conversations got started. Well, that was over with quickly and relatively painlessly. Except for calling him a dickhead, which is neither here nor there because everyone calls him that, I didn't really say anything bad to him. Until …

Lou brought out the desserts – her two delicious masterpieces. Emma's eyes lit up.

"Ooo, I'll have a piece of each please."

"Em," Lennie said, "Are you one of those chick's who's just gonna get fat now you've got a husband?" He mimed the Michelin Man. "Why do chicks do that? I bet you're wearing big cotton knickers and I bet you've stopped shaving too. I won't even mention s-e-x."

He guffawed, of course, but there was an edge of venom in the way he said it so Emma couldn't even playfully tell him to get fucked. She just looked down at the table. That man really does have an entrenched prejudice against women. He manages to say something so sexist and so hurtful every time we get together. He can't help himself. He's got some major issues.

Lennie handed her two big pieces of cake. "Here you go, Em. You know I'm only joking." Subtle Michelin Man again for the benefit of Heath and Rusty.

I don't know why I leapt to her defence. Maybe because I could see Brenton wasn't going to. Maybe because she looked so hurt and I didn't trust she could stand up to him. Maybe because Louise was trying her best to pretend nothing oppressive had been said so she didn't have to speak up.

"Lennie, you can't say hurtful things to someone and follow it up with 'I'm only joking'. It doesn't cancel out what you've said. I'll demonstrate - You're a fat-gutted, freakishly hairy, brown-toothed, bad-breathed, loud, obnoxious, boorish, stinking sack of steaming sexist crap. Tee hee. Just joking. Geez Lennie, where's your sense of humour."

I could see what Lennie was thinking, and it wasn't, 'Thanks for drawing my attention to my piggish attitude. I appreciate the chance this gives me to learn about myself and to, hopefully, grow and evolve'.

"Jodie, if you drank Dr. Jekyll's potion, you'd turn nice."

That's a surprise. I thought he was thinking, 'Fuck you, bitch'.

Lennie officially hates me.

Monday 13th
2.00 pm

On the way home from the dinner, Louise asked me why I can give Lennie a mouthful but I can't tell Liz to shut up. It's a good question. I didn't know how to answer her but I've been thinking about it.

I feel intimidated by Liz. She's just so … dominant. I always feel nervous around her. Basically, I'm too weak to confront her. And I can't bear the thought of upsetting Mick because I know how hurt and embarrassed he'd be if I did speak up.

In the case of Lennie – for me, he's an easy target. He's full of bullshit and bravado but, really, he's weak too. He doesn't have that alpha energy. If we lived in the wild, I would have eaten him years ago.

But even before Liz came along – there was the Fuhrer. He alpha pecked me into submission so anytime I come across a similar energy, I'm screwed.

Seriously, how do you undo years of abuse? Because once it's been witnessed/experienced, it's there forever. It would be like trying to rid your brain of the alphabet or numbers. You can't just decide one day that you can no longer count. You could choose to never count again, but you would always know how. And chances are you'd do it, even if you didn't want to.

Is it even worth going through this Feel:Deal:Heal thing?

Tuesday 14th

Too sad today.

Wednesday 15th
4.45 pm

I've been brewing and stewing for quite awhile now and on Monday night I was in a fighting mood so I got stuck into Bernie with my alphabet/numbers theory.

"That's a relevant point," she cooed. "You've been doing some excellent thinking, Jodie. You won't forget about the things that have happened to you. You won't forget how you felt and you won't forget how those things have impacted on your life. What does happen is that these things become a secondary force in your life. They no longer take prime position in your brain and influence every choice and decision you make.

"You'll go for weeks and months without once thinking about how you were hurt when you were younger. Inevitably, something will come along and trigger a memory and all the old feelings will rush forward and feel as fresh and painful as they were the day you originally felt them. But you'll recognise when it happens. And instead of being reactive and automatically regressing to a state of despair/shame/guilt, you'll understand what's happening and you'll know how to deal with it.

"By talking about your feelings and dealing with them in a safe, nurturing environment, you will heal the wounds that keep you injured. You learn to manage your reactions and responses. You learn to understand that you are intelligent and capable. You learn to understand that you are a free individual who has choices. You learn that the ties that bind you are, in fact, non-existent. You learn to please yourself – not everyone else. And, eventually, your past becomes a history lesson containing some emotion but little relevance to your life today."

"Well how come I've been coming here for nearly three months and I'm still angry and tired and shitty and weak? Nothing's changed. When will I feel better?"

"How much actual expressing have you done?"

"I write in my journal. And I did cry. Once."

"Have you cried again, when you've needed to? Have you screamed, stomped your feet, punched a pillow? Writing is excellent because it helps you analyse and understand, but it won't release the actual emotion from your body. You need to do something physical for that."

"Why? The shit's in my head," I snapped.

"The shit is also held in your body. This is why we sweat, cry, shake, vomit, kick, punch. This is why unexpressed stuff can manifest into physical illness."

She stood up. "Stand up. Face me."

I stood but my body wouldn't stay still. I was fidgeting terribly and my right leg was trembling. I was suddenly sorry I'd opened my big mouth. I felt nervous. My face was hot and my eyes stung. Why is the act of expressing a feeling so bloody hard? My resistance was causing me actual pain. What's the big deal, I was asking myself? It's just a feeling. People have them all the time.

"Get out of your head, Jodie."

She then laid her hand ever so gently on my chest.

"Come on. Tell me something that's been bothering you."

It took me three deep breaths, but I finally said, "My mum irritated me when she said that we dealt with our dad's death at the time and that I had a good childhood."

"You obviously don't agree. So what do you want to say to her? Yell it. Scream it. Punch my hand. Come on."

Even though I've got a thousand things I'd love to say, the thing that spewed forth was, "I hate that you replaced my dad with that fucking arsehole. You didn't even wait a year. I was still grieving and you just slotted another man in as if it was a production line. No one asked me if that was ok. No one asked me if I wanted my father replaced. No one …"

And then I howled. I felt my body collapsing and Bernadette held me up. She moved to a chair, sat down, put me on her lap and held me like I was a child. I cried so much I thought I wouldn't stop. I cried snot and tears all over her top.

She rocked me and soothed the desperately sad 12 year old who missed her father - the man who loved her when no one else did, the man who was interested in her, the man who found her funny, the man who took her to the movies, the man who adored her weird, mousy hair, the man who enjoyed his children, the man who would never grow old.

Thursday 16th
8.30 am

When I walked into group last night, Bernadette took one look at me and immediately hugged me. "I'm glad you're back."

I looked like crap. My eyes were puffy and I looked really old and exhausted. Every woman there gave me a warm, nurturing hug and I cried softly through each one of them. Di held my hand all night.

Tuesday was a tough day for me. The grief that came up in an endless stream was overwhelming. I cried for Dad. I cried for me and Mick and Donna because our mother took to her bed and forgot about us. We were beyond devastated and there was no one to hug us and tell us everything was going to be ok. We spent that first night all alone, terrified and heart-broken, and crying more than we thought was humanly possible.

And I cried for Mum because I understand how devastated she must have been and that she didn't really have anyone to help her either.

The Grandparents arrived for shifts, but Nanna and Pop were too devastated by the loss of their son to be of much use to anyone and they had a bit of a strained relationship with Mum anyway. They quickly retreated back to the safety of their home so they could grieve the loss of their only child. Nan and Grandad stayed for four days and Nan forced Mum out of bed and made her behave like a parent – something, apparently, my Nan failed miserably at, according to the grief-stricken wailings of her daughter.

Grandad heated up soup as Nan and Mum argued about responsibility and self-indulgence and selfishness.

"Laura, your children need you."

"I'm your child and I need you but you don't care about that."

"Grow up. You're an adult. I did my job, now it's your turn."

"You think that, don't you. That it was a job. I'm sorry I was such a chore for you ..."

On and on they went.

Through no conscious decision - the neglected daughter became the neglectful mother. The same cycle of want and need continues.

Thinking back on it, the thing I'd never noticed or considered before was the lack of friends. The few they did have drifted in and out but they were awkward and unsure and couldn't really offer much. And we never even saw Mum's brother and his family. That didn't surprise me though.

Nanna and Pop did most of the funeral arrangements, with minimal input from Mum. She was too distraught to deal with details.

After the funeral, we barely saw anyone and we were expected to carry on as usual. The rule seems to be - the funeral's over so now it's time to get back to life. But how do you do that? There's a gaping hole in your world. It really feels like you've had a limb cut off. It takes ages to adjust.

It was so quiet in the house for a long time. We hardly spoke – only when necessary, and every day at five, around the time Dad usually got home, I would go outside, sit with Lucky and cry because I knew he wasn't going to walk through the door. Mum always retreated to her room for about half an hour.

And I know I felt more alone than Donna and Mick did. Dad was my ally. Mum and I never had the best relationship. We just didn't connect. Even though I was her first born, there was something missing between us. I needed Dad. He was the one who made me feel as if I mattered. He stood up for me and protected me if Mum was being too hard.

Days turned into weeks into months and we walked through our lives like disconnected aliens. And I hated that Dad was only ever spoken about in whispers; as if people were afraid to mention him lest we suddenly remember he was gone. We knew he was gone – every second of every day, we knew. It would have been nice if someone had spoken his name out loud and reminisced about him. It would have been even nicer if his life had meant more than his death.

So, no, we didn't deal with Dad's death at the time at all. We merely got through the days and the years, suspended in an inadequately expressed bubble of grief.

Friday 17th
3.28 pm

I still look bad and I feel kinda fragile, but I also feel calmer. Louise has been so awesome. When she got home from work on Tuesday she crawled into my bed and spooned me while I cried for my dad. She remembers when he died but most of the next few years are vague to her. She was dealing with her own loss at the time so it's not surprising she can't recall much.

I got the photo albums out and had a laugh and a cry. Why did everyone take photos from such a great distance in the '60s and '70s? Where are the close-ups? So many photos show plenty of uninteresting backgrounds with specks for people, usually squinting or shading their eyes from the sun. And any shots Grandad took are terrible. He never centred anything and half of us are cut off or out of focus!

There are some bad shots of Dad. At one stage he had an atrocious '70s porn mo and big sidies! Not a good look but it was the norm, so he would have looked sensational. He never even got to the '80s, so no mortifying mullet! He was a good-looking guy. I wonder what he'd look like now? I bet he would have aged well. And I know he'd be an excellent grandfather.

I've made a decision to mention Dad every day from now on. Even if it's just a sentence or a word, I'll talk about him out loud so I can finally express all the unspoken words inside me. Death of a person shouldn't mean death of their memories or of their meaning.

Saturday 18th
10.25am

I've just had a look back over some of my early entries and I feel bad that I called Tina a victim because I can see now, she wasn't. A victim indulges their hurts and never, ever lets them go. They use their wounds to their advantage. They use them to control and manipulate others and as an excuse for bad behaviour. They cry and complain, but they never change.

Tina flowed with her pain and with the releasing of it and she's gone through an amazing transformation. All she needed was some knowledge, some awareness, some nurturing, and some love. She didn't resist what was offered to her. She took it and she worked with it. And she got to the heart of herself. She got back to who she truly is, before she got weighed down by the layers of crap everyone ever dumped on her over her life. She is Tina again. And she looks alive.

I feel sad that I thought mean things about Di too. Di is gentle and sensitive and she deserves to be applauded for that. I'm not surprised I was mean though. My first response to things is often so judgemental and hostile. I'm not a peaceful person. I'm petulant and pouty. I'm disconnected and I'm uncomfortable with people. I want my first response to be love – the way Bernadette's is. She sees the best in everyone.

It was Emily's 12th birthday on Wednesday so we're getting together today to celebrate. Family gatherings push all my buttons but I will try and see only the best. To help with that, Bernadette told me to make the day about Emily, not me. I think I can manage that.

8pm

I took the albums to Mick's and showed Emily and Sarah their real grandfather. Told the girls a few Dad stories and Donna, Mick and I had a laugh about the bad photos. And how everyone wore so much brown back then. Even Mum squealed and cringed at her hair and clothes.

I'm thrilled that Mick and Donna want copies of the photos. No one realised I had all the albums. Forgot to tell anyone I'd snaffled them when I left home. Oops!

I asked Mum a few questions about how Dad was when he was younger and she was happy to talk about him. Even the presence of the Fuhrer didn't see her put a lid on it. She was quite generous to me today. She must have realised something had happened to me during the week firstly, because of the way I looked and, secondly, the photos and questions. She handled the situation well. I'm glad she didn't dismiss me and refuse to engage.

Mum's the only one I can rely on for info now that Nanna and Pop have gone. I wish I'd thought to ask about Dad's life years ago when they were still alive. All his history, and theirs, is now lost.

Liz was an utter bitch a few times to both the girls but I did something positive. I took them aside, gave them hugs and told them that I thought they were wonderful and that I would always look out for them and they could come to me for anything, anytime. I don't have the guts to confront Liz yet so I did what I was capable of. I'm proud of myself for giving them some support. Sometimes an ally is all you need.

No scenes were made. Avoided the Fuhrer and Craig so I didn't feel like committing mass murder and I kept everything upbeat. All in all, a good day.

Sunday 19th
6.47 pm

Dan and I were hanging around like a couple of loose threads so we decided to go to lunch. He said I looked like I needed a good drink and a good feed. We were going to go to the beach but it was too cold so we went to the Willow and Ash. I love that pub. It's so cosy when the fire's roaring. I pretended I was at a ski resort.

I love winter. Probably because I've got a body better suited to big coats and fleecy fabrics than shorts and slip dresses.

Dan was so chatty and funny. He was what Bernadette would call 'attention away from your hurts'. That's anything that keeps you in the present moment and keeps you from dwelling on all the crapola in your life.

He told me about his misspent youth and he asked me lots of questions about mine. We've shared a house for three years and we know next to nothing about each other. I didn't even know he'd been to Europe.

I told him I want to go to Spain and walk the road to Santiago. Ever since I read 'The Pilgrimage' by Paulo Coelho and 'El Camino' by Shirley MacLaine, I've been in love with the idea.

We both ordered fish and chips because it was the only thing on the menu that didn't contain garlic. He hates it too. Aaah, a kindred spirit. I wish someone would open a garlic-free restaurant. It's almost impossible to eat out now because it's in everything. Why? Who decided it was the herb of the century and so had to be used lavishly in every dish ever created? There'll be garlic coffee next!

I downed a few glasses of red and I felt quite giggly at one point. When I started touching Dan's hand every time I came to the end of a sentence, I stopped drinking. A couple more and I would have started touching more than his hand because I was feeling rather horny.

He's so good-looking and now I'm wondering if I fancy him or if I was just in need of some attention? I've confused myself????????????????????

No, I haven't. I do like him, but not like that. He was attentive and I responded to it, that's all. It's natural. He made me feel … nice.

Monday 20th
10.45 pm

Tonight, Bernadette reminded us about the importance of expressing our feelings. She told us that even though it's the first thing we're encouraged to do when we start Feel:Deal:Heal, we somehow 'forget' about it as the weeks go on. We forget because it's not something we've been trained to do. We've always done the opposite, so not expressing feels more natural.

"I'd be willing to bet that no one in this room was ever encouraged to keep on crying. 'Good work on those tears. Keep it up'.

"This is because people tend to make your feelings about them so in order for them to feel more comfortable, they try to shut you down quickly. The biggest mistake we make is we think that by stopping the expression of feelings it somehow eliminates them. 'Stop crying about feeling scared and the fear will just magically disappear.'

"But it doesn't. How can it? All we've done is stop the healing process in its tracks. The fear/shame/guilt/grief/disappointment, etc., just gets stuffed back down ready to erupt another day. Feelings are part and parcel of who we are yet none of us are equipped to deal with them. Everything starts in utero so once we've arrived into the world we should be immediately encouraged to express, express, express. If it was as normal as learning the alphabet then the world we live in would be a dramatically different place indeed."

I'm glad she reminded me because this morning I was thinking that ever since I had that big cry about Dad, I'm fine. Nothing else to work on because everything stemmed from that. Which it didn't, because I remember a lot of painful stuff from when Dad was still alive. Sometimes it feels never-ending and I'm back around to it being too hard to bother with.

I said to Bernadette that I wish I was like one of those people who don't care about feelings and what's happened in the past.

And she said, "What, a person with an addiction or a person who tries to control everything or a person who is so full of anger they can barely interact with someone without wanting to punch them or a person who says to their children, 'This is your fault, you made mummy upset/angry/sad/stressed. You're bad for doing that', or a person who says, 'I beat/raped her because she was asking for it', or a person who lacks the ability to say anything positive or a person who is full of aches, pains and illness or a person who never understands how wonderful meaningful connection can be? Jodie, I'd rather more people were like you – those who realise they're not doing as well as they could, those who are willing to go to the hard places; willing to risk feeling vulnerable and embarrassed, and those who are willing to take responsibility for themselves and the way they behave."

Fair enough when you put it that way, Berns. But it doesn't make the process any easier.

Tuesday 21st
8.09 pm

Last night, Bernadette set us a challenge. "You're all in this group voluntarily and you all knew what you were in for when you signed up, yet most of you still hide and avoid and choose petty things to focus on rather than getting down to the nitty-gritty of why your lives aren't the happy, sunny things you want them to be. On Wednesday, I want you to come to group with a couple of words that describe how you feel the moment you wake up in the morning. I want you to notice your first thoughts."

When I woke up, I felt low. But that's how I feel every morning. My first thought was, 'I'm still tired'. Then my brain realised it was a new day and that I'd have to go through the shower/breakfast/teeth routine, which all seemed like a chore. This was followed by the 'how am I going to fill my day' thought which was followed by the 'you could exercise, you fat cow, and do some writing, you lazy cow' thought which was quickly followed by a groan and a desire to lie in bed all day so I don't have to 'do' anything or 'be' anything. Then I thought, 'you're expected to contribute and participate, it's how the world works'. Then my rebel kicked in. 'Fuck that. I should be allowed to do what I want when I want. It's my life. I don't agree with the way society operates anyway so I'm being true to myself by not participating in the ridiculousness of it'. Then I realised I have a lot of thoughts in the morning. I lay there for a while longer and just before I fell back to sleep, I thought, 'It doesn't matter if I get out of bed or not. No one will notice anyway'.

I asked Louise about her first thoughts. She bounces out of bed because she loves her job and she found that her thoughts kick in, in the shower. "What if I've run out of ideas? What if I can't come up with anything new or fresh? What if they realise I'm not very creative and sack me? What can I wear so I look good for Liam? Is Liam going to run off with Sophia today when he realises she's beautiful and talented and I'm boring and old? Of course he's going to leave me. It's just a matter of when. How can I make sure Liam doesn't leave me?"

Wow! She's a brilliant graphic designer, a chef extraordinaire, she can sew, knit, and crochet. She's fit and healthy and works to maintain her looks. She's funny, well-read, caring, and always looking to improve herself emotionally. If she's boring and old and sackable then I'm really screwed!

We talked about the group again because Bernadette is right. Most of them have been skirting around things for the past few weeks, afraid to get in there and go for the jugular. Louise included. She still hasn't talked about her mum leaving. She said she's getting to it and that I'm just as bad because I haven't even mentioned the Fuhrer.

Arrabella still rocks up stoned even though you're not supposed to indulge in any of your addictions before, during, or after group because addictions are what we form to stop ourselves from feeling.

Heidi hides behind Spirituality and the idea that 'everything happens for a reason', as an excuse to never broach anything deeper than her body's energy systems. She claims she was guided to the group and is waiting to find out why.

Marion puts up with a humourless man who bores her senseless and Gretel thinks sex is the answer to everything.

Di is fixated on women's clothing – as if the only thing to being a woman is what you wear. Eva had her meltdown but it was just the tip of the iceberg. She's still angry and hostile and she's as cold as ice to Di.

Tina's doing well but she's started to express anxiety about her new job because she says they're taking advantage of her and she's finding she's falling back into being a people pleaser. I thought she was all empowered now and this wouldn't happen to her again but Bernadette said this shows Tina where she needs to build her strength. She exercised her 'power' muscle once. To become really strong, it needs to be used. We're all going to get tested by life to see how well we're doing and Tina's changed enough to recognise instantly that she's feeling weak and that she doesn't want to put up with being manipulated, which is what it's all about. She'll scream and cry it out in group and go to work better able to deal with things.

Finn's always doing something to her body. She had hot pink and lime green hair yesterday. It was like a neon sign on her head screaming, 'Look at me'. Then, on the flip side, she goes out of her way to avoid attention! Bernadette calls it the head and tail of the need. One half of Finn is desperate for attention because her sickly brother consumed it all so she never got a chance to shine or express her individuality. Every major moment of her life was quickly overshadowed by him and his needs. She said that if it looked like a hint of attention was going to go her way, he'd suddenly have a turn of some sort so she was promptly forgotten. However, if you fill her need for attention, she goes nervous and teary and cries that she's got nothing to offer anyway so don't bother looking her way. Bloody hell people are complicated. You give them what they want and they don't know what to do with it!

Meredith's a perfect example. She's the biggest talker in the group and Bernadette often has to cut her short otherwise she'd never stop gabbing. She spent half her time crying that she had no one to talk to so she volunteered for Meals on Wheels and now she's crying that all the oldies talk too much!

And Nicole. The most down-trodden of us all. She's scared to death that if she so much as says boo, the earth will stop spinning and everyone will fall off! Apparently, saying 'no' and doing something to suit yourself causes others to leave, become ill, or suffer great pain. Death may even occur, and she wouldn't want to be responsible for that now, would she? You don't have to be a genius to see what shit she was subjected to as a child. After she hung up on the Telemarketer a few weeks ago, she's been afraid that something bad is going to happen.

Lou and I looked at each other and we sighed the sigh of the exhausted.

"The gnawing agony in our gut won't kill us but the suffocation of our fears will," I said. "Seriously, do you want to live like this forever? How hard can it be to feel secure and unafraid? So what if you run out of creative ideas. What's the worst that can happen? You'll get a job in advertising! So what if Liam runs off. What's the worst that can happen? You've survived being left before, you'll survive it again."

"And you," she said, "what's the worst that can happen if you never get published and you have to go back to work? And what's the worst that can happen if you open yourself to love. Real love; real connection. A man the opposite of Olli?"

Wednesday 22nd
10.42 am

"A man the opposite of Olli." Six little words, yet I can't stop thinking about them.

Oliver Conrad Blake. Selfish bastard.

A man the opposite of you would be faithful, attentive, loving, interested in me, honest, and connected. And he'd enjoy having a chat.

On the down-side, he'd prefer big breasts, be lousy in bed and have non-sexy hair. So I'll settle for mostly opposite.

His hair. I loved his hair – all shaggy and dark and glossy. And the sex was always amazing. The lust factor was breathtaking, before the cheating killed it.

I think for a little while he was content. He kind of 'nested' and seemed happy to slow down. The first few years of our marriage were good so, including the engagement, I figure I had him to myself for four years. Although I can't be sure.

When he was all 'nested' out, he just decided that he'd go back to his single man ways and come and go as he pleased and shag anything that moved. He must have remembered he was still married because he did it all in secret so he knew he was being an arsehole.

And I just took it. Too afraid to confront him. Faking ignorance. Happy to have him home whenever he deigned to stay. I felt ill for five years and he aged me about twenty. My insecurity and stupid pride kept me stuck. I didn't want to get divorced. It's embarrassing, it felt too hard and I didn't want to give the Fuhrer the satisfaction. Then Lou and Charlie split so things started to look different.

Olli had been away all weekend "hiking" and when he waltzed back in I was ready to speak, but he beat me to it. Seems he was about a week away from becoming a father so he thought he should go and live with the mother.

I surprised myself because I just said, "Ok then. Thanks for letting me know."

I just couldn't be any more broken by him and I was all cried out. He'd taken me to the lowest point I'd ever been and I was a shell.

He may have been expecting a scene and when I didn't give him one he looked awkward and unsure about what to do next. We stood in silence for ages, looking everywhere except at each other. He finally said, "I'll go and pack."

I grabbed my keys and Cool, drove to Lou's and stayed for a week.

I contacted him a month later to discuss the house and he told me he and Jill had a son – Lucas. His guilt must have kicked in because he apologised for being a bad husband and he felt I deserved compensation, so he gave me the house. And I took it. The bank still owned half of it and I couldn't afford the mortgage on my own. I didn't want to live in it anymore anyway so I sold it for a very healthy profit. He'd told Jill we were only renting so she never knew he had an asset and he just started paying his share of her mortgage. So there he was, still telling big, fat lies.

Three months ago, Brenton hired him to landscape their garden so I know he's now got Lucas, Amy and baby Jasmine. He asked Brenton to say hi.

Thursday 23rd
10.08 am

Another huge night at group. A lot of healing took place. We were told to go to the hard places but we were also told to have a bit of fun with it, if it felt appropriate. If you make light of fear, it dissipates

Bernadette got us to pair up and talk about our waking thoughts. The thing I love about Feel:Deal:Heal is that it doesn't just 'fix' us and send us back out into the world. It also teaches us how to be counsellors at the same time. The idea of pairing up is so we can begin to act as counsellors for each other. We get to put into practise some of the techniques we've been shown.

This time when we paired up, we all went into separate rooms so we wouldn't disturb anyone else with our yelling and crying, or get distracted by theirs.

I went with Marion. We scored Bernadette's bedroom and got comfy on the bed. We faced each other and held hands.

Her first thought was, "I'm hungry."

"Anything else?"

"Nah, just that."

What the hell was I supposed to do with that? How was I supposed to counsel her around being hungry? That's not even an emotion!

Then I remembered one night when Gretel said she was tired and Bernadette asked her, "What are you tired of?" and Gretel was all "Huh?" and Berns said, "Tiredness is a result of holding in feelings." And Eva weighed in with, "Of course it is! Fucking feelings."

So I thought I'd go with that, seeing as Marion wasn't offering up anything else.

"What are you hungry for?"

"At the time, it was breakfast. Right now I could go for a cup of tea and a tasty bit of cobbler. The peach kind, not the shoemaker kind. Although …"

Marion's habit is to use humour to control her emotions and avoid feeling any hurts. She makes everything a joke and her frequent use of laughter stops her from having to reveal her true feelings. Bernadette told me I had to encourage her to break this pattern. If she started being glib, I had to say, "Marion, I welcome your feelings."

I looked into her eyes and said it.

It was the simplest of things to say, and even though Marion knew it was coming, it had a stunning effect.

"No, you don't. No one does. Everyone hates my feelings. Let's just pretend everything is a-ok so we can keep things nice. I was hungry. Big deal. Let's talk about your waking thoughts."

"Marion, I welcome your feelings. Your feelings make life interesting and fun." (*Going opposite of what she believes.*)

"No they don't. My feelings make life messy. They ruin parties. They embarrass people and make them feel bad. They get you locked in your room until you behave. They alienate your husband."

With great delight, I said, "Marion, I want to throw your feelings a party, that's how much I celebrate them. Woo hoo, big party, this Saturday. BYO anger, sadness, fear, husband. We'll invite the media so they can put them on the news for all to see. We'll take them on a world tour. Audiences everywhere will cheer and applaud. We'll release the DVD." (*Being happy and relaxed about her feelings and showing her they are worthy of being expressed; they are valid; they are real; they are welcome. They're not a nuisance or an inconvenience.*)

When someone is paying you good attention and is actually listening and encouraging, the feelings that erupt from nowhere are amazing. Her face fell. She put her head in her hands and started to cry.

I reached for her hands and gently took them in mine. "Look at me," I said. "I'm here for you. Connect with me." (*Break the feeling of being alone.*)

Slowly she lifted her head. She looked at me and sobbed harder. It is very challenging and confronting to look at someone and cry because we are so used to hiding away in shame. It is a powerful method of release.

I encouraged her feelings and held her the way Bernadette had held me. Somewhere inside so many of us is a child that needs to be nurtured. It's never too late to give that level of love.

When she calmed down I asked her again, "What are you hungry for?"

"Honesty."

"Where in your life is there no honesty?"

"Everywhere. My whole life my mother's mantra was, 'Never reveal anything of yourself to anyone because they'll use it against you. If you react to things, then people can pick your weaknesses and hone straight in. Smile through everything so no one can tell where you are vulnerable. Never cause trouble. Keep things nice'. Basically, put up and shut up."

I was more than familiar with that!

"Neither of my parents could bear confrontation so they got walked all over and pretended they didn't mind. They let people treat them badly and talk to them however they wanted and they made a joke of it. But behind closed doors they took out their frustrations on us. They were aggressive, sarcastic and cruel. And if my brothers or I didn't take it in good humour, we had to stand against the wall until we did."

"Pretend I'm your mum. Tell me the truth about something." (*Role playing – good for expressing what you'd love to say, but know you can't or won't.*)

"You've got thick ankles."

I burst out laughing. "Thank you dear daughter. Please tell me more."

"Did you and Dad think you were in the effing KGB with your endless covert shit? The biggest secrets you had were that you were pregnant before you got married, you couldn't stand each other and he had one ball."

I laughed again. "Excellent. Tell me more."

"When I was 16, I stole $10 from your purse, bought some condoms and had sex in your bed. Then I smoked afterwards."

"Fantastic! I appreciate your honesty, daughter. I hope you've put these facts onto the internet so everyone in the world knows." (*Over-exaggerating the enthusiasm for the truth to help take away any fear.*)

That cracked Marion up. She laughed the first real laugh I've heard from her. I knew it was real because it sounded quite different to the laugh she usually does. It was … unaffected. She was sweating too, so I knew the technique was helping her release stuck feelings. For the first time, she wasn't using laughter to mask her feelings, she was using it to release them.

"Anything else?"

"Pretend you're my husband now."

"Wife, I welcome your honesty and your feelings. I am here for you.

Please reveal everything."

"You are so boring I want to cut you up, pop you in a vindaloo and serve you with a pappadam just to make you interesting. With you, sex is the new dull. Fish, chips and sex - I'm sick of all three. I'm sick of assuming the missionary position and I'm sick of you pretending to miss my vag and trying for my bum. If you want to try something new, you could try touching me or listening to me or not shutting me out anytime I show a real emotion. I wouldn't care if we never had sex again. I hate your taste in shoes, I wish you didn't have chest hair, and that you consider calligraphy an extreme sport and beige a loud colour really says it all. I haven't listened to a word you've said for the past decade and I intend not to listen for the next decade either. If I work up the courage, I'm likely to leave you."

She started to cry again. "Now I feel bad for saying those things."

"You can feel whatever you want," I said. "I welcome all your feelings."

"My parents were so effing paranoid. I didn't see the world the way they did so I always felt confused and frustrated and stifled. Being honest got me into trouble and upset everyone so I just gave up. It got too hard to fight against. It was easier to comply."

(*Tell the truth about the situation.*) "That's what we all do – if we can't beat them, we join them. We put our true selves to sleep but, luckily, a part of us stays aware of who we really are and, one day, when we can't deny our true selves anymore, it steps out of the shadows. This is why people do healing work. We suddenly wake up and we realise the nightmare wasn't a dream, it was our real life taking place as we slept-walked through it. We work to get ourselves back in sync so we can live our lives wide awake, instead."

After a few minutes, Marion stopped crying. I bought her attention back to the present moment by having her name five things you'd buy at a supermarket. Then she was ready and able to focus her attention on me.

It's easy to tell if someone isn't ready to give you their full attention. Once, Bernadette asked Gretel to name five things you'd find at the beach. Gretel said, "Sand, water, seaweed, wallpaper, tiles." She started well but her emotions were still not fully expressed so her thinking was muddled. Bernadette gave her more time to release the feelings and she was fine after that.

"Jodie, what was your first thought?"

Because I had so many thoughts, I decided to condense them into one statement. "I can't be bothered doing anything."

"What do you mean?"

"I've got all this time on my hands and I do nothing with it. I have no motivation, I'm uninspired, I barely leave the house, and I don't even care. It's as if I'm numb most of the time. I just go through the motions of existing. Life holds no thrill for me."

I wish I hadn't said numb because she pinched me. And she wasn't gentle about it either. It's a ploy used to demonstrate that you aren't numb and you do feel. A sharp poke works just as well.

I could see she was on the verge of apologising because she was worried she'd hurt me so I said, "Thanks for that. Scratch numb off the list!"

To break a pattern of boredom and lethargy, it's good to be active and perky so Marion said, "With great gusto, I want you to say, 'I'm excited!'"

Unable to muster much enthusiasm, I repeated the words in a dull monotone.

So Marion did it for me. She started jigging around all excited and hyper and she spoke a mile a minute. "I'm so excited. Excited, I tells ya! I can't believe there's so much to do and not enough time to do it. I wish the days were longer. Tomorrow I'm going to climb a mountain, swim a sea, do macramé, start an herb garden, knit a jumper, fly a plane, save the Amazon, save the animals, save the whales. And that's just in the morning. In the afternoon I'm going to learn the piano, jog 5k, protest against everything bad, become a Buddhist, sing on stage, build a boat, renovate my house, cook a five course dinner, cure cancer."

She was so funny and I was marvelling at how fast her brain came up with activities. I started to laugh.

Her smile was huge and she kept her expression and manner delighted and energised.

"And that's just the beginning. On Friday, you're going to skateboard to my house at 5am and I'll give you that day's list of activities."

"I wish," I laughed.

I went quiet so she moved her body in closer to mine and took my hands.

"Can you remember when the feeling first started?"

My brain took me straight to the Doc. "I think it was after my boss died. I took some time off and I never really got going again. It suddenly felt too hard and too meaningless and the less I did, the less I wanted to do.

And it soon became evident that the world didn't miss me. It spun around just fine whether I got out of bed or not."

"Jodie, you can be bothered. You bothered getting dressed. You bothered coming here. You bothered listening to me and helping me. You bothered working on the fact you can't be bothered. I'm glad you're in this group. I would miss you if you weren't here. You have been so valuable to me, especially tonight. Without you, I wouldn't have been able to be honest. You made me feel safe. Thank you."

Such kind words. Such positive feedback. I cried as she held me and melted some of my pain with her warmth.

Friday 24th
3.25 pm

Mum called and asked me to go and visit Nan with her. She always does this because she can't stand to go alone. I notice she doesn't mind my unemployed status when she needs something! I haven't seen Nan since Mother's Day, so I went.

Mum is so weird around Nan. It's always the same - she walks in with an air of tragedy and drama around her hoping that Nan will notice and ask her if she's ok, which she never does. Then Mum spends most of the visit purposely talking to me. It's the only time I get any attention! Nan tuts and sighs because she's being ignored so she just launches into a tirade of negativity about what's wrong with everything.

Today, when she finally had our attention, she told Mum she looked old and tired – which she doesn't, then she asked if she'd put on weight – which clearly she hasn't. Mum hasn't aged or changed an inch in forever. The tension became palpable.

Nan then gushed about how wonderful No. 1 son is because he pops in at least once a fortnight. Big deal. He stops by for 20 minutes, says two words, then nicks off. And none of his lot ever visit. But Nan doesn't see any of that. She only sees where her daughter fails her.

Seems this is how first born daughters are treated in this family – with little or no regard and as if they're inferior to their siblings, particularly the male ones. And I fear I would have done exactly the same. I would have convinced myself I'd be nothing like them; that I would do better. But I wouldn't have been able to escape my programming because I had nothing new to replace it with.

Nan has got small eyes and thin lips. She looks mean. To be honest, I don't think I even like her much. She's miserable and selfish. She never did anything for anyone yet she expects everyone to pander to her needs and fawn all over her. Each time Mum was pregnant it was met with a roll of the eyes and a disapproving sigh. She never said congratulations. I know this from the four days of hell they spent with us after Dad died. I also know it was Grandad who dragged her there. She's just so cold and disconnected. I never remember her babysitting either. Nanna and Pop used to look after us all the time. Really, she probably shouldn't have had children. I get the sense she just did her duty, and then resented every long second of it.

Nan asked if I had a boyfriend yet.

"Don't leave it too much longer. Women need men."

OMG that's exactly what Mum said. What is their obsession with having a man? It's so bloody old-fashioned. I'm sure there's a man out there living a very nice life that he doesn't want ruined by introducing into it a neurotic, depressed woman.

I'm doing men everywhere a favour by leaving them alone at the moment.

Mum was making small talk about Emily's birthday and Nan was obviously peeved about not being invited. "At least your brother took me out on Mother's Day. Nice to know he cares."

By this stage I was staring out the window wondering when we were leaving but I looked at Mum in time to see her jaw clench.

She turned to me and straight out of left field said, "Rob thought you looked really bad on Saturday. He thinks you're unhealthy and that you've indulged yourself long enough. He says you need to get a job. People who don't work aren't much use to anyone. I hope I can tell him you've got a job soon."

I went into shock. I was literally speechless. What the fuck!?

I looked like crap because of the release I'd had in group. I was emotionally drained. I was exhausted. I was fragile.

God, look at me. Justifying myself in my own journal!!!! Fuck that!

All I can think is - Why would she tell me that? Does she enjoy hurting me?

Saturday 25th
10.30 am

At lunch last Sunday, Dan and I made a pact to tell each other a dad fact every Saturday. Dan told me his father loved jigsaw puzzles, and I told him that when my dad danced, he moved only his lower legs in a kind of backward flick motion while the rest of his body swayed side to side. It was so funny to watch.

Dan asked if I wanted to go to the pub tonight. He's got birthday drinks for a work mate. My first response was to say no but all I've got to look forward to is big, fat nothing so I stopped myself and said yes instead. I need some good company to stop me from obsessing about what the Fuhrer said. He will not ruin my life any longer. I'm taking it to Bernadette on Monday and I'm going to scream and swear until I'm empty.

3.10 pm

Lou dragged me out for another mountainous hike. Liam's playing golf today so she won't see him until tonight. We talked about group, of course. We were both quiet on the drive home on Wednesday and too drained to compare notes. We needed space to process our sessions so neither of us had mentioned them yet.

She worked with Arrabella. Her first thought was, "If I get up now, I'd better be really, really quiet."

"I thought she lived alone."

"She does, but old habits die hard. Her loser teenage parents would party half the night and when she got up, if she was noisy or went to them for say, breakfast, they told her to shut up and piss off. She had to be so quiet all the time so as not to disturb them. If she did speak, they would say, 'No one's interested in what you've got to say. Shut up."

"That explains why she's so quiet and her voice trails off."

"Yep. Absolute bastards. Her dad pissed off when she was three and her Mum dumped her at her granny's when she was nine because she met a bloke who didn't want a kid. Granny drank, so she pretty much raised herself. Granny croaked when she was 16 so she's been on her own for the last seven years."

"That is shit. What did you get her to do?"

"First I gave her some desperately needed nurturing. I felt real love for her and I never wanted to let her go. Then I got her to tell me a full story. It took her three goes but she got there. She couldn't think of anything to tell me so I asked her where she buys her clothes and how she chooses them because she has excellent taste. I acted really interested and thrilled and begged her, on my hands and knees, to tell me more. She laughed and then she cried.

"After that I got her to stomp around the room being as noisy as she could and yelling that she wanted her breakfast. Every time she yelled I gave her a hug and told her I loved her and her noisiness. She cried a lot after that. I felt like crying too. I felt so sad for her and the shit she's had to endure.

"I held her and told her she was interesting and fascinating and clever and the more noise she made, the more I loved her. I suggested she get a job as a town crier, a megaphone tester or a spruiker. To help smash the pattern once and for all I told her that the moment she gets out of bed she has to stomp her feet and yell, 'I'm up'."

"Good work."

"Yeah. She responded well to it."

"And what happened with you? You looked really drained "

"I was. I went with 'How can I make sure Liam doesn't leave me?' Arrabella said, 'Chain him to your leg'."

"That's funny."

"I know. I laughed. Then she asked, 'Why do you worry about him leaving?' And, of course, straight away my head made it about my mother."

"All roads ultimately lead to our parents. There's no escaping their impact."

"I felt agitated and I didn't know what to say. Arrabella held me and reminded me she was there and I wasn't alone; that together we could get through anything. It was only feelings. Whatever I was in pain about had already happened and I'd survived it, so I'd survive releasing the feelings.

"I kept thinking – go for the jugular, it's time. But then I worried that Arrabella wouldn't be able to handle it if I had a complete meltdown. In the end, I told her if she needed to, to get Bernadette.

"I started by saying, 'My mother abandoned me', and I just about got that out before I bawled. I don't know if it was because I knew Arrabella understood exactly how that felt, or if I was just relieved to finally say the words out loud, but the grief that rolled through me was overwhelming. It came from as far down as my toes.

"Arrabella cried with me. I knew she was crying for herself but it didn't matter. There was comfort in it. She was so gentle and she kept saying, 'Tell me again what happened'. I ended up repeating 'My mother abandoned me' about 10 times and each time it got a bit easier to say. It really is true that when we express something, it loses its power. It's like that saying, 'The truth will set you free, but first it will piss you off'.

"She was the perfect person to work with. Even though our stuff was similar and it could have been a disaster for both of us, we felt more connected as if, together, we could move on from it. There was another human being in the world who truly understood.

"I went through, 'Please don't go, I'll be good', 'How dare she leave me. I'm her daughter', 'Why didn't she love me? What's wrong with me?', 'Everyone will leave me. I'm too hard to love'.

"Arrabella was fantastic. Through her own grief she nurtured me and loved me. But the best thing she did was get me to say what I wanted to say at the time. I just screamed, 'Don't go', over and over and we both cried so hard. She kept her focus on me though and she just kept saying, 'I'm going. I'm leaving. I can't stay. I won't stay'.

"That was hard to hear because I wanted her to say, 'Ok. I won't go', but not giving me what I was desperate for really tapped into the deepest grief. It was a good tactic. My mum left. I was heart-broken. It can't be sugar-coated. It can't be changed. What can be changed is the effect it has on me. All I can do now is accept love, nurturing and patience until the hurt goes away.

"When I'd calmed down, she said we needed to get a bit of lightness going so we stood up and had a 'weirdest dance move' competition. It took a few moves but we were soon cackling like old ladies. She was doing these really amazing moves and I saw before me a brilliant, lovable woman who deserves to be happy. My guess is, she saw the same in me. I told her she was an amazing counsellor and that she should do what Bernadette does. And I told her she's got the most beautiful hair I've ever seen.

"I feel lighter but inside I still wish my mum hadn't left and I still feel hurt and insecure. Time will heal that though. As Bernadette said, 'When an old wound is opened and cleaned out, it's raw and it needs time to heal.

This time though, it will leave only a tiny scar, the type that fades until it can barely be seen'."

Pain does have a residue – like a ghost image of the actual thing. It can linger long after the 'solid' is gone. Maybe it hangs around to remind us of where we've been and how far we've come. Humans are very resilient. Considering what some of us are put through, we manage to carry on and achieve many wonderful things. By some miracle, we find our way to people who can help us and if we allow it to happen, we can recover our intelligence, zest for life, and natural capacity for love.

I never knew Lou's mum. She left a month or so before we met. She's the reason we met at all because, after the split, Lou's family moved and she ended up at my school. She had it a lot easier than Arrabella though because she's got a brother and sisters and a dad. Logically, her mum didn't abandon her. Her parents got divorced because her mum had an affair. Her father was the better choice of parent because her mother was unstable.

But emotions aren't logical so Lou wouldn't have understood it like that. All she saw was that she'd been abandoned. She was 11. She's allowed to be shocked and confused and feel that way. No one ever explains anything to a child so it's little wonder we make up our own stories that then become our reality. A lifetime of hell could have been avoided if someone had just told her the truth.

And back then, fathers left, not mothers. It was unusual, so people always looked at her with such pity and sorrow. They almost behaved as if she had done something to cause her mother to leave. That just added a layer of shame to the grief.

My dad died a few months after we met. No wonder we cling to each other. We're connected by grief. Besides our families, we have been the only constant in each other's lives since our shit began. I'm glad I've got her. She keeps me going.

Sunday 26th
12.22 pm

Last night at the pub was fun, but it was also a bit uncomfortable. The only person I knew was Dan and I felt like a fish out of water. Everyone was really friendly and they were a fun group. I thought I'd be ok but I felt really out of touch and unable to say anything of any interest. Dan looked out for me but I acted super happy and struck up a few animated conversations just so he didn't feel obligated to spend the whole night by my side.

I learnt a good trick from the Doc – always ask people about themselves and the conversation will never end. If they've travelled – ask if they'd recommend it as a holiday destination. If yes, why? If no, why not? Ask where they'd love to go in the world, and why? Where did they grow up? What did they want to be? What's the most interesting or unusual thing they've done or seen? I was kept busy finding out all about these people so no one got much of a chance to ask me any questions. I'm quite masterful at the art of deflection, especially when I don't feel like revealing anything.

Doing Feel:Deal:Heal expands your thinking and the way you see the world. I'm finding it harder and harder to make small talk about inane things. I like my conversations to be deeper, with more substance. I can pick people's patterns and I know where they are hurting and how it can be healed. I listen for repeat words and phrases – a dead give-away of an issue crying out to be acknowledged and healed. But it's not something you just launch into with a beer guzzling dude. "Hi, I notice you keep saying, 'It's not about the money'. This means it's about nothing but the money. If it wasn't about the money then you'd never mention money. Tell me … what is your earliest memory around money?" Bernadette told us, "If they don't ask, don't tell."

Dan spent half the night chatting up the friend of some bird from work. I think her name's Stacey? I thought for sure he was going to bring her home, but he just took her number. At least he didn't ditch me at the bar and expect me to find my own way home. That's happened to me before, and it sucks.

We got in just after two. I drove because Dan was drunk. Lou and Liam got home from his sister's 40th about five minutes before we arrived so we had coffee and birthday cake. Liam was drunk as well and they were doing macho stuff like underarm farts and chest-beating. A bit more body hair and we could have dropped them at the nearest jungle! Lou was laughing so much she shot coffee out of her nose.

Liam taught us swear words in Spanish, German and Klingon, and Dan played 'Stairway to Heaven' on his air guitar! Lou did her Shirley Bassey and I burp talked. Always the lady!

We wrapped it up about 3.30 and I reckon Liam would have been snoring even before his head hit the pillow.

Monday 27th
10.25 pm

Bernadette asked her usual question, "Does anyone have anything they need to get off their chest?"

I didn't hesitate. I was stirred up good. "I'm fucked off with the Fuhrer."

"You mean your step-father?"

"The Fuhrer is not my father, step or otherwise. He's just a dictator my mother married and I had to endure."

"What happened?"

"He virtually said I was lazy and a waste of space. Not to my face. Oh no. He just got Mum to relay the message. And she wouldn't have defended me. She would have just nodded and said, 'Yes dear, you're so right. I'll let her know'. I've been working since I was 17. I worked for 21 years at the same job. He doesn't know shit about me or my life or ..." My voice cracked. "Why won't he leave me alone?"

I didn't get to scream or swear. I just melted into another river of tears. Bernadette held me like a child again as I sobbed. All the while she kept saying, "I'm sorry he hurt you."

When my sobs turned to sniffles, she stood up and started goose-stepping around the room, arm in a 'Heil Hitler' pose.

In a German accent she said, "I am zee Fuhrer und I am zee dickhead. Jodie, you vill agree zat I am zee dickhead. Agree. Do vat I say. I order you."

"You're a dickhead."

"Zat's right. I am zee dickhead und you vill not forget it. I am also zee smelly pooh pooh head und zee loser. I vill vatch you wiz my beady peepers all of zee time until zey pop out of my head from staring so much. Can you see my peepers popping? Zen you vill carry my peepers around wiz you in a jar so zey can stare und stare und stare.

"You vill go to vork in zee factory until your fingers are vorn to little stubs. You vill make zee little plastic schticks for zee lollipops. If zere are not enough little plastic schticks, the vorld will end. Lollipops need schticks. Wizout schticks, how can ve eat ze lollipops? Ve can't. You vill sleep at zee factory so no one steals the little schticks."

We were in stitches as she marched and rambled and made him look absolutely ridiculous. But best of all - she took away his power.

Tuesday 28th
11.02 am

I slept well and I feel a lot lighter today but the intensity of the anger and hatred I have towards the Fuhrer is still there. Bernadette said I'm likely to feel this way for a while yet. Issues are like onions and each time we deal with an aspect of it, we peel a layer. And those damn onions have lots of layers!

I'm sick of him looking down his nose at me about work. It's none of his fucking business, yet he's made my whole life his business. When it comes down to it, he's kinda fixated on me. That's not natural. I am forever grateful he never laid a hand on me. I don't even want to imagine what that hell must be like.

I haven't worked for two years. In the grand scheme of my life, that's not that long. I wish I was still working because it'd mean the Doc was still alive.

Doc Brown – like the Doc from 'Back to the Future', except a Dentist, not a mad scientist. For three years I rather formally called him Dr. Brown. When the film was released, I immediately changed it to just 'Doc'. In my strange little fantasy world it made me feel connected to Michael J. Fox because I loved him, and that film. I was 20 going on 10!

That man had the patience of Job. Why he didn't fire me in my first month, I'll never know. I'd been in for my check-up and he offered me a job on the spot. I'd never even considered being a dental nurse. I said yes because I'd just left school, had no other prospects, and I could tell the Fuhrer a job just landed in my lap, easy as that! That felt sweet. And I'd be able to leave home. Even sweeter. Except that was soured by the reality I simply couldn't afford it.

Everyone hates the dentist but I always liked going. I liked how clean it smelt and how quiet it always was. And Dad was big on nice teeth. He made sure we brushed twice a day and had 6-monthly check-ups. Doc Brown had been our dentist for 15 years so he'd known Dad. The connection had a nice feel to it.

But I was 17 and a party animal. I smoked and drank and stayed up to the early hours of the morning. I was always tired. There were times when I nodded off holding a sucker in someone's mouth! I was also very unhappy because of the Fuhrer.

The straw that very nearly broke the camel's back happened on a Saturday. I'd been out most of the night and I forgot to set my alarm. At 9.15 the phone rang. It was work wondering where I was. Fuck! I dragged myself up, picked my uniform up off the floor and staggered out the door. I rocked up to work hung over, stinking of stale cigarettes, alcohol, and sweat and wearing last night's make-up. I looked trashed.

The Doc didn't say anything as I sat down. We finished with the patient and I started cleaning up. He closed the surgery door. Here it comes, I thought. A barrage of abuse. Head hung, I stared at the floor. I was too ashamed to look at him.

"I don't understand what's going on with you. You're a good nurse. You're intelligent and funny and all the patients like you. You're skilful. Yet you go out of your way to sabotage yourself. You have got enormous potential and you could achieve anything you set your mind to, but you seem to be on a path of self-destruction. If you don't want to work here, that's fine. But you're a good nurse and a good person. I'd hate to lose you."

He was the first person since my dad to say something nice to me. I'd endured nothing but endless put-downs and bullying. I cried. I couldn't help it. I desperately tried not to, but I couldn't stop it even if I wanted to. He stayed with me and when I pulled myself together, he told me to wash my face, brush my teeth and carry on.

From that day on, I changed. I partied less during the week and got enough sleep. I cared about the job. He encouraged me to study to become a hygienist. He believed in me.

He worried when I got too thin and never, ever said anything when I put all the lost weight back on – which was a continual cycle with me. He knew I was unhappy but I always refused his offers of help. "Really, I'm fine," I'd say. He knew there was no point pushing it. He'd just say, "You know I'm here if you need me." I guess I just didn't know how to accept help or kindness.

The Doc was one of the loveliest men I ever knew. He was generous and kind and intelligent. He would do anything for anyone. All they had to do was ask. He was charitable and humble. When I told him I'd started writing, he bought me a dictionary/thesaurus. That book is one of the best gifts I ever received. He always asked what I was writing and the few times I got published, he bought a copy of the magazine. I promised him I'd finish the many books I'd started.

He was there for my marriage and he supported me through my divorce. A year later, just when I thought my life was on the up again, he was diagnosed with prostate cancer. It spread to his bones and he was gone in six months. He was 62.

It was like losing my father all over again. I was so completely devastated and I kept thinking about how he loved France and red wine and it was his plan to retire to Bordeaux. But he never got the chance. I felt angry that good men die and that dreams go unfulfilled; that our jobs rob us of life and, many times, choice.

After his funeral, I went to bed and I couldn't get up. I was inconsolable. I wish he'd retired at 55 then he could have had seven wonderful years in the wine country. These are the things that life should be about. Not four walls, day in, day out, doing nothing but making enough money to feed and house yourself one week at a time.

For some people, their work is their life. For a person like me, it was something I did to pay my bills. I didn't mind my job because the Doc made it easy to go to. But without him there it held no pull, so I quit. I told myself I'd write full-time instead.

But grief is a thief. It steals from us sense and reason. It robs us of function and self-preservation. It takes a piece of our soul.

I've barely written anything in two years. I should have churned out at least three books by now. I've let myself down big time. But I'm going to cut myself some slack because I see now that I was very badly broken. I'm just now starting to mend.

Wednesday 29th
10.30 pm

Heidi's made peace with the potential disruption to her lower chakras and she's agreed to go out with the meditation dude. I think she said his name's Raven, but that can't be right, can it? Maybe it's Raymond??

Raven/Raymond told Heidi that the lower part of the body needs to be used otherwise the energy of the chakras stagnates. That's clever – using the chakras as an excuse to get laid! Beats the usual pick-up lines that rarely work, so points to the 'R' man for originality.

Arrabella looked really lovely tonight and she spoke up - a lot. And best of all - she wasn't stoned! She sat with Lou and they held hands most of the night. Connection is encouraged because it reminds us we're not alone. She told us that she's getting out of bed and stomping around the house. Her dog and cat were a bit wary at first, but now they couldn't care less. She said she's enjoying making noise.

Bernadette said, "What was that? I couldn't hear you."

Arrabella laughed and shouted, "I'm enjoying being noisy."

When the thrill of making noise wears off, her other hurts will resurface. But as it is with all of us – one day at a time. For now she can just enjoy feeling good.

Bernadette asked us to bring our journals and I shared the last entry about the Doc. Bernadette picked up on the 'I guess I just didn't know how to accept help or kindness' line.

She explained that my inability to accept help or kindness was more common than the cold! It begins when we're stopped from having a feeling. Because no one is willing to allow us to express, we feel alone with our stuff. We put up walls to stop any further feelings from getting out because they're unwelcome and inconvenient. But they also stop anything from getting in. We become prisoners within these walls and we lose the ability to give and receive. We become isolated and unable to be close to people.

Closeness has been a key technique all the way through Feel:Deal:Heal. We're encouraged to hold hands, sit close, hug, make eye contact. We need to do whatever we can to help break our isolation patterns. By being close, it helps reveal the stuff we need to work on.

Like everything else we do in this group, real closeness is very confronting and it can be bloody uncomfortable! It's a terrible thing that we lose the ability to connect. As babies, most of us are so cherished and adored and fussed over. When we cry, we're soothed – predominantly to stop us from crying because 'crying is bad', but at least there's a semblance of care and attention for the feelings. But as time goes on, it all falls away. We're barely touched anymore and there's zero soothing for our crying. We're forced into immediate shut-down. No wonder we're a terribly confused lot.

Gretel is the least comfortable with closeness. She never reaches out to anyone and she makes sure there's a gap between her and the person she's sitting next to. When you hug her, she struggles to hug back. For a woman who has orgies, she's a contradiction in terms!

Bernadette asked her to stand up. She actually looked afraid.

"Why me?"

"I want to be close to you."

"Why?"

"I love you. You're worth being close to."

Gretel scoffed and looked sceptical.

Bernadette took a few steps towards her. Gretel suddenly looked like a cornered animal. She sank back into her seat. Bernadette said, "What stops you from being close to me?"

Gretel blinked furiously. Either she didn't know or she didn't want to know.

"Umm … you might tread on my toes."

"And that would hurt?"

"Yeah."

"So being close might cause you pain?"

Gretel looked irritated. "If you leave yourself open to it, you're going to get hurt. It's as simple as that. I did my big release weeks ago so you should demonstrate this technique with someone else."

She looked at Eva when she said that. Which is a fair call because Eva has got a problem being close as well. I think Berns honed in on Gretel because she's always on about sex and the way in which she indulges in it completely lacks intimacy.

"I want to be close to you."

Gretel snapped. "Well I don't want you to be close to me. Back up."

"I love you. You're worth being close to."

Gretel was sweating and her breathing was heavy.

"Don't bullshit me."

"What stops you from being close to me? Remember, they're just feelings. I'm interested. I care."

Gretel couldn't fight against Bernadette's love. "You'll break my heart."

The grief she had long ago buried and denied, erupted.

Darren, the love of her life, left her at the altar. Before he did that though, he undermined her in every way, shape, and form possible.

Gretel was a traditional girl. She came from a small rural town and had an oppressive religious upbringing. She wanted to be a virgin when she got married.

In 1975, when she was 21, she moved away from home for a job in the city. She'd never had a boyfriend. She was shy and naive. She was full of self-doubt and insecurity from years of being ignored and blamed and unfairly compared to her 'far superior' siblings.

Then along came Darren, the first man ever to show Gretel a hint of attention. She was smitten.

They started going out and she loved and adored him; thrilled that someone loved her too. But he was your hot and cold type. At times, he was affectionate and charming. At others, he was cruel and dismissive. He made her feel as if she was lucky to have him because she was plain and boring. And when the sex issue began, she never knew from one day to the next how he was going to be.

He nagged her to have sex. She told him she had strong feelings about remaining a virgin until she was married, but he kept nagging anyway.

He was always pawing her and trying to convince her it was no big deal. "I won't think you're a slut," he romantically declared. "It's the 70s. Everyone's doing it."

After months of nothing he asked if she'd consider it if they got engaged? "Maybe," she said.

Even with a ring on her finger, Gretel's conditioning was too strong. She begged him to wait. They'd get married quickly and everything would be fine.

"It would be better to do it before the honeymoon, so the honeymoon is fun and not painful," he reasoned.

Still she asked him to be patient.

"I've been patient long enough. If you won't have sex, I'll find someone who will."

What could she do? She loved him. She wanted to keep him. She sucked it up and had sex. It was terrible and awful because he was rough and she was just too guilty to relax and let go.

Worse than that, he started treating her with contempt because he decided he wasn't impressed that she gave it up so easily! His contempt didn't stop him from having further sex with her though.

On the morning of their wedding, as she was getting ready, he popped in and unceremoniously dumped her. His parting words were, "I've been thinking about what my life would look like with you and I've decided it would be dull. You're frigid and I don't want to marry a frigid woman. Men want good sex. You let me down."

And that old thief grief, which we give way too much power to, hit Gretel so fiercely in the chest it knocked her over.

She had a breakdown, got pumped full of 'these will stop your feelings' drugs and lived like a brain-dead zombie for a few years. The psychiatrist she was seeing helped her sort through some stuff and one morning she woke up, decided she was going to look for alternative healing therapies, threw away her cocktail of drugs and set about getting better.

As the fog cleared, she started to feel the sting of her ex's words. I'll show him, she thought. In an extreme move, she became a swinger. Orgies and swinger parties became her main activity. And she took to them like a duck to water. Physically, she indulged every wild and weird fetish, used every toy and accessory and tried every position. Emotionally, she was off-limits. Sex became the only thing she could relate to. It had ruined her life so now it was going to fix it.

As Gretel told her story, Bernadette moved towards her slowly, all the time reassuring her that she loved her and that she was worth being close to. Bernadette sat herself next to Gretel and then encouraged us to move closer to her as well. We formed a circle around her and made non-sexual, loving contact with her body. We connected with the woman, not the object.

We took turns to tell her we didn't want to have sex with her, we'd never want to have sex with her, we just wanted to love her and be close to her. To us, she was a beautiful woman. Gretel could not stop crying.

Afterwards, Gretel admitted to us that she told herself she had come to Feel:Deal:Heal to work on the sadness she felt around not becoming a mother. She would have quite liked to have got married as well. Other than that, she believed she was happy with other areas of her life and that maybe she might look at some childhood stuff, if it came up. Talk about denial with a capital D!

This is how we keep ourselves functioning though. We can only handle so much at any one time. Something inside of us must know that in order to heal, we need the support of others. For any of us to try this stuff on our own, without knowledge and support, would be difficult. It's the connection to the other people who encourage our feelings and make us feel ok about them that really helps us push through the shit and go to the hard places. We see each others patterns and we work to get rid of them so we no longer live our lives through them. We work to become free.

Bernadette achieved in two hours what years of psychiatry and pills hadn't managed to touch. She got Gretel to express the agony she had been too shocked and ashamed to admit and she gave Gretel what no one else ever did – love, compassion, understanding and attention. She re-started her heart.

Thursday 30th
12.02 pm

Last night, as we were walking to our cars, Finn sidled up and asked about the sensitivity she's having in one of her teeth. I forgot that this happens the moment someone learns you know stuff about teeth. I was forever giving boozy advice about oral hygiene. I diagnosed the likely problem as a bit of chipped enamel but recommended she see a dentist for a thorough exam. She seemed happy with that.

Gretel's story got me thinking about sex and the unhealthy attitude people have towards it. It's actually quite frightening. TV and movies are full of sex and it's nearly always dysfunctional. There's a strange obsession with guys losing their virginity and girls keeping theirs. If the girls hold onto their virginity, who exactly will the boys have sex with? Bernadette's right, we do need to ask why sex is seen as being degrading for women?

And the way womanisers are portrayed, especially on sit-coms, is weird. They're always misogynist bachelors who have a sense of entitlement and all they talk about is getting laid and how many women they've had sex with, yet the way they act when they see a gorgeous woman, you'd think they'd never had sex in their life! It's all so infantile. Kind of like young boys seeing a picture of a naked woman for the first time.

And the movie, 'American Pie'. A guy can stick his dick in baked goods and that's comedy. If a woman shoved a banana cake up her twat, that'd be porn. The world has lost the plot.

How the hell did sex take on a life of its own? It's like it broke away from us and formed itself into a living, breathing entity and the more we feed it, the more it grows. Porn is a raging, rabid beast all its own.

It shits me to tears that women aren't allowed the same luxuries as men. We're raised with a completely different psychology. We're trained to deny our sexual urges because if we indulge ourselves the way men are allowed to we get harshly judged and called names, and we're trained to use 'self-respect' and 'sex' together in a sentence. Men aren't. No wonder they can see sex as being only a physical thing – just flesh and bone. They're allowed to. Women are conditioned to attach emotion to everything because we're told that we're the gender with all the feelings and so everything in our lives has to have some kind of emotional context.

Our natural urge for sex and what we're told about it just doesn't correlate. Sex is a part of nature and something we do as a species. Our non-oppressed selves know this. The part of us that has been brainwashed into believing it's sinful, however, overrides nature. In a way, we are constantly fighting against ourselves. No wonder we're confused! The oppression suppresses our natural instinct and we become repressed.

Oppressed, suppressed, repressed. So much pressing!!

If we just accept sex as being as ordinary as brushing our teeth, we'd no longer be obsessed by it and we'd get over our need to sexualise everything. Sex is not dirty, or bad, or wrong. If a person treats it like that then they need to see Bernadette so they can figure out why and get over it!

Friday 1st July
6.30 pm

It was freezing today. Dan had a sickie and Cool curled up on his lap as he dozed in front of the telly. He makes such a fuss of her. I love a man who loves cats. It says a lot about them.

He went out with Stacey last night and didn't get home until this morning. Dan's never on his own for very long. He doesn't maintain a relationship for long though. I think he's a little gun shy after Miranda walked. He told me he and Miranda started going out when they were both 16, got married at 22 and had both boys by 26. By 37, they were divorced. For the past four years he's kept things pretty casual with his girlfriends and if it starts to look serious, he ends it.

Bernadette would soon sort him out and open him up to love again. She'd probably get him to work on the shock of Miranda leaving and when that wall was down, take him through the gazillion feelings. And that would be the tip of his iceberg because he would have to have a shit-load of unacknowledged grief around his dad. It would be impossible not to.

I've talked about Dad every day since I promised I would. Most of the time it's to Cool, but she's a good listener and that's all I want. I'm enjoying talking about him. It gives me a sense of peace.

I can't believe I'm saying this, Journal, but … I'm glad Lou dragged me along to Feel:Deal:Heal! Even though the first four weeks were agony. One of the first things Bernadette said was if any of us wanted to quit the group, could we speak to her about it first. She predicted we'd be uncomfortable and afraid and that we'd prefer doing time in a Russian labour camp to sitting in her counselling room and having a feeling.

And she wasn't wrong! She did promise the resistance wouldn't last and to give it a fair go because the results would be well worth it. I remember, I sat as stiff as a board, arms folded across my chest, unresponsive. I wouldn't look at anyone and I spoke only when I had to. I felt nervous and self-conscious a lot of the time.

It really helped that Bernadette never pushed me. She was patient and gentle and when she sensed a crack in my wall, she knew it was time to coax me out of my reverie. And it was hard. I can't deny that. It was hard to feel my grief. It still is.

I regret that it took me four weeks to pick you up, Journal. I wish I'd started writing in you straight away so I'd have a record of those first weeks. I can't remember much that happened. Except a lot of crying by Tina and Di!

Lou found out about Bernadette from a woman she met at a yoga retreat. She told Lou that Feel:Deal:Heal changed her life and that she urged everyone she came across to do it. I have a feeling I'll be doing the same.

Saturday 2nd
12.49 pm

Dan dad fact: His name was Patrick Daniel Rogers. Everyone called him Pat. He loved black liquorice.

My dad fact: His name was Christopher Winters and he read film star autobiographies. He liked that his surname was the same as the actress Shelley Winters and that she was a best friend of Marilyn Monroe.

"I always thought Winters was your married name," Dan said.

"Nah, I never changed it. I like my name. Hey, your surname's the same as Ginger Rogers."

"Oh yeah."

"And you know what they say about Ginger – she did everything Fred Astaire did except backwards and in high heels!"

"It's the same as Buck Rogers too. You know – from the 25th Century. I don't think he danced though."

"Pity, it might have improved the show."

We talked about movies for awhile. I asked what his favourite was. He doesn't really have one, but he prefers sci-fi and comedy. He was surprised when I told him my favourite film was 'Fight Club'.

"It's so brilliant what it says about materialism and consumerism and corporate greed and how were are all just so numb and controlled and oppressed. We fall for whatever propaganda we're fed. We do everything by rote. We're on permanent auto-pilot. Our lives are the same thing, over and over and over again and we all follow the pack. Whatever's popular and 'now' – we run with it. As Jack says, 'Everything is a copy of a copy of a copy'. We're half alive and we've forgotten how to really live and really feel. Jack just wants to feel something and he has to go to great extremes to get through his layers of conditioning and armour."

Dan said, "So it's not just about a bunch of guys beating each other up? I think I need to watch it again."

I laughed. "Well, it's in the DVD rack. Right next to 'Elvira, Mistress of the Dark'."

Dan's eyes lit up. "I love Elvira. We have got to have a movie night."

"Whenever you're free, pencil me in."

"Cool."

Sunday 3rd
5.44 pm

I caught up with Donna. She's still not pregnant. She thinks it's because she's 36. I think it's because her eggs are repulsed by Craig's sperm. But that's just my non-medical take on it!

It's an interesting phrase, 'I want a baby'. Why don't people say, 'It's my desire to create a human being so I can share the joys of life and all the wonders and beauty the planet has to offer. I want this new human to experience tastes and smells and textures. I want them to exert their individuality and bring their uniqueness to a world that needs it. I want to create new life to keep hope alive'.

Nope, everyone just says, 'I want a baby'. To me, it's like saying, 'I want a car'.

Donna wishes she'd started trying on her honeymoon instead of letting Craig talk her into waiting. Six years later and she's having trouble. They say if you just relax and stop being anxious about getting pregnant, it will happen. I hope it happens for her soon. She'd be a great mum. I just pray she won't let Craig be a controlling dad who takes over his child's life. That is no fun at all for the new human.

I often wonder about parents. I imagine they start out thinking they'll let their child be an individual who will fully live its own life, but somewhere along the way that gets forgotten and so many kids are forced into living an extension of their parents lives and fulfilling their parents wishes. Be this, do that. Control, control, control. Kids are subjected to the fears of their parents and their lives are restricted because of it. Do we ever really know exactly who we are and what we're capable of?

And how does a parent go from the birth of their child being the happiest day of their life, to yelling and abusing that child at the supermarket? What happens?

Old, buried, unexpressed feelings happen, that's what. Kids push all our buttons so those long ignored feelings sneak on through, hoping they'll get some attention so they can be resolved and released once and for all. But for that to happen, people need to be aware of what they do and pay attention to what they say so they can get the vital clues as to what needs healing.

And, most importantly, they then need to do the healing work.

Monday 4th
11 pm

Gretel came in quite distressed tonight. Over the past couple of days she's started feeling a deep sense of shame and remorse about her sex life.

Bernadette explained this was normal. Her original oppression around sex was bound to come back up now that her armour has been pierced.

"When people don't get the chance to express their hurts, they tend to go to extremes of behaviour. The 'all or nothing' pattern. With release, we eventually find our way to the functional middle ground. This is what Gretel is now working towards. She'll then be able to make a clear, non-distressed choice about sex. She might carry on as she has been, or she might form a more intimate relationship. Whatever she chooses, she'll choose from a place of empowerment."

One of the F:D:H techniques used to help someone release crap from their head and body is to say the opposite of what they're feeling. Gretel was feeling remorse and shame so Bernadette ever so lovingly said, "I'm proud of you."

Gretel started crying. "What for? I'm disgusting."

"Why?"

"Because of the things I've done. I feel so dirty."

"You had consensual sex with consenting adults. Is that right?"

"Yes, but the things we did and the things we used …" She shuddered and sobs racked her body.

Bernadette held her and soothed her in her gentle, loving way.

"So it was interesting consensual sex?"

Gretel's shiny eyes looked up at Bernadette and at first it looked like she was going to sob again, then her face relaxed just a hint.

"That's one way of putting it."

"Did you use garden gnomes?"

"Garden gnomes? No!"

"Jodie's used gnomes. Haven't you?" Bernadette nodded for me to play along.

Casual as you like I said, "Gnomes, flower pots, shrubs. And I know that Louise has used tinsel. It was Christmas though, so she was just being festive."

"Yeah, and it gave me tinsellitis!" Lou laughed.

"I've swung from a chandelier," Di enthusiastically added. I'm thinking that's not far from the truth!

Marion brought the house down with, "Three-headed dildo. Whatevs! I once used a sock puppet that had a lisp!"

Running with the theme, the others each shouted out something that would take a lot of imagination to use. We had: a piano accordion, an egg whisk, a cat toy, a staple gun, a packet of frozen peas, a pair of slippers, and a plank of wood!

Marion said, "Plank of wood! Have you been screwing my husband?"

Gretel was laughing and crying at the same time. But her distress was clearly reduced. We all acted so casual, as if using bizarre stuff for sex was no big deal.

This is one of the first things we're taught: not to react in a shocked or surprised way at anything anyone says. We're to remain relaxed and neutral and unworried - 'At the altar, in my wedding dress, I suddenly got my period. Blood gushed everywhere and everyone saw it'. - No gasping, cringing, empathising. Their stuff is not about us and how we'd feel. It's about them and how they felt. If we react, then we've made a judgement call and doing that will shut a person down. They won't feel safe enough to release their feelings.

Some of the best techniques are the one's where things are kept light and funny, as if there's no drama. It really just dispels the fear and shame. It's a good technique to use after the person has been given a chance to release some of the heavier feelings, like grief. I think the lesson in that is the less drama we make of everything, the easier life becomes.

It's so interesting to watch Bernadette work. She never tried to tell Gretel she shouldn't feel the way she feels. She acknowledged and accepted her feelings as being real – which they are. She didn't agree or disagree with anything she said. She was just, 'Yep, you feel like crap. Let's work on that'.

Bernadette said all Gretel can do now is continue to work on her feelings of shame and remorse until she clears them. Express, express, express.

I've just noticed 'express' is ex press as in 'no more press'. So no more depress, suppress, repress, oppress. Interesting!

Tuesday 5th
1.09 pm

Guess what, Journal? I sat down this morning and wrote two pages of my book. A miracle, I know! It's been so long since I've looked at it, I've forgotten what I had planned for the story. And of course I don't have any notes. I figure if I just start writing, it will flow and whatever ends up on the page is meant to be there. I will make a promise to try and write at least a page a day. That's not unreasonable.

Mum has cropped up in my head again. I was thinking about how she struggles with Nan and resents her for being the way she is, and it occurred to me that they are exactly alike. Mum never baby sits Em and Sarah and once, when I asked her if she could cat sit for a week so Olli and I could go on holiday, she said she didn't think so.

Her reason, "I might have plans."

"Might? Do you or don't you?"

"I'm not sure but I need to be free to carry them out if they happen."

Thanks for nothing! She's so selfish. The only pain she sees is her own and she doesn't mind letting you know if you've hurt her. She goes all victim-y and says, "You've really upset me." However, if she hurts your feelings and you let her know, she's all, "You're too sensitive. I've said nothing wrong. Toughen up."

Grrr, mother. Grrr.

Mick, Donna and I have a terrible rescue pattern when it comes to her. After Dad died, she was hyper-fragile. Every little thing got on her tits and her favourite saying was, "I can't cope. If you kids don't start behaving, I don't know what I'll do."

We were frightened for our lives. Would she leave us? Would she kill herself? Either way, it wasn't good. We shushed and hushed each other. We shut each other down. We dared not express our feelings in case they upset her. We did everything we possibly could to accommodate her and her needs. And we still do it today. If she shows a hint of distress, we panic and set about fixing it.

This is exactly how Mick is with Liz. He keeps her happy. He placates her. He takes on all the responsibility in case it all becomes too much for her and she can't cope. It's a pity he couldn't break free of his patterns and marry a woman who treated him as an equal, who respected his kindness and sense of humour, and who looked after him anytime he might need it. Damn unexpressed feelings!

Donna's the same. Craig's needs come first. As long as he's happy, then everything runs smoothly. She goes out of her way to please him, as well. And he rarely appreciates it. He criticizes a lot and her efforts are ok, but she could have done better. He refers to her as 'she' as well, which absolutely infuriates me. Her name is Donna. Fucking use it! If Donna stopped trying, their marriage would shatter into a million pieces in a second.

I wasn't any better. I put up with a loveless cheat who I clung to for fear

I'd die without him. At the time, it felt real. Everything we're told we are becomes a self-fulfilling prophecy. The Fuhrer was always letting me know I was unlovable. I believed it easily enough because Mum had never really liked me, so it must be true. But I had been well-loved by my father for 12 years so a small part of me knew that I wasn't a complete write-off. Pity the loved part didn't find its voice a lot sooner.

The worst thing is, I know I'm rescuing Mum, and I bloody resent it. I'm an adult. If she leaves, I will survive. If she can't cope, I will survive. If she takes to her bed, I will survive.

But I'm stuck in a pattern from the past when I relied on her for my survival. It doesn't matter that we didn't get on very well, she was still my mother and my lifeline. I just have to get my brain to comprehend the truth of the situation, that I am an independent, financially secure adult who can sustain herself.

I'm going to write that on a piece of paper and carry it around with me so every time I forget, and I will, I can remind myself. Saying the opposite of how we feel is a great way to interrupt a pattern. Coupled with releasing the hurt feelings that set the pattern up in the first place, it's a winning combo. The pattern gets all huffy because it loses its power and it dissipates into the ethers, never to be seen again.

I don't know if F:D:H would be any good for Mum because endlessly indulging your hurt self is not encouraged. The techniques are in place to heal our hurts and break the patterns of behaviour that don't serve us. 'Yeah, you're sad. We're all sad but that doesn't mean you should drag out your shit just for the attention'. If you find you need constant attention, then that's addressed. There's nowhere to hide in F:D:H. Whichever pattern is playing is the pattern you work on.

Wednesday 6th
10.25 pm

Gretel was much better tonight. She looked rested and was quite bubbly. She sat close to Nicole and held her hand. I bet she feels about 30kgs lighter after the week she's had. Feelings have a literal weight.

The 'R' man's name is Raven! During a meditation he saw a raven, took it to be his animal totem and promptly changed his name. I'm glad he didn't see a dik-dik or a pink fairy armadillo. That'd be awkward if the cops pulled him over and asked his name! I always think of all the John Smith's of the world booking hotel rooms. I bet no one ever believes that's their name.

Finn revealed that her name is actually Cassie. She calls herself Finn because her favourite book as a child was Huckleberry Finn. We also found out Di's male name is Mitchell. He chose Diana to pay homage to Princess Di.

Eva rolled her eyes when Di told us that. Not everyone saw it, and luckily Di didn't, but Bernadette's feelings radar honed straight in. That woman is like a frickin' clairvoyant when it comes to our stuff. She knows us better than we know us!

"We are all intelligent, happy, capable people," she said. "The patterns of behaviour we have formed as a result of being hurt make us come across as being unhappy, vague, irritated, angry, scared, hostile, confused. We are not our patterns. Our patterns are separate from us. When we release all our hurts, we won't cease to exist but our patterns will.

"We are so used to hearing and saying negative things about ourselves so what we're going to do is praise ourselves. I want each of you to stand in the middle here and say as many nice things about yourself as you can. Start each thing with, 'I value …' For example, 'I value that I am a loving person'. Any volunteers for first?"

As if! Is she crazy? She knew no one would put their hand up so she chose Eva. Eva dragged herself up and she had instant sweat.

Eva looked at the floor, at the ceiling, at the walls. She didn't say anything. Bernadette stood in front of her. "Look at me, Eva. Good. Can you praise yourself?"

Eva shrugged. She didn't look at all well and she was trying to swallow but it looked like her mouth had gone dry.

"It's ok. I'll praise you first. I value your sensitivity. I value your patience. I value your beauty. I value that you have a soft, shapely, feminine body. I value your womanliness."

That hit the spot. Eva's red, sweaty face collapsed and her bulk was reduced to child-like proportions again.

Through the tears and the rage and the shouting and the hot sweat, we learned that Eva's parents had two girls, so they wanted a boy. They even had his name picked out – Ethan Henry. They hadn't bothered with a girl's name so when Eva arrived it was most inconvenient! The nurses ended up naming her.

However, the small issue of incorrect anatomy wasn't going to get in the way of the folks having their boy.

Eva was quite a girly-girl and she wanted to be exactly like her sisters. She wanted to wear pretty dresses and play with dolls. She wanted to host tea parties and wear jewellery and lipstick. She wanted long hair.

But she was dressed in masculine clothes, forced to have short hair and was encouraged to do 'boy' things. If she cried and said she didn't like her hair or clothes, she was told, "You look ridiculous in a dress. You're not pretty like your sisters. You're not petite like them. You're big and strong. Toughen up and stop being a sissy."

She was little. She had no power. It was no use fighting because all it got her was a pile of insults about how unattractive and ungrateful she was.

She was picked on at school for looking like a boy. She got into a lot of fights. Just for acceptance, she played sport and hung out with the boys. She went through puberty and ended up with a great set of boobs and curvy hips. She had a really hot bod but she hid it under baggy clothes. She looked shapeless and continued to be treated like one of the boys. She liked guys but never got asked out. She was always passed over for the pretty girls. Everyone assumed she was a lesbian.

She left school at 17 and got a job as a forklift driver. At 26, she met her loser hubby and it wasn't much of a courtship. They shared a love of drinking at the pub and that was pretty much it. When they started going out, she attempted to feminise herself by growing her hair and wearing more fitted clothes. She thought she'd feel like a princess, but she just felt awkward.

When they got married, she wore her first dress and even though she was slim, she felt so big and unwieldy, she had a miserable day. She felt ugly in her make-up and her hair irritated her so much she actually ripped a lump of it out.

Once married, she had to take on the female role and she didn't know how. She felt stressed and unsupported. The hubby would say, "You're the woman. You're supposed to know what to do." But she didn't. He was unsympathetic and no help. "I'm not gonna do it. It's your job."

She cut her hair, went back to her familiar clothes and started to put on weight. She was too far out of her comfort zone. Her unhappiness and anger escalated to the point where she was crying or yelling every day. She felt out of control. She got bigger and bigger and her hubby told her she looked like a truck-driving lumberjack.

When he walked out a few weeks ago, they'd been married for two and a half years.

It's little wonder Eva can't stand Di. He's an actual man and he's more feminine than she is. Seeing Di would put Eva in a permanent state of irrational feelings; feelings that are overwhelming and out of proportion. If Di giggles, the rest of us delight in it. Whereas Eva gets irritated and looks as if she wants to kill her. It's a giggle, but to Eva it's nails down a blackboard. Di reminds Eva of what she was denied and it would be so painful. To add insult to injury, her horrible hubby did a runner with the type of woman Eva is on the inside. So cruel.

Bernadette got Eva to say, "I am female. I always have been. I always will be." She struggled with it but she got it out.

"Ok, let's reclaim our power." With no warning, Bernadette started to sing, "I am woman, hear me roar …" She got us up on our feet and we started slow but before long we were dancing and singing like we were at a karaoke night for unashamed feminists! We were having a ball and Meredith had this funny quaver in her voice which cracked us up. Bernadette was a full-on rock star and her passion was so infectious. Eva stood like a statue at first but Bernadette soon got her moving. She shook her ample booty and she had some seriously good moves. The dancing loosened her up and her face looked really happy and relaxed. She surrendered herself to the moment.

Thursday 7th
9.38 am

On the way home last night, Lou cracked it. "If Eva's stupid husband prefers someone who looks like Di, why the fuck did he marry her in the first place?"

"Who knows? Why do any of us marry the people we do? We're all screwed up. Maybe he had some gay thing going on and he sorted through it. Eva had served her purpose so he moved on."

"And how fucked were her parents? Look at the enormous damage they caused. All Eva wanted was a dress, some curls and a doll. The simplest of things. What an absolute waste of 30 years."

"In all reasonableness, how could they have not known they were being completely psychotic?" I said.

"Did they think, 'We created her so we can do whatever we want'?"

"Selfish fuckers made it all about what they wanted and never once considered what Eva wanted."

"It's not just the clothing/hair thing, it's all the other stuff as well – feeling like you're a big mistake, being bullied, no friends, no boyfriends, terrible job. I feel overwhelmed for her."

"Me too. How good's Bernadette though? She wrenched every last tear and drop of sweat from Eva and then she got her laughing. That woman is a gift."

"Do you think that when you sort out a big thing, a lot of the other stuff falls away with it?" Lou asked.

"Yeah, I think. I reckon that's happened to me."

"I kinda feel that too."

"I hope that happened for Eva and I hope she finds her way."

"I hope she grows her hair, loses 30kgs and buys a dress."

"And a doll."

Friday 8th
2.58 pm

I hardly know myself! In the last couple of days I've written five more pages. I'm on a roll. Woo hoo! I also remember my plot but now I'm thinking it's lame so I might have to rethink it. Not long before I stopped writing it, I spent half a page describing the agony of lemon juice on a paper cut! I must have been struggling for ideas that day!

I will officially note in you, dear Journal, that I am proud of myself for getting up at 9.30, performing my ablutions, writing for two hours, then going on an hour walk.

I will also note that it is my intention to do this every day. With potentially many more hours spent writing.

My brain has just said, 'Yeah right. You'll do it for a day or so and then go back to being a sloth'.

Shut up brain! You're not the boss of me.

Yes, I am.

I'm going to put my iPod on so I don't have to listen to you anymore. Ha! Now who da boss!

Saturday 9th
11.36 am

Dan dad fact: When Dan was seven, his dad took him to the zoo. After they'd walked around for a while, they stopped in front of the lion enclosure. His dad looked as sad as the lions. "I've brought you here to show you that zoos are wrong," he said. "People have no right to imprison these beautiful creatures; to rip them away from their homes and deny them their freedom. It's exactly like being in jail. Never let yourself be caged like this. It's no way to live." (So much subtext!)

My dad fact: When he was 18 and stumbling home drunk from the pub, he stopped for a rest and fell asleep in someone's front garden. In the morning, the family found him, took him in and gave him breakfast!

Obviously my dad wasn't as deep as Dan's!

Dan got up especially to tell me his dad fact, then he went straight back to bed. He had another late night/early morning. Half his luck!

Dinner's at Brenton and Emma's tonight. I love going there. Emma has such good taste. Their house feels so inviting and comfy – all soft and plush and cocoon-y. And it always smells gorgeous.

Before Emma came along, Brenton was a lost soul. When Meg walked out, we thought he'd never recover. He loved and adored her beyond measure and although he loves Emma, I can see the difference in how he is with her compared to how he was with Meg. We are capable of loving again but it's true that the first cut is the deepest and I don't think we can love with that same level of purity or intensity. We develop an edge of wariness.

Emma's a decade younger than B so that makes her … 32. They met at parent/teacher night when she was Toby's teacher. They've been married three years and they're trying to get pregnant. Brenton's got Toby and Tilly but he's keen for a couple more.

It'd be good being a teacher. All those holidays every year. Maybe I should look into it??

Why would you do that, Jodie? You're a writer, remember!!!!

Oh, yeah. (There needs to be an emoticon for 'sheepish'.)

I went to help Lou with the cheese platter but she'd already done it. Bless her cotton socks. Liam's coming tonight. I'm beginning to feel like a third wheel. I'll be the only single there.

I am determined to be on my best behaviour. I will not be reactive. I will not be the evening's entertainment.

I'm going to dab a drop of orange oil behind my ears. It's good for joyful communication.

Sunday 10th
9.45 am

Except for coming to the realisation that if one of our dinner party's was filmed it would be more banal than Big Brother, last night went fine.

We arrived, and Brenton immediately showed us Olli's handy work. He'd landscaped both the front and back. I can't give any landscape-y descriptions except to say that, aesthetically, his designs were colourful and beautifully realised. He's still as talented as he ever was.

Liam was warmly welcomed and everyone bombarded him with questions. Rusty and Alice weren't there. They're on a Mediterranean cruise, lucky bastards.

There was a hint of tension between me and Lennie so I made an effort to be relaxed and friendly – thanks to my orange oil and its built in joyfulness!

"Look, Lennie, I don't want you to think you have to watch what you say around me. But know that if I don't like it, I will say something. It's only fair that I get to defend myself."

"You know I'm only joking about stuff, Jodes. I don't mean nothin' by it."

In his deluded way, he would think that's true. This is the same lack of accountability that causes parents to fuck up with their children.

It seemed quieter without Alice. She's always good for a bit of gossip and she makes me laugh. When you have a history with someone, you can speak in half sentences and key words that set off a flood of memories. I love that. And you don't have to force yourself to think of things to talk about. Everything just flows. I think I missed her because Lou was looking out for Liam and without her to fall back on, I noticed that I didn't have much to say and, really, I wasn't all that interested in what was being said. It was a lot of kids, work, and sports talk. All of which are foreign to me.

As usual, the food was amazing. Penny did the main. It was a gorgeous vegan thing. The only ingredient I recognised was chick peas. If ever I don't have Lou to rely on to do our share of the food, I'm going to be royally screwed. The best I can offer is something pre-packaged and an apologetic smile.

As the night wore on and the alcohol kicked in, lips got looser and voices got louder. Except Lennie's. He was the designated driver so he was forced to stay sober. He's a lot less obnoxious with only lemonade in him. He looked bored out of his head most of the night.

There was barely any sex talk, no marked sexism, and no one got picked on. So nothing for me to get fired up about! It was so nice to arrive home without a knot of fury in my stomach and indigestion. I slept like a log.

Monday 11th
10.45 pm

Because Eva ended up taking up all the class time last Wednesday, we all had to take our turn praising ourselves tonight, and only a few of us got away without crying. It is so hard to say something genuinely nice about yourself without being flippant about it. It's especially hard when you have to say it while looking into someone's eyes. Appreciation for ourselves shouldn't be that bloody challenging. But it is! I think it's because we're effectively saying things we do believe about ourselves - that we do rock, we are awesome, we're way special - but we struggle to admit it because we've been hurt or belittled or abused — 'go away, you're not funny', 'shut up, you're not smart', 'don't bother, you suck at sport', 'get lost, you're ugly'. And no doubt, if we were ever proud of ourselves, we got accused of being conceited and inevitably knocked down a peg or two.

To praise ourselves is to admit our goodness and we don't know how to do it without hearing the echoes of the past and feeling its sting. Bernadette was the only one of us who was truly comfortable saying good stuff about herself. It was actually nice to see. I admire her.

With great discomfort and a lot of deep breaths, I managed: I value my intelligence and humour. Then I was relieved that my ragged brain found something I could say with absolute confidence – I value my deep and abiding love for animals and nature.

Tuesday 12th
6.52 pm

Heidi was ready to share last night. She's said all along that she was guided to Bernadette for a reason she wasn't yet aware of and that it would reveal itself when the time was right. I guess the stars aligned last night.

She went out with Raven and it went ok, but she felt a deep mistrust for him so she couldn't fully relax. He was lovely all night and he obviously thought things had gone well because he made a move on her. She refused his advances and told him she'd call him if she wanted to go out again.

The thing is, she actually really likes him and she'd love it if they were in a relationship. He's spiritual and vegan and he's got a lovely serenity about him. She's even found herself thinking that she'd like to have sex with him. Which is a bloody big deal for Heidi. She's never had a boyfriend to speak of and she doesn't want to be alone anymore. She wants to find out why she felt so uncomfortable.

The first question Bernadette asked was, "What was your relationship with your father like?"

"I didn't have a father."

"Why not?"

"My mum got pregnant when she was 18 and he, the guy who did it, didn't want to know her after that."

"So you were raised by a young, single mum?"

"Yeah."

"Did she ever talk about your father?"

"Not really. I think she hated him for dumping her. And when she told her parents, they were furious and they made her leave home. She really struggled for a few years until her parents came back into her life and started helping us out."

"Do you have a good relationship with your mum?"

"I did, but she died just over five years ago when I was 19. She was 38. She had ovarian cancer. I'm not surprised, considering the way she was treated. Cancer is caused by longstanding hurt, grief and resentment eating away at you. Her ovaries, which are tied in with the energy of the sacral chakra, were the affected organ because she felt so used up by the guy who got her pregnant and then was completely abandoned by him and her parents."

"How do you know she felt used up?"

"She always used to say to me that I need to be on my guard because men will use you up and throw you away. They only want one thing from you so not to trust them, no matter what they say. She warned me not to give them the chance to hurt me."

Bernadette gave Heidi a 'right there, you've answered your own question' look, but Heidi wasn't getting it.

"Heidi, all your mother ever exposed you to was warnings about men and how they can't be trusted. Then she died young of something that you believe was caused by her having been hurt. No wonder you mistrust Raven and can't relax with him."

Heidi actually seemed vague! "Do you think so?"

"I do."

She looked upset. "I can't believe I didn't figure that out. It's so obvious."

"When you say it out loud it is, and when you connect your mother's words to an actual event in your life you can see how her words, thoughts and feelings have had a very profound influence on you."

Heidi suddenly burst into tears. "I can't believe I'm so stupid. Why did I not see this before? Why would the Universe guide me here when I already knew the answer? It doesn't make sense. It's so obvious."

"Heidi, what's obvious? First thought."

"It's obvious I'm stupid."

"Who called you stupid?"

No one called her stupid. She just decided she was when she wasn't able to cure her mum's cancer.

"I was stupid and useless. I just stared at my mum for nine months as she got sicker and sicker. I can't remember speaking or even moving. If I hadn't been so stupid, I would have researched things like alternative healing methods, anti-cancer diets, yoga, meditation, healing workshops.

Louise Hay cured herself of cancer. My mum could have worked on the emotional trauma that caused her cancer and she could have healed herself too. I can't believe I didn't help her."

"Did you know about any of these things when your mum was sick?"

Heidi shook her head and fat tears spilled down her cheeks.

"You were 18 when your mum became very ill. You hold the surreal idea that you didn't move for nine months. That's not possible. Tell me what you did do to help her."

Heidi did everything. She became the parent and her mother, the child. She nursed her, nurtured her, fed her, bathed her, took her to appointments. They moved in with her grandparents because they had no money and, together, the three of them devoted themselves to doing everything they could to make her mother comfortable.

"I tried to save her. I wanted to save her so much … but I didn't get the proper information. Why didn't I know …"

Bernadette held Heidi's face. "Look at all the things you did, every day, for nine months. When did you have any time to research anything?"

"That doesn't matter. I should have known."

"When did you have time, in those nine months, to research an ideology that you didn't even know existed until a couple of years ago?"

"I should …"

"When did you have the time or the energy?"

Heidi sagged in Bernadette's arms and cried.

"Heidi, it's not your fault your mother got sick. It's not your fault she died. It's not your fault you didn't know about other healing methods. You were 18. You were in shock and deep grief. You did the best you could with the knowledge you had. You made your mother's last months on this earth, comfortable and loving. You couldn't have done any more."

"Is that true? Is that really true?"

"It's true."

"But it is my fault she got sick. If she hadn't got pregnant …"

Bernadette looked deep into Heidi's eyes. "We can't know the whys and wherefores of a soul's journey, but what I do know is that your mother would have been so grateful for you. You showed her real, unconditional love. You were her greatest lesson – that love exists, and she learned it well. Without you, she would never have known it. For her, you were a gift from the Universe."

Wednesday 13th
1.05 pm

Bernadette is so accepting of everyone's beliefs. When she spoke to Heidi, she used words that Heidi could relate to and would offer real meaning. She made Heidi's beliefs relevant. I'm always so impressed by how loving she is. Maybe she's my greatest lesson – proof for my cynical head and wary heart that real love exists and not every human is a scourge.

About a year after her mother died, Heidi was in a second-hand bookshop and 'You Can Heal Your Life' sprang out at her. That book was the start of her spiritual journey. She went to the library and borrowed 'A Beginner's Guide to Spiritual Stuff and Alternative Healing', followed by every new-age book she could get her hands on. She learnt about the body's energy systems and how illness manifests. She studied acupuncture, massage, aromatherapy, crystal healing, got attuned to Reiki I & II, and at the moment she's studying naturopathy. She also did a vegan cooking course. She literally found her calling and she went for it.

In a few weeks, she's going to start a Feel:Deal:Heal course to learn the techniques in greater detail so she can include them as part of her healing repertoire. She's realised its importance in helping us release the stuck energy from our bodies. She and Arrabella are going to study with Bernadette, which is so awesome.

A part of Heidi still believes that if she'd known all this stuff before her mum got sick, she would have been able to save her. But I don't think we can work backwards like that. Each event occurred so the next one could. Heidi would call it her soul's journey. Everything happens exactly as it should, in the perfect time and space. A lot of the time it doesn't feel that way, but apparently everything is working in perfect order.

Speaking of perfect order, I did my three W's – woke, wrote and walked. Good for me! Now I'm off to the shops to get a birthday pressie for Mick.

4.30 pm

I bloody hate shopping! While I was out I thought I might buy some new jeans or something. Big mistake! I tried on two pairs, got depressed by the fact they didn't fit properly – tight legs, no bum room, loose waist - and the change room mirrors made me look four foot high and eight foot across. You'd think they'd make better mirrors. It's like hairdresser mirrors. They should be banned as well! Or else they need Hollywood lighting so you only see yourself in soft, flattering light.

Hating my body with a passion and wishing I was long and lean, I sulked my way around the centre, managed to buy Mick a book and a couple of DVDs, and to ease my pain, I bought myself baggy tracky daks, flannelette PJs and fluffy slippers.

Fucking shit body. It's the bane of my life!

Thursday 14th
2.09 pm

Last night I asked Bernadette, "Can we yell at the people we're pissed off with? Can we confront them?"

"That's why you come here, so you don't have to. You do it by proxy. The people you want to yell at probably won't be able to hear you anyway. They'd get defensive and shut down. Most of them don't have a clue they've hurt you. And if they do know it, they'd be in denial about it. If there's something wrong with you, they reason, it's because you're difficult or strange or you always were a bit odd. They'd never admit it's because they hurt you. By releasing the feelings here, at least you know you're heard and understood, and considered to be perfectly normal."

"Sometimes I just don't want to be that polite about it. I want to hurt them as much as they've hurt me. Why shouldn't I be allowed to?"

"You are allowed to, but is that who you are?"

I sighed. "I don't know. Sometimes. Maybe."

"Who do you want to hurt?"

"The Fuhrer. I hate him."

"Let's do it then. Pretend I'm him. Hurt away."

I stood there. Now that I had permission, I didn't know what to say.

"You're a spiteful bastard," Bernadette started for me.

"Yeah ... and fuck off and Leave. Me. The. Fuck. Alone. I don't know who the fuck you think you are but to me, you are nothing. You have been nothing but mean and nasty and hateful towards me ever since we met. Why did you have to be so fucking miserable? You didn't have to make everything so hard. I missed my dad ..."

And the tears just sprang from nowhere. I didn't stop though. I cry yelled, which looks a lot like hysteria.

"I missed my dad and you could have made it easier. But you didn't. Why? Why did you hate me? Do you have any idea how hard you made my life? Do you have any idea how much I hate myself because you told me I was fat and unlovable? Are you pleased with yourself? Are you glad that you managed to destroy a young girl? Does it make you feel good? Do you feel successful? Was it your life's ambition to intimidate a child? When you're on your deathbed will you look back and say, 'I'm so glad I fucked up Jodie. What a great achievement'?

"I feel so sorry for you that you don't have any love in your heart. How fucking sad are you? How much of a waste is your life? You are a lonely, cold, spiteful man who could have had a family. You would never have replaced my dad … but that didn't mean I didn't need one. It would have been nice to feel protected and cared about. I might have let you in."

The grief rolled up through my body like a tidal wave. I was all snot and sweat and tears like the first time I cried all over Bernadette. But god it felt good to say all that. I've been holding that shit for years.

Bernadette held me and then she pretended to be the Fuhrer. "I'm sorry I let you down," she whispered. "I didn't know any better. Someone hurt me too. I didn't know what I had. I'm so very sorry I hurt you."

It's really amazing how much pain the word 'sorry' can dissipate. Even though it's not coming from the source who needs to say it, it's still very powerful because I know that, in her heart, Bernadette is sorry on his behalf.

I'm a bit blocked and puffy today, but not half as bad as I have been previously. I feel tired, but not to the point of exhaustion. Nurtured myself in a nice, warm bubble bath. It felt cosy. And I'm wearing my new PJs and slippers. They're cosy too.

They might become my writing uniform. I love loose and comfortable.

Friday 15th
3.35 pm

As I pulled on my baggy tracky's and prepared to go on my walk, I thought about my body. My horrible, horrible body. In F:D:H, I have avoided it like the plague. I worry that the feelings that come up will be so awful, I won't be able to get beyond them. It literally feels that hard and that dramatic because I have to live with my body every single second of my life so I know I have to learn to accept it and reconcile my feelings for it. I can't just rant and rave and it'll magically go away. No, it will still be here, taunting me with its odd shape and cellulite.

I don't know what to do. Ignore it, and pretend I'm just a head. Or deal with it and then go back to pretending I'm just a head!

It sucks because our physical self is the thing we're judged on. It's the thing that other people see. They can't see our hidden talents or interests, our brilliance for cooking or music or words or science. They can't see the love in our heart for family, friends and nature. They can't see our childhood or any of our experiences or who we are or where we've been. All they see is how we look and what we're wearing.

We're scrutinized for wrinkles, lines, blemishes. Have we had Botox or surgery or lipo? Are our boobs and lips real? Have we been chemically peeled? The focus on our physical body is beyond ridiculous and it's limiting because we're reduced to the sum of our hair and make-up.

I often wonder if I would have become dysfunctional around my body if the Fuhrer had never picked on me. It's hard to say. Up until that point, I don't recall giving it any thought. Mum bought all my clothes and she prepared all my food. I must have looked ok because she never made any negative comments about it.

I possibly would have become obsessed by it though because of the way we're bombarded with body image and who's thin and who's not. Magazines can't wait to show unflattering shots of female celebrities and discuss their weight gain and tut tut it saying how unhealthy it is. In the very next edition, they show unflattering shots of all the celebs who are worryingly thin and tut tut it saying they're promoting unrealistic body images. Too fat, too thin. Either way, they're screwed. I notice they never put fat male celebrities all over the magazines and shame them. What is this fixation with women? It's strange and worrying.

I know women have always been judged on their physical appearance but did this ongoing and relentless obsession with it begin after the sexual revolution? Were the ruling patriarchy worried we were getting too big for our boots so figured out how to undermine us and keep us insecure and apologetic? How ever it all came about, it clearly shows that women are very easily manipulated. That's scary.

The '80s were a particularly bad time. I think that's when all the eating disorders began. Even Princess Diana had bulimia. I often did aerobics twice a day and ate once a day. I'd binge and starve in a never-ending cycle. I went on every fad diet and I was so dehydrated, I'm surprised I didn't turn to dust! God knows what damage I've done to my body. My bones could crumble at any moment.

When the Fuhrer decided I was fat, Mum must have looked at me for the first time since Dad died, because she agreed. I've looked at photos and I can see that I was overweight when I was 13. After Dad died, I comfort ate. We weren't allowed to express anything so I stuffed my feelings down with food – especially lollies and chocolates. I still comfort eat now. It's a hard habit to break. If Alice is depressed, she goes to the gym! Wish I'd developed that pattern.

Mum put me on my very first diet and I lost weight. Didn't change the Fuhrer's attitude towards me though. I was still thick-set and that was most unfortunate because, "That will never change." And because I was still full of unexpressed feelings, and the Fuhrer was adding to my distress every day, I put the weight back on. So began the yo-yo. During puberty I took on my permanent shape – small boobs, thin torso, fat arse, fat legs. What a fucking nightmare.

I used to envy those gorgeous girls with their boobs and lean legs. They'd pop on a little black dress that ended mid-thigh and they'd dance the night away, happy to be alive. I'd wear long jackets with shoulder pads, which hid my ill-fitting pants. I just drank and smoked to feel happy. I was pretty though. I'll give myself that. I found a hair cut that suited me and I made the most of my face.

But I was never happy with my body - fat or thin. I was unhappy the whole time I was dieting because it was one big head-fuck. Measure this. Avoid that. Don't you dare have that. And if I 'cheated' and had something 'forbidden', I'd abuse myself with, 'You're pathetic'. You're a fat bitch'. 'No one will love you'. 'You're not eating tomorrow because of that and you can exercise all day'.

Then, one day, I'd suddenly find myself thin. Happy that I'd achieved my goal, I'd be on a high for about a week then the stress and worry would kick in - how was I going to maintain the weight loss? If I keep doing what I'm doing, I'll get even thinner, which was always tempting, but if I introduce extra things into my diet, I'll get fat again. All I knew how to do was lose weight and then put it back on. I never learned how to maintain.

The stress of keeping the weight off was a bigger head-fuck that losing it. My brain was never, ever at peace. My body consumed all my waking thoughts. And that is so utterly exhausting it has the potential to cause an actual mental breakdown.

I'd look in the mirror and all I'd ever see was my odd shape – boobless, bony upper with thick, ugly legs and protruding butt. At times I was a size eight but, in my head, I'd achieved nothing because I'd just become a smaller version of the same horrible shape. It's not like I ever got a set of fabulous legs or a high, tight bum, because I didn't. Consequently, I still couldn't wear a little black dress.

Shopping for clothes was always hard, no matter what size I was. Dresses never fit properly. Too big up top. Too small down below. I had to go for A-line styles which made me look shorter and thicker and about a hundred years old. Might as well have just bought myself a set of bowls and gone down to my local green! Jeans just about fit on the legs but were always too big on the waist so I had to wear a belt. I loved the high-waisted, baggy pants in the '80s. They were the only things I could wear with ease.

When I stopped going out, I stopped shopping all together. I wore a uniform for work and at home it didn't matter. I took to fleecy tracky daks like a duck to water and I never looked back. I'd think about dressing nicely but then I'd think, why bother, I still look like crap. This thought occurred at every size.

I've got one pair of jeans which are at least five years old and I pray for cold weather if I have to go out because I've got plenty of long, baggy tops to help cover my bum and thighs. I've worn those jeans to every dinner party, family gathering and pub date for the last three years.

Summer is hell for me. I expand in the heat and I feel like I'm broiling like a lobster. My thighs rub together because of their blob shape so wearing dresses and skirts can be uncomfortable. Shorts are a definite no-no. Three-quarter pants are my best option but I need to find ones that have an elasticised or tie waist. I've got one pair of those as well.

When I walk, my bum wobbles up and down, but not in a sexy, jiggly way. In a boombada, boombada way. I wish J-Lo had been a sensation when I was a teen. I might have felt less embarrassed about how far my bum sticks out. Mind you, her butt is tight and cellulite-free. Mine is not!

I often wonder - if my body obsession had been of my own making would I have gotten over it by now? It's hard to say. But the Fuhrer planted seeds of self-loathing, and those fuckers are perennials! He made me feel like crap and I may have felt that anyway, but it would have been self-inflicted crap which, I think, has a completely different psychology.

In my occasional rational moments, a small part of me does know that, in reality – I'm neither fat nor thin. I'm a funny kind of in-between but as far as I'm concerned, my body is ugly. Olli was forever trying to get me into lingerie. I never succumbed because I couldn't bear the way I looked. Lace top stockings and bustiers emphasised my misshapen flaws and made me feel desperately self-conscious. Oddly enough, I always felt sexier naked.

And now I'm older, I'm flabbier. My body doesn't bounce back like it used to. For the past few years, I've been consistently about 10kgs too heavy and most of that resides in my arse and thighs. I'm thankful my body seems to have a stop point. It settles into this size and shape and, if I don't force it, it hardly changes. But I bloody hate how it looks. Grrr. I've never been more than 15kgs overweight. It might not seem a lot, but 15kgs is as hard to lose as a 100 because it comes off slower and requires a lot of work to get it moving. And it's just enough weight to make someone my height and shape look chunky. A 5'5" pear is not exactly the stuff of catwalks!

I used to think that if I had a decent set of boobs to balance out my bottom half, I wouldn't have made such a fuss. In my head I imagine that I look like one of those thick-ankled, thunder-thighed, uptight women from a Marx Brothers film who ends up being ridiculed and covered in pie. I'm the comic relief and I always wanted to be the willowy leading lady.

Lou says I suffer from body dysmorphia. The fact I can shop off the rack and I'm a size 10 – 14, which is average, should give me a clue that I have a very distorted view of myself. She's probably right because even after I've lost weight, I can never comprehend the difference in my body. Photos tell a different story and I look at myself and can't believe that's me because I look thin. All I know is that I've never felt thin. Maybe that's the problem.

Sigh. I don't know where to begin on this issue. It feels too big.

Saturday 16th
12.24 pm

Dan dad fact: Pat was an engineer but when his mother died of a heart attack at only 58, he left his high paying job and got an apprenticeship as a pastry chef. It was the job he had always wanted, but was 'talked out of' as a teenager. Dan was 11.

My dad fact: He was a great supporter of the arts. He loved the cinema, theatre, musicals, and concerts. He had an eclectic taste in music – from jazz to opera to pop. He loved it all. Because of Dad, I'm familiar with actors and musos from every era.

When Lou and I were shopping this morning, there was a guy in a wheelchair making his way around the supermarket. For all the complaints I have about my body, I am grateful it's healthy and it's 100% functional. I do know it could be worse. But everything is relative. We all live in our insular little worlds where our issues, which are petty to someone else, are big to us.

We all have a point from which we start our desire for a thing. Someone in a wheelchair would love to be able to walk. They wouldn't give a toss about the size and shape of their thighs. For me, I'm starting my level of desire from a completely different place. My legs work just fine, so I'd love to improve on that and have them be slender, firm and tanned. I know I'm lucky I'm not disabled, but that good fortune doesn't just make the dysfunction disappear. I wish it did.

7.30 pm

Lou and Liam came with me to Mick's birthday. Mick and Donna were so excited to see Lou because they haven't seen her in ages. Lou made Mick his favourite fruit and nut biscuits, which he was stoked to get. It's Lou's secret recipe and she makes him a batch every Christmas. He eats them all in one day and complains when they're gone. Getting a mid-year fix was like manna. Especially 38 of them. Heaven in a cellophane wrap!

Mum and the Fuhrer gushed all over Lou and Liam. Such was their gushing, Liam could be fooled into believing they are the greatest people on the planet. Liz behaved herself a bit more than usual too because of the extra company. At least the girls got a day off from being yelled at.

The Fuhrer asked me directly if I had a job yet. I thought he might because he always talks to me if there's any non-family present. Tries to make it look as if we're one big happy family! I'd prepared my response.

"No. I don't need to work. I'm quite wealthy because I have savings from my 21 years as a dental professional and I made an enormous profit from the sale of my home."

Mother was most unimpressed!

The Fuhrer tried to one up me. "With all that money, you could dress better."

"I dressed down so you wouldn't feel alone. I'm considerate like that."

That shut him up.

We purposely ignored each other after that. Just the way I like it. Lunch was good and everyone was chatty. Having Lou and Liam there gave everyone a different focus so there were new things to talk about.

Liz brought out the cake and we sang happy birthday. Em and Sarah were allowed to have a sliver. I used to think Liz was so mean but for the first time today I felt glad that she won't let her girls go through the hell of being overweight sugar addicts. In the long run, she's doing the right thing. I know the girls will be very glad of their nice, healthy bodies. I won't buy them lollies and stuff anymore. Using the girls to undermine Liz is really immature.

As we scoffed down our cake and coffee, Donna was telling us about a guy from work who was thinking about starting his own on-line shop selling the stuff he makes himself, like dream catchers, runes, inspirational wall hangings, aromatherapy candles, that type of thing.

The Fuhrer looked straight at me. "So he'd work as a bank teller, a craftsman, and a salesman. One person with three jobs. That's inspiring. And here's you Jodie, you won't even get one job." He actually sighed and shook his head.

I knew he'd been biding his time since my last remark, so I was prepared as well. I fixed him with a steely stare. "Tell me, Rob, why are you so fixated on what I do or don't do? Honestly mother, don't you think it's odd the way your husband has concerned himself with me since I was thirteen? I'd almost suggest he has a unnatural fascination for me."

If it was a scene from a movie, the only sound would have been crickets chirping. She said nothing. He said nothing. Liz looked a mix of shocked and impressed. Craig looked nervous. He actually went pale! Lou and Liam looked at each other, then their shoes. Donna and Mick both spoke at once. Always the rescuers and peacemakers.

"This is great cake, Liz. What is it?" from Donna.

"Would anyone like anything else to eat or drink?" from Mick.

The cake was a vanilla and raspberry something and, no thanks, everyone was fine.

For a man who doesn't mind controlling, Craig obviously doesn't like witnessing confrontation. Spilling his words out, he asked if anyone had seen 'The Princess Bride'. Yep, we'd all seen it at least 15 years ago. He and Donna got it on DVD the other night and it was the first time he'd seen it and wasn't it excellent and so funny and how's that scene where they're trying not to drink the poison. So good. They also watched 'The Lost Boys'. Another oldie, but so good. They were thinking of getting 'Flatliners' and 'Throw Momma From the Train' next. Yep, we assured him, they're both excellent too.

Craig really got the ball rolling on films, so we chatted about our favourites and all the ones Craig just had to see. The tension was sort of dispersed and all subsequent conversation was non-threatening.

Mercifully, home time rolled around and Mum didn't say goodbye to me. Oh well. Let her stew.

On the way home, Lou laughed and said she couldn't believe I'd said that.

"I wanted to say he had a perverse fascination but I thought that could be taken the wrong way and I didn't want Mum to think anything too yuk. But it had to be said. He needs to leave me alone and he needs to know I'm not scared of him anymore and that I don't give a tinker's cuss what he thinks."

"Tinker's cuss, hey," said Liam. "Monty Python fan?"

"Geez Liam, it's only an expression. I didn't expect this kind of Spanish Inquisition."

He laughed. "Noooooobody expects the Spanish Inquisition. Our chief weapon …"

Sunday 17th
4.30 pm

Mick rang me this morning to see if I was ok. Bless him. He couldn't believe what I'd said to the Fuhrer but he was so glad I'd said it.

"That guy's been an arsehole to you forever. Good on ya for standing up for yourself for once. Liz is glad too."

Liz! Bet she wouldn't be so glad if I stood up to her.

"Thanks Mickey. I'm trying not to put up with any more crap. You, me and Donna were treated pretty badly sometimes and I hate that we still let it happen. We're good people and we deserve to be treated accordingly."

"Yeah, we do. We did it pretty tough for a while there. It's good we've got each other."

"I am thankful every day for you and Donna."

"I'm thankful too. And tell Lou – I'm out of biscuits."

Donna rang a bit later. "Are you ok?"

"Couldn't be better. What I said was long overdue."

"I know. He's a tool. I just can't believe you said it, and Craig was amazed you finally had a go at him. Mum's pissed off. She asked me if you were on drugs. She said, 'Why would she speak to him like that. He didn't say anything to provoke such a tirade'."

Typical Mum. Support the abuser. "Tirade! Please. And she's always pissed off with me so this really doesn't make much difference. I gave them both something to think about. I doubt they will though. She's probably hoping you'll tell me all this and I'll feel bad so I'll ring, full of guilt and remorse, and make everything ok again. But not this time. I'm allowed to stand up for myself. If he can say whatever the hell he wants, so can I. I'm not responsible for her reaction. All she can do is have her feelings. Same as me."

"Are you like this because of the course you're doing?"

"Yep. I'm finding my power."

"Wow. It must be a good course."

"It is, and although it's been tough sometimes, it's been worth every tear. And let me tell ya, there's been a lot of them!"

It's so nice to know that Mick and Donna support me and that they don't think I've done anything wrong. That means the world to me. And even Liz and Craig have got my back! They aren't blind to the Fuhrer. They just do what we all do – keep things nice.

Monday 18th
10.30 pm

I told Bernadette what had happened with the Fuhrer. She was ecstatic. She got everyone up on their feet to give me a standing ovation. I laughed and laughed. It feels pretty good to get a round of applause; like you're something special. Now I know how singers and actors feel. It could become addictive.

Bernadette went around the room and asked us to sum up what we wanted from the people around us when we were children. Some of our answers were: To be loved, wanted, seen, heard, appreciated, respected, supported, to have the freedom to make our own choices, to be accepted for who we are, to feel safe and secure, to feel happy.

Bernadette then asked us, what do we want now – as adults. And the answers were exactly the same.

"What you have just discovered are unfulfilled needs. These are needs we had as children that were never met. Because of their own hurts, our parents and caregivers weren't able to give us unconditional love and attention. Not getting what we need leaves us with a sense of unfulfilled longing - as if something was, and still is, missing from our lives. Unfulfilled needs are also things we hope for, wish for, and are waiting for. Another clue to our needs is indicated if ever we ever find ourselves saying, 'You always …' or 'You never …'. Like – 'You always ignore everything I say'. 'You never do anything for me'. 'You always put yourself first'. 'You never give me compliments'.

"These needs often cause us to compromise ourselves just so we can attempt to fill them. For instance, the person who has a need to be appreciated might spend all their time doing stuff for other people, often to their own detriment. And they don't do it because they're altruistic, they do it so someone will say thank you and tell them they're valuable and generous. The problem is, they hear the words, but they don't sink in. The need, ultimately, goes unfulfilled so the cycle of needing to be appreciated continues. It's a vicious circle.

"There are moments in our lives, of course, when we are getting exactly what we need. We start a new relationship and feel loved. We have a baby, and feel happy. We assert our independence and feel in control of our choices. But once the honeymoon period is over, we revert back to feeling lost and empty and unsure.

"This is because the need is like a bird trapped in a cage. It calls out to us, we feed it a little, but we can never set it free. It's trapped because the cage is locked and someone else holds the key.

"What we need to do is bust open the cage and release the bird. In other words, we have to give up the need - give up the need to be loved, wanted, seen, heard, etc. To give up a need often feels like giving up hope and it can be painful. We tell ourselves, 'If I just hang in there long enough, I know my father will approve of me'. But it never happens. And it's never going to happen. Especially not in the way you want it to.

"People rarely understand that they've hurt you. They behaved a particular way. You reacted a particular way. There's no way they could predict how you were going to feel. You wanted your mother to hug and adore you. She didn't. You hoped every day it would happen. It didn't. You felt so hurt and unloved and unwanted because of it. Yet she believed she was doing the right thing because it would toughen you up and prepare you for a cruel world. However, to you, it meant only rejection. You just weren't lovable. Consequently, there is often a lot of grief attached to an unfulfilled need.

"We work to accept that the need can't be filled. Once healed, we'll see through clear eyes and we'll suddenly notice all the places in our lives where the need is actually being met all the time. And it will sink in. The perpetual cycle of 'trying, getting, failing to see' will be broken."

We paired up and spread ourselves around the house again. I went with Nicole. We chose to go to the kitchen because Nicole wanted a glass of water.

Of her many unfulfilled needs, Nicole chose to work on her need to be appreciated.

Inside of Nicole is a very confused and frustrated child. She was a good girl. She followed orders. She went out of her way to be helpful. She took charge of her younger brothers and kept them in line so her parents needn't feel 'stressed' by them. She was a top student and a great organiser. A model, dutiful daughter. But it all went completely unacknowledged. Nothing she did ever earned her any praise and any attempts for attention were met with, "You're very selfish. It's not always about you, you know."

That's because it was all about her father. He was the centre of the household and everything revolved around him. Moods were matched to his. Conversation was dictated by him. If he wanted quiet, he got it. If he wanted a party, he got it. The TV was his. You ate what he ate, whether you liked it or not. You spoke only when spoken to.

Her mother's rule was that you look after your husband first and children second because your children eventually leave. What she didn't bank on was that the husband would actually leave first, so she was left with three neglected children and no understanding of why her husband walked out. She'd done everything for him. Where had she gone wrong? She didn't remember saying 'no', but maybe she did? Did she not do enough? Wait, maybe it wasn't her fault. Maybe it was the children. Did they do something to upset their father?

Then her mother remembered. Nicole had refused to go on an assigned family day out because she had a project due and she didn't have the time. Well, there's your problem right there. That would most certainly have caused her husband to leave. So her mother took it upon herself to make it clear that Nicole was responsible for their broken home.

Nicole worked twice as hard at everything to make up for the terrible thing she'd caused. Whenever Nicole got wore down and it looked like she might rebel, her mother would become unwell. "I was always so strong until your father left, then I just suddenly got so weak."

So as to avoid any further distress to her mother or anyone else in the world, Nicole became an over-achiever who took on every task going. She never asks for help. She handles everything seamlessly so, for all the world to see, she is highly efficient, in control, and doing well. But inside she's screaming and slowly drowning.

At home, her husband is happy to let her do everything. He set high expectations and insists she meet them. Her sons follow their father's lead. At work, she's PA to a demanding CEO. She runs the joint and he gets the top dollars and all the credit.

Nicole is an intelligent super woman yet she's a slave and a pushover. All because she has a need to be appreciated. Those unfulfilled needs have a mighty powerful influence on our behaviour, that's for sure.

I said, "I want you to give up the need to be appreciated."

When she told her story, Nicole looked sad. Now her face flashed anger. "Why should I? I've worked hard my whole life. I've done everything anyone ever asked of me, and more. I deserve some thanks for that. I deserve someone to say, 'Nicole, you've done amazing things. And you did it all yourself, against the odds. Well done'."

Bernadette warned us that we'd all have a thousand and one reasons why it's a stupid idea to give up the need. We've invested our whole lives trying to get this one thing, why the hell would we abandon it now? It just doesn't make sense.

"Nicole, just say to me, 'I will give up the need'."

She drummed her fingers on the kitchen table. "No. I shouldn't have to."

I took her hands in mine and I gently persisted. "I will give up the need."

"How come I'm the one who has to make the sacrifice here? How come my mother or husband or boss can get away with never having to appreciate me? I've earned the appreciation and I've sacrificed enough."

"I will give up the need."

"Bullshit. They should appreciate me."

"I'm really sorry Nicole, but it's never going to happen. Your mother is never going to appreciate you."

"She might, if I ask her."

"It's never going to happen."

Nicole squeezed my hands and the tears fell. "It's bullshit. Such bullshit. It's not that hard to say well done or thank you or it's not your fault or you're a wonderful daughter …"

Nicole's cried a few times but what suddenly erupted was her 'all the way down in her toes' grief. As she sobbed and spluttered, she spoke, but it was mostly incoherent so I only caught odd words. I managed to get that she was furious that she had to give up wanting to be appreciated. She was furious she had to compromise, yet again. She was furious she even had an unfulfilled need to be appreciated. If her parents had done a better job …

Her grief was so deep and I was watching her thinking, shit, I have to do this next.

I nurtured and loved her broken child and I said I was so sorry that no one had ever told her how wonderful she is and how clever and creative and intelligent. I told her I appreciated that she was a brilliant daughter, a hard worker and a wonderful wife and mother. And through it all, I told her the hard truth that no matter how much she wanted it, no matter how much she needed it, her mother was never going to appreciate her. It was never going to happen.

As her crying subsided, I switched to the other technique of 'over-filling' the need. I started to appreciate every single centimetre of her. "I appreciate every strand of hair on your head. I appreciate the shape of your head. I appreciate that little freckle above your left eyebrow. I appreciate the shape of your nostrils. I appreciate your ear lobes. I appreciate …"

The act of appreciating minute details made her laugh. She laughed a lot when I appreciated the perfect concave of her armpits.

It's a big thing to bust open that bird cage and encourage the bird to go free. There is a definite sense of loss about it. But we know this before we begin and Bernadette prepares us well so we understand that we'll feel fragile for a while.

I brought Nicole's attention back to the present moment by asking her to name five sports you play with a ball, and then it was my turn.

To be continued ... gotta get some shut eye.

Tuesday 19th
8.45 am

I've just read what I wrote last night and I'm in awe of the fact that a few simple words can cause a person to cry a river. I don't think it's the words, necessarily, that set us off though. I think it's being aware that someone is close to us, they're interested in us, they're paying us 100% of their attention, they really care about our stories, they want us to be the best we can be. They see us as the good people we are and not the broken, frightened people we present ourselves as. They touch our heart and our heart has no choice but to respond. In half an hour they give us, in a very concentrated dose, what we needed when we were little. The child within is grateful that, finally, someone is listening and someone cares.

Nicole smiled at me. She'd put some balm on her lips so they were moist and shiny. Her lips always used to look dry but she's taken to moisturising them. For some reason, dry lips annoy me. She's got nice teeth, too. I studied her face for a moment. She looked a bit tired from crying, but her eyes looked really clear. She asked me what unfulfilled need I was giving up.

"My need to be supported. My mum never stood up for me or defended me."

Before the attention got turned to me, I'd been thinking that I was just gonna agree with Nicole and say, "Yep, I give up the need." Easy as that.

So she says, "Jodie, I want you to give up your need to be supported."

Suddenly, I couldn't speak! What the hell? My head started thinking the exact same things Nicole had just expressed. It was protesting. It was pissed off. It was indignant. I wasn't expecting that! It came from nowhere.

"Ummm …"

"You don't have to give it up right this second. Can you just make a decision to give it up?"

No, I bloody well can't! Shit. This was not going as planned. I was determined not to say the same things Nicole had just said. I would give up the need with no drama and no problem. But I literally couldn't.

I looked into Nicole's loving eyes and I said, "If I give up this need then I'm saying that I accept the fact my mother never stood up for me. I don't like how that feels. I feel so let down by her. Aren't mothers supposed to protect their children? If we can't rely on our parents to look out for us – who do we have? No one. It feels so lonely …"

The word lonely made my heart skip, and I just wept. I remembered how hollow I felt after Dad died and how desperately alone I was when I was married and, when the Doc died, how grief-stricken I was that the last person who cared for me like a daughter was now gone. But mostly I remembered how Mum just switched back off when she married the Fuhrer.

After Dad died, she reverted to a child-like state. She relied heavily on me and Mick to take responsibility and behave like adults. She changed towards me. Instead of being distant, she pulled me in close and made me her rock. I felt so grateful that, for the first time in my life, we were connected. I nurtured her and I realise now I didn't get much back, but it didn't matter at the time. It felt nice. I had a mother who wanted me. I was there for her anytime she needed me. I put aside my own grief to accommodate hers. I tended to her every need.

Then she met the Fuhrer, and in a whirlwind they were married. In 10 months I went from being a mere presence to being the be all and end all then back to being a mere presence again. But a part of me really believed we had finally established a relationship and that it would continue to grow.

Not so. This I learned when I needed her and she was nowhere to be seen. She never told the Fuhrer to leave me alone. She never defended me against his tirade – and his literally was a tirade. She let me run off crying, full of hurt and confusion and grief, without ever once coming after me or even checking on me hours later. She never tried to support me or reassure me when the Fuhrer wasn't around. If I tried to broach the subject of his bullying with her, she shrugged it off and seemed irritated that I was unable to defend myself. I was 13 for fuck's sake. What's a 13 year old supposed to do? She left me alone to cope with a situation I shouldn't have even been in.

I don't know why I was surprised though. She was cold to me when Dad was alive. Just because we'd had a few months where we had a relationship – one-sided as it was, why would I really expect anything different?

Nicole held me as I sobbed. Sweat, caused by the heat of my anger, poured down my arms. I felt a bit sick too. I realised that was due to feeling nervous. Why was I nervous? My head immediately said, 'You're afraid of your mother'. I don't think I'd realised that before. Grief, anger, fear. That's a lot of big feelings.

Nicole was encouraging. "You're doing well. I'm here."

"I just wanted her to defend me. Just once, defend her daughter. Protect me. Support me. Look after me. Just once …"

With a loving, gentle voice, Nicole told me what I'd told her. "It's never going to happen. Your mother will never support or defend you or protect you. I'm sorry."

I didn't want to hear it or believe it. I wanted to bargain for it the way Bernadette said we would. I wanted to hang onto the hope.

Nicole reminded me it was never going to happen.

I cried because I knew it was true. I cried because I didn't want it to be.

I don't know if my bird flew free. It's probably too early to tell. I hope it did though. And I hope it enjoys the exhilarating feeling of liberation.

Bernadette finished off the night by teaching us how to juggle, which got us laughing. By the time we got home and had a cuppa, I felt a lot better. Lou, who'd worked on her unfulfilled need to be wanted, went off to bed looking a lot lighter as well. It's pretty evident that the more work you do, the quicker your recovery time. And it helps that Bernadette has us leave with a smile.

In the car, Lou said, "Have you noticed that we all feel the same way and we all deal with the same stuff. We can pretty much put our own names and faces to each other's stories. The scenario might be different, but the hurts that need healing are always the same."

I did notice. The good thing about a group situation is that you end up doing a lot of work vicariously. As they deal, you deal.

8.30 pm

Donna just rang to tell me that Nan's in hospital. She's been unwell for a couple of days. Her leg is badly swollen which means her fluid tablets aren't working and her heart is struggling. I'll go and see her tomorrow.

Wednesday 20th
4.30 pm

Just got back from seeing Nan. Mum was there. I behaved as if everything was normal and Saturday hadn't happened. She was off with me and doing her best to try and let me know by overtly ignoring me, but I ignored her childishness and pretended not to notice. It very much irritated her.

Nan could see there was something going on between us, but she never said anything. I gave all my attention to her and she lapped it up. She's a major hypochondriac so anytime something goes wrong with her health, she's in her element. She literally becomes the happiest woman on the planet!

She loves to describe her symptoms and tell you what meds she's on. She excitedly told me that the doctor is concerned about her heart. She actually chuckled and looked so proud when she told me her kidney function was down. Going by that, having her thyroid removed would have been like winning the lottery and the next greatest day of her life would have been when she had her hysterectomy!

The doctor came around and told us Nan really was very unwell. They'd changed her tablet to try and get her leg down but her heart wasn't pumping efficiently, which was hindering the ability of her body to eliminate the fluid.

Nan has had something wrong with her all the years I can remember. She's been in hospital on a few occasions with fairly minor things. She's 92, eagle-eyed, and sharp as a tack. To me, she looked pretty good. Fair enough, her leg was massive and a horrible red/purple colour, but she's always had fluidy legs. The only difference with her today and how she normally is, is that she seemed happy!

Mum hovered around Nan and tried to be helpful. She handed her a drink which she didn't want. She offered to brush her hair and was refused. She asked if she could get her anything or do anything and was told no.

When she started to adjust her pillows, Nan snapped.

"Stop fussing Laura. You're annoying me."

So sharp was her tone, Mum actually jumped and looked scared. She quickly backed off. Her eyes cast downwards and she looked like a wounded child.

And right then, I saw the nervousness I had felt on Monday night. My thought to explain the feeling was that I was afraid of my mother. And I was, in exactly the same way she is afraid of Nan. It's not the scared for your life fear. It's more a feeling of trepidation which comes from being eager to please but consistently failing and disappointing and being told so in a very harsh tone. A victim of emotional torture, I'd flinch at the smallest thing and felt anxious if I had to approach her for anything.

I'd spent my life walking on eggshells for fear of upsetting her so I don't think I ever recognised it as intimidation. I just always felt wary. Her method was subtler than the Fuhrer's. Tuts and sighs and disapproving looks can be just as devastating as outright meanness.

Every now and then Mum can still get the better of me but it's not anywhere near like it used to be. Thinking back, I reckon I got over her intimidation when I was married. For all the ways in which I was weak and pathetic, a part of me grew strong. After 30-odd years of being treated badly by various different people, I was so very tired of it. There came a day when I decided enough is enough. It took me awhile to stand in my power with her, but I got there. Much of the time my power stance comes across as anger, but I'm working on being reasonable.

For 66 years, my mother has been trying to please her mother. I felt like saying to Mum, "It's never going to happen. You will never please her. Give up that need right now."

I bet she'd cry an ocean of tears over that.

10.45 pm

Group was so loving tonight. There was a real nurturing energy in the room and everyone seemed really relaxed. Often half of us are tense or full of feelings. Tonight we were all pretty chill.

Arrabella hasn't rocked up stoned since the night we worked on our first thoughts in the morning. She looks more and more amazing each time we meet, really healthy, and there is a glow about her. She was gorgeous anyway but now she's stunning. I feel so happy for her.

Tina said her parents paid a surprise visit and brought loads of food so she knew they were making a peace offering. They actually miss her! They wanted to know why she hadn't been to see them in weeks. When Tina had gone around to them and told them she wouldn't be visiting anymore for this and that reason, they didn't pay any attention to her. But as the weeks went on and no Tina, they started to think that maybe she'd meant what she'd said.

Tina calmly explained about all the hurts they'd caused her and they defended themselves and said it wasn't true. They had no concept of what she was talking about. Tina was loved. How could she think she wasn't? Tina could see she'd get nowhere so she changed tack and said this is how she felt. They may not have intended any harm, but that's how Tina took it. That sort of got through, but they were still not fully convinced they'd done anything wrong. Even still, they apologised and agreed to treat Tina better. That woman just goes from strength to strength.

One of the things we did tonight was say a couple of words or a sentence to everyone about what we value in them. It was an amazing exercise. The things the others said to me were so beautiful and loving. Some of the things I was valued for were my kindness, empathy, intelligence, bravery, honesty, and beautiful, sparkly eyes!!! Apparently I laugh a lot and when I do, my eyes light up. I admit I wasn't fully aware of how much I do laugh so it's nice to know I don't come across as a sad sack.

When Eva had to value Di, she said she valued her femininity, courage, and humour. And she meant it! Di told Eva she was a Goddess and she valued her beauty, and her ability to feel deeply.

We all cried (of course!), because it was so touching to hear such wonderful things about ourselves. It's so nice to know that others see me in such a positive way.

Thursday 21st
5.00pm

Just got back from the hospital. Nan's not as good today and she looks drawn. She wasn't enjoying her illness anymore. Mum and Donna were there. Mick had been in earlier. Lou had stopped by as well. So had Uncle Jeremy. Glad I missed him. Mum was still huffy with me but because Donna was there, she was full of bravado. Honestly, we were there to see Nan and Mum just made it all about her.

From nowhere, and with no prompting, she goes, "I'm not going to pay any mind to what you said to Rob. Next time you see him, apologise and we'll forget it ever happened."

Deep breath. "Well you should pay it some mind. Your husband was always concerning himself with me. He was cruel, and you never stood up for me. Not once. Had you bothered trying to stop him, I wouldn't have had to say what I did. I've got nothing to apologise for. He needs to apologise to me. And so do you."

If we had been anywhere but a hospital, she would have screamed at me. Through gritted teeth, she hissed, "I am so tired of your 'poor me' crap. You were over-indulged by your father so anything that doesn't meet that standard is abuse, according to you. You need to buck up your ideas and stop blaming everyone for your problems."

Before I could attack back, Nan said, "So do you, Laura. Now leave Jodie alone."

Mum's face was like stone. She picked up her bag, turned on her heel and stormed out.

"She'll be back," Nan said. "She just needs to calm down. The two of you are so alike Jodie. That might be why you don't get on. She's too much like me as well. I think that's why we've had our troubles too. It's hard to look at a reflection of yourself if you don't particularly like what you see."

Wow. That is the deepest, most meaningful thing I have ever heard Nan say. EVER.

"You're a lot more like your dad, Donna. So is Mick. And she loved him. She really, truly did."

Mum came back but only to say 'bye to Nan. She told her she'd be back tomorrow. She kissed Donna and ignored me. Sigh. I'm too old for this shit!

8.30pm

That was interesting. Just got off the phone with Mum. I picked up and straight away she starts with, "All Rob said is that it's time you got a job. Where is the offence in that?"

That man has been the bane of my life (along with my thighs!), and he has caused such a rift between me and my mother. It didn't have to be this way.

"I have a job. I'm a writer."

"That's not a job, and you know it. You need a real job. Something where you contribute to society."

"You're not listening. I have a real job. I'm a writer. Writers contribute in more ways than are ever recognised or appreciated."

"How can you say you contribute? You've never been published."

Instantly I could feel the bile rising in my throat. I need worry about Eva's gall bladder. Mine is so engorged with vitriol it's now officially my biggest organ!

"I have been published, just nothing major – yet. I should be supported for who I am and what I do. Other people get supported for their occupation choices – bakers, doctors, lawyers, whoever. Artists don't. They're expected to work at a proper job and be creative in their spare time. It's not fair. Imagine if Michelangelo had to scrub toilets to fund his work. Would the Sistine Chapel be what it is? And imagine if Leonardo Da Vinci had to pick fruit! When you're tired after a long day at work, the last thing you want to do is be creative.

"Mum, I don't care if you don't support my choice. I care about what makes me happy. Seriously, what does it matter what I do or don't do? I'm financially independent. I pay my own way. Does it really matter if I don't work? Does it?"

She was quiet for a minute. What could she say? When she spoke, she said, "I just don't like to see you disappointed when you get rejected. That's all."

"Thank you. But that's for me to worry about. If I'm disappointed, I'll work out how not to be."

We hung up and I must admit, I feel a lot better. She must too.

I do feel a lot of disappointment. It's hard wanting something and not getting it. I see where other people have been successful in ways that I want to be and it makes me feel so jealous and I start to believe the world is unjust.

It's a tough gig being an artist. Most of us don't get paid week by week for the work we produce. Most of us will never get paid at all. People take art for granted, as if it somehow produces itself. That's why people don't mind pirating movies and music. They don't seem to understand that they're denying someone their livelihood.

I knew a guy who copied movies and then sold them for 10 bucks. I said to him, "How would you like it if someone followed you around at work all day just copying what you did and at the end of the week, the boss handed your pay packet over to him and you got nothing. That's what happens when you pirate movies. You did nothing to earn that money. It's grossly unfair."

He didn't care because he wasn't directly disadvantaged. Arsehole.

Friday 22nd
10.45 am

Donna's just rung to ask if I'm ok after yesterday. I told her Mum rang last night so everything's fine. Donna does worry. Fights and hostility stress her out. She was so happy I'd spoken up again though. She sees the value in it after the event. Said she'll pop in on Nan after work. I'm heading there now.

5.30pm

I'd just missed Mum by about 10 minutes, so it was me and Nan by ourselves. Nan told me she'd had a dream about her younger brother Reg. He was killed in a work accident when he was 41. It was before I was born so I never knew him. He had a cat that would spend hours draped around his neck and when he died, the cat disappeared. Nan said that in the dream, Reg had come to see her with his cat. He told Nan he was coming to take her home.

A shiver ran down my spine. I felt so overwhelmed, I burst into tears.

"It's ok, Jodie. I'm ready to go. I miss your Grandad and I don't have much of a life anymore. I'm stuck in that home all the time and I don't like it there."

"Death is so hard, Nan."

"I know. I'm the last member of my family. It was hard losing everyone."

"Do you have any regrets?"

She thought for a moment. "I regret not becoming a nurse. That would have made a difference to how I was, I think."

"Happier?"

"Happier."

We talked for ages about stuff she did as a kid and what Mum was like as a child and how Nan really loved Dad but when they first met she thought he wasn't husband material. Thought he was too happy-go-lucky to be capable of real responsibility. He proved her wrong. She told me, just between her and me, that she never liked the Fuhrer and she was always pleased when I called him that.

"You're a good writer because you've always been able to see situations and people how they really are. Except maybe your mother. Try and see her differently, if you can."

Just then, Uncle Jeremy turned up and ruined the moment. When he walked in, Nan's eyes lit up. Her baby boy. She adores him, always has. He adores her much less. Mum always used to say the way Nan fussed over him irritated him. He felt stifled and smothered by her. She made him the centre of her world. He could do no wrong. Quite the opposite of her daughter. That must have stung, watching that play out your whole childhood.

Of course he was alone. No wife, no daughters. Wouldn't expect them to visit though. There's no love lost between Aunt Janet and Nan. They'd never even met until Jeremy brought her home and announced she was pregnant. That went down like a sack of shit! Naturally, Nan blamed Janet. Wouldn't have been her precious boy's fault. In the moralistic and judgemental year of 1962, at the tender age of 17, Janet had Denise, followed two years later by Sharon.

I stayed for another couple of minutes and made polite with Jer, then I left. As I kissed Nan on the cheek, she said, "I'm glad we had this time. It's been nice."

In that hour I spent alone with Nan, she was mellow and accepting. How I wish she'd been like that all her life. Seems impending death changes us quite dramatically. Is it a chemical reaction in our brain that causes it, or do all our patterns and needs fall away and we become the very thing we began our life as – pure love?

Saturday 23rd
11.22 am

Dan dad fact: He loved Alice Cooper and his favourite song was 'I Never Cry' because he loved the line about the tear on his face being, '… just a heartache that got caught in my eye …'

What a brilliant lyric. Now I love it too. I'll have to put the song on my iPod.

My dad fact: He was always laughing. Especially at his own jokes! And when he told us a story, he would do voices and accents. He was very entertaining.

Dan slept in his own bed last night – alone. Either Stacey was busy or they're through already. I wanted to ask because I'm nosy, but I didn't. Might get Lou to get the goss.

I'm off to the hospital.

5.30 pm

Got there and Mick, Liz and the girls were there. Donna, Craig, Mum and the Fuhrer came half an hour later. It was a full house.

Nan's rapidly deteriorated and the prognosis isn't good. She looked exhausted but every time she closed her eyes, they'd suddenly shoot open and she'd grab for our hands and say, "I'm falling. Keep me from falling."

None of us really spoke much. We just sat with each other, happy to share the closeness. Nan looked at us one at a time and she nodded quietly to herself, as much to say, 'that's my family and I'm proud'.

When it was time for me to leave, I leaned in to kiss her. She touched my cheek and held her palm softly against my face. My tears wet her hand. After I pulled away, she took my hand and the way she held it and looked into my eyes felt so final. I have never told Nan I love her. She just never let you get that close. But I found it in my heart to say it. Unable to say it back, she just nodded.

Nan wasn't perfect and I won't pretend she was. I won't even pretend that I regret saying mean things about her. I felt how I felt, moment by moment. But when someone we care about is dying, we feel real love for them and all the bad just falls away. That's how it should be. This leaves us to remember the best of who they were.

I know I won't see Nan again. I am eternally grateful I got to say goodbye.

Sunday 24th
6.30 am

Mum just rang. Nan died at 4.30 this morning.

7.30 pm

Lou drove me to Mum's and she stayed with us all day. We were all there and we cried and laughed and told stories. I didn't realise just how much time Lou had spent with Nan and Grandad over the years. She had so many 'remember when's'.

We all took comfort from the fact Nan had had a long life and that she didn't have to live every day anymore without Grandad.

We were grieving but it wasn't the same kind of grief you suffer when someone is taken from you with no warning. It's a kinder grief. It leaves you hurting, but whole.

Monday 25th
3.30 pm

I feel tired today. Very drained. It was decided I'd write a eulogy from us grandkids. Mum will write one on behalf of her and Uncle Jeremy. I really don't know what I'm going to say. I'll talk it through with Bernadette.

10.30 pm

Bernadette gave me excellent attention for my grief. She got me to talk about Nan's last days and how I felt. I told her she'd stood up for me against Mum, that she said I was a good writer and that she didn't like the Fuhrer! In her last moments she became my ally and I was ecstatic, but I was also sad that no one else would hear her say those things. And I seemed to be grieving a lot over the fact she was my last grandparent and that I'm nobody's granddaughter anymore.

Bernadette said, "Throughout our lives we wear many hats - daughter, sister, granddaughter, aunty, cousin, friend, wife, mother, etc., and each thing we are makes us special and unique to someone else. You're grieving the loss of that thing that made you special to your grandparents. It's a normal response."

Heidi talked about her beliefs around death and how death in the physical realm means rebirth in the spiritual. She believes our spirit goes back to the spiritual realm, rests up, considers the life it's just had and then prepares itself for its next incarnation. No one ever dies before their time. Not even if it's an accident. Years ago, she read in the Beginner's Guide that 'Death' is an acronym for 'Departing Earth And Travelling Home'. I like that. Especially because of what Reg said to Nan in her dream. Heidi also said that just because someone has left the physical world doesn't mean we can no longer communicate with them. If we talk; they hear.

There's a lot of comfort in Spirituality. Thinking of someone we love as being eternal and having a nice time somewhere helps ease the grief.

When I said I wasn't sure what to write in Nan's eulogy, Bernadette said, "Don't remember her as her patterns. Talk about what she was like when she was coming from a more real place. You'll know those times because they'll be the moments when she was happiest."

That got my brain ticking. I think I know what to write.

Tuesday 26th
Nan's eulogy:

Our Nan. She wasn't big on emotional expression and she played her cards close to her chest. She took a no-nonsense, practical approach to life. She was hard-working, loyal, strong, resilient, and independent. She was a shrewd observer and she weighed people up pretty smartly. She didn't suffer fools gladly.

These may have been the traits Nan revealed the most, but they don't make up the full picture of who she truly was.

She took ages to choose us a birthday card, making sure the wording perfectly expressed her deepest feelings. Cards were important to Nan, probably because they said so beautifully what she couldn't.

She loved to knit and the click-clack of her needles, as she whipped us up a jumper, sang out that she was thinking of us with every stitch. The finished garment, which she proudly presented, said, 'I love and care about you. I want you to have the best'.

She nurtured us with delicious, home-made treats and she remembered each of our favourite things.

She lovingly tended plants, flowers, and fruit trees, which thrived under her care. She threw seeds onto her lawn to feed the birds.

She had a playful chuckle which showed her cheeky side. Her caring nature often expressed itself as worry. Her softness showed itself when Emily and Sarah were babies and she held them close.

We all hold our own memories of Nan and in those memories we'll be able to see that she showed us her heart and her love every day.

It has been our privilege to share Nan's life for so long. Her passing marks the end of an era and we will miss her so very much but we take some comfort in the fact she's with Grandad.

We hope that Nan had a good life and I know, without a doubt, she was so proud of her family. She told me the other day that we were her greatest achievement.

Wednesday 27th
7.38 pm

Mum rang. She was crying.

"I can't do the eulogy. I asked Jeremy to do it, but he won't. He said I'll be fine but I don't know what to write."

I let her cry. If she knew F:D:H stuff, I would have reassured her I was there, I was listening, and for her to keep crying and telling me all the reasons why she couldn't write it. Instead, every now and then, I just said, "We'll figure it out."

"What am I supposed to say?" she spluttered. "She was hard on me, you know. I don't think she ever hugged me. I remember when Sarah told me that riddle: What has arms but cannot hug? And the answer is, a chair. Straight away I thought, my mother the chair."

Her sobs grew more intense.

"Hang up and I'll come over."

I got to Mum's and the moment I was in the door, fresh tears started. "I don't know what to do."

We stood a few feet apart and I felt awkward just staring at her. If she had been anyone at group, I would have immediately hugged her, sat her down and held her hands. Ok, that's what I'll do. I sucked it up and grabbed her in a hug. She responded gratefully. She desperately needed the contact.

We sat down and I held her hands.

"Why are you struggling with this? What's hard?"

"I didn't think I'd miss her, and I do. I thought that because we never really got on, I'd be ok when she went. And I'm not."

She laid her head in my lap and let her grief flow.

My own tears landed in her hair. She was the child again, but I didn't mind this time. Her grief was deeper than mine. She'd just lost her mother. She needed to be nurtured.

I stroked her hair and wondered if this is how I'll be when she dies. Probably. I decided that, if I can, I'll work out how to fix our relationship.

"I'm here," I soothed. "I'm here."

"She broke my heart so many times. How am I supposed to stand up on Friday and talk about her with love?"

"The truth is, she wasn't an emotionally connected woman. She struggled to express her feelings. A lot of people do. To demonstrate her love, she did stuff instead."

She sat up. "Is that good enough, Jodie? Is it? It feels like a cop out – I can't care about you but here's a little something to ease the neglect."

"It may not have been what you wanted from her but it was the best she could do. So let's think about all the things she did and find that sense of love in her practical actions."

I could see she was trying to think of something but I knew her distress was too deep for her to think clearly at the moment. I prompted her.

"Nan told me you had a holiday away every year."

"That's true. Not everyone could afford a holiday. We were lucky. She saved hard for those holidays."

"She taught you how to knit. She came to all your school concerts."

"We always had the best shoes."

"She paid half of Dad's funeral."

"She did. Your Nanna and Pop paid half and she did the rest."

"She always made sure you were well provided for. You had a good education, good food and a nice home. She struggled to meet your emotional needs but she compensated in other ways. She told me the other day that in spite of her, you turned out really well and she was very proud of you."

"Did she really say that?"

"She did. She was aware that she had always been hard on you and she was aware she didn't know how to stop herself. Something inside her just wouldn't give. She wishes she could have been different, but she couldn't. She wanted me to tell you."

10.30pm

At group, I told Bernadette that I'd half expected to hear an apology from Mum about the way she's been with me, but it never came. Bernadette said it probably never will. It's an unfulfilled need so I'll have to set that bird free as well. Seriously, I've got an entire aviary! Lou said she'll go through the release exercise with me at home if I want. I said next time we've got a spare hour or two for blubbering, I'd take her up on it.

Thursday 28th
11.35 am

That's … a surprise. Just got off the phone with Olli. He asked if it's ok if he and his parents come to Nan's funeral. I was shocked when I heard his voice. He kind of threw me.

"Of course it is. It's nice that you want to."

He told me that Brenton had told him about Nan and how sorry he was. I was incapable of making small talk so he wrapped things up quickly and said he'd see me tomorrow.

Alice called earlier as well. She said everyone would be there. It's strange. They barely knew Nan, and Lennie and Emma never met her. Why would they come to her funeral?

6.52 pm

Oh, I get it … they're coming to support me. Wow. That's huge.

Friday 29th
8.30am

Liam's just arrived and Dan's just out the shower. Lou was up at seven, got ready and now she's cooking breakfast.

I've been up since six. I didn't sleep very well but I feel ok – just a bit restless.

I got organised last night. I've got the eulogy and plenty of tissues. Lou did a fantastic thing for me. She took my words and put them in a layout with photos of Nan and printed it like a booklet. She made five copies so Mum, Mick, Donna, Uncle Jeremy and I could each have one. It looks amazing.

Lou's just called us for breakfast. Cool, who was fast asleep in the middle of the bed, opened her eyes, stared at me, yawned, then promptly went back to sleep.

Oh to be a cat!

11.15pm

It's been a long day and I'm tired but I can't sleep so I thought I'd empty my head.

There were a lot of people at Nan's funeral. About 50, I'd say. Which is really impressive for a woman who didn't have many friends throughout her life. Aunt Janet and Sharon sat stony-faced and unmoved the whole service. Uncle Jeremy and Denise shed a few tears though.

That family is weird. Sharon is nearly 41 and she still lives at home. Her and Aunt Janet are more like creepy best friends than mother and daughter. Uncle Jeremy works full time then gets home and does all the cooking and the housework because Aunt Janet lies around like Lady Muck all day, getting fatter.

Sharon's got irritable bowel syndrome. Can't say I blame her bowel. I'd be irritable too if I had to live in her. She's got that air of superiority about her and she's a bossy little cow. On the rare occasion we got together as kids, she'd have us all organised and doing her bidding within five minutes. And selfish! It was her way, or no way. Spoilt brat.

That's because she was the prize in that family. Poor old Denise was the unwanted, unloved child. She was to blame for Jer and Jan having to get married all because she magically created herself inside Janet's uterus.

The resentment for Denise was palpable and when Sharon came along, Aunt Janet made such an over-the-top fuss of her it was embarrassing. It was her way of making sure Denise understood just how unlovable she really was. Yeah, because the neglect and complete lack of attention and care didn't demonstrate it quite enough!

When Denise was 16 she ran off with Graham, who was pretty whacked-out at the time, and they went on to have nine kids!!! Nine!! Who does that? For 21 years, no one heard a word from her and when Grandad died six years ago, she suddenly re-emerged with this full-on family. Nan tutted and said, "She's a glutton for punishment."

I always liked Denise. She was kind. She must have been so desperately wounded, but you wouldn't have known it. She always came across as doing ok. Until she ran off, of course. Her and Graham are still together, which is amazing. He's missing most of his teeth and is balding. She's 43 going on 63. All those kids have made her haggard.

Olli sat directly behind me, with Bev and BJ. It was so nice to see my ex in-laws. They were always so lovely to me. Bev is still gorgeous and they looked genuinely thrilled to see me. They asked me to drop in for a coffee. I said I would but I feel a bit odd about it. They've got a new daughter in-law now. I'd feel as if I was intruding. I'll think about it.

Olli gave me a big hug and he lingered a touch too long for my comfort. He looked fit and sun-kissed, even in the middle of winter. The benefit of working outdoors. He gave off a schmoozy kind of energy and I didn't like it. It felt inappropriate. I immediately thought of Jill and felt for her.

Alice and Rusty were sun-kissed too, and uber-relaxed, having only arrived home a week ago. Alice was quite upset and she cried when she hugged me. I ended up comforting her.

Nan wasn't religious so the service was really simple and the priest was a young guy who wasn't at all like a priest. He didn't push God. In fact, he spoke in more general spiritual terms, which was really nice.

Mum read her eulogy first and it was lovely and heartfelt. She went with the whole 'she did stuff for us' theme, so her eulogy was in the same vein as mine. She managed to come from a loving place and she said some really beautiful things. Her voice broke once, but she held it together.

I did my eulogy next and my hand was shaking so badly I could barely read it. The same thing happened at Grandad's funeral. I shake when I'm highly emotional. Bernadette says it's just a form of release. After me, a friend from the home spoke, as did a carer.

When Nan's coffin was carried out of the church, that's when the most tears fell. There is something so devastating and so touching about the sight of six men hoisting a coffin onto their shoulders and walking it slowly down the aisle. To me, it's symbolic of holding the person aloft and elevating their status and their meaning. It always reminds me of the Hollies song, 'He Ain't Heavy, He's my Brother'.

Nan's pallbearers were Uncle J, the Fuhrer, Mick, Graham, her great grandson Ryan, and Olli. Olli asked if he could do it so Graham and Denise's other son, Will, said he'd step out.

We followed the hearse to the cemetery and the priest said a few words before the coffin was lowered into the ground. She was buried next to Grandad.

We went back to Mum's for the wake. Uncle J organised it all.

It was a good four hours before things started to wrap up. Everyone was so busy catching up, the time just flew. Bev and BJ told me they loved being grandparents. Olli's kids were just beautiful and Jill was a great mum. They were taking a couple of holidays a year now they were retired and they were off to New York next. Now that's a nice life.

As numbers dwindled, Mum came and sat with me and thanked me for my help the other day. She said she'd felt a lot lighter after I'd left and she then found it easy to write. Again, I'm amazed at what a bit of good attention can achieve. Bernadette has been a blessing.

I made an effort to speak to Aunt J and Sharon and they were so fake pleasant it was painful to watch.I had a decent chat with Denise who was a bit vague, but friendly, and I gave Uncle J his copy of the eulogy. He thanked me and gave me an actual hug, which took me by surprise so I stood there stiff, unable to hug back.

The Fuhrer shat me off, but I didn't let him get me down. After I gave Uncle J his eulogy he said, in such a facetious tone, "That was rather magnanimous of you."

Why the fuck would he even say that, sarcastic prick? I just said, "Yes it was, considering the abuse and blame we've put up with from them over the years."

The Renshaw's have not been a pleasant lot. They blamed Mum when Denise ran off! How she caused it remains a mystery, but they refuse to see how they did anything wrong. That caused a bigger rift than the one that already existed because Uncle J blamed Mum for Janet's brief affair with some African guy who sold jewellery. Mum didn't know him or anything about the affair. Via Nan, we often heard the latest round of bad-mouthing. We didn't even see them anymore, yet they still found things to blame us for. It was very strange.

And Olli … he waited until Bev and BJ left before he made his move. He stood way too close to me and spoke quite softly so I had to move my head in closer to hear him. He started telling me how good I looked and how sorry he was things didn't work out but that maybe we could, you know, get together for old time's sake and, who knows, maybe things could be different for us. Then he started running his finger up and down my arm and he attempted to kiss my neck.

It took a moment for my brain to register and when it did, I pulled away from him. I must have looked uncomfortable because Dan came over and put his arm around me, "Is everything ok?"

"Yeah, Oliver's just saying goodbye. He's going home to his wife and children."

That man is such a shit-head.

Eventually, it was just us kids and co. We had one last drink to Nan, helped Mum tidy up, then we headed. Mum looked really drained by the end of it.

Louise had arranged for Alice and the others to meet us at the pub.

We had a really good laugh. It was so nice to be distracted from my emotional week. We called it a night at 10ish and I thought I'd crash the moment my head hit the pillow, but I didn't. I'm tired now, though. I'm ready to sleep.

Saturday 30th
12.04 pm

Dan approached me tentatively and asked if I wanted to hear his dad fact today.

"Yes please. It's a favourite part of my week. And Dan, I'm fine. You don't need to tip-toe around me."

"Cool. Ok, my dad was really skilled with his hands. He designed, built and upholstered a chaise lounge and gave it to my mum for her birthday."

"Nice. Did you inherit any of his skills?"

Dan shook his head sadly. "I am my mother's son. Nothing but good looks and a winning personality."

"Still a good set of skills. Ok, here's my dad fact: Every Saturday morning was housework time. We each had a job. Mine was vacuuming the lounge, Mick's was mopping the kitchen, and Donna's was making our beds. Because we were always half-arsed about it and whinged about having to do it, Dad rather cleverly made it into a contest. Whoever did the best job, got a prize. The competition was on. We worked our little butts off doing a perfect job. I even started dusting as well! Of course, we each won it in turn but for some reason, we never twigged. He tricked us good."

I got the albums out and showed Dan a few photos. I pointed out Dad, Nanna, Pop, Nan, and Grandad. There are photos of them spanning several decades.

Photography is a truly phenomenal thing. By some fantastic means, we point a rectangle thing with a lens at something, press a button and it captures the moment in perfect detail and perfect colour. Photographs are a version of time travel.

It never ceases to amaze me that someone had an idea to capture an image via mechanical means. How did they even think of that? Then how did they even know how to bring it all to fruition? In the old days the image was imprinted onto a plate then someone improved on that with film. Not only did they capture an image, they figured out how to get it onto paper using a set of chemicals. And now we've got digital cameras so the image is saved to a tiny card. This stuff is mind-blowing!

I am eternally grateful for the brilliance and innovation of the man who invented the camera because, without it, all I'd have of my Dad would be an idea in my mind.

I won't even start on how blown away I am by movies because I just don't have the words to adequately express my awe. Or music and musical instruments, for that matter.

It's funny, people wish they could do magic for real. For me, these things prove we do.

Sunday 31st
6.58 pm

Lou, Liam and Dan took me out to lunch as a post-funeral 'check-in'. They were probably worried I might end up like I did after the Doc died. They should have known not to worry because I was out of bed and functioning.

No amount of begging, pleading, coaxing or cajoling could get me out of bed after the Doc's funeral. I really worried Lou and Dan and after a week they got Mum around to see if she could shift me. When that didn't work, they called in Donna and Mick. They seemed to understand the level of my grief though so they told Lou and Dan I'd be fine and to just let me come around in my own time. Donna and Mick called me every couple of days and after three weeks, I slowly emerged for hours at a time. It took me a full six weeks to get out of bed in the morning, and stay out.

I told the three of them that I felt really well and that I had expressed my grief during the week so it wasn't lingering anywhere in my body. I'd received excellent attention from the group and Nan's death wasn't a terrible shock. I didn't feel fragile or delicate so they needn't be wary or careful around me.

Liam said, "That's good to hear, you snotty-faced heap of parrot droppings."

"Shut your festering gob, you tit."

Liam and I guffawed.

Dan looked confused.

"Monty Python," Louise explained.

When the boys were playing pool, I asked Lou if she had the goss on Stacey and she told me Dan and Stacey are no more. They were never really a 'thing'. Just a bit of fun for both of them. That would explain Dan's availability.

Monday 1st August
10.49 am

Just got back from my walk. Hour and a half today. I felt like looking at trees and nature. It was nice.

I was thinking about grief. I think there is an expectation that we have to grieve forever – not full-on like in the beginning, but always and forever there must be a sad or pensive tone when we talk about the deceased, to suggest that we've never gotten over their passing and we never will. 'My sadness proves my love'. It's as if we think the person who moves on is insensitive or cold.

I thought that about Mum. I never understood how she could lose her husband then re-marry within a year. Nan told me that Mum did it out of need, to begin with. She didn't want to be alone and she didn't want to raise her children alone. The financial side of it was a factor too. The Fuhrer was cashed up. All Mum had done was ensure our security.

When Nan told me that, I remembered something Mum had said to me during an argument, "You do what you have to, to survive." Sometimes it's a pity our most basic instinct is for survival. It makes us compromise ourselves.

I suppose it was the last thing Mum ever wanted to do. She probably believed she'd be married for life and that she and Dad would grow old and grey together. She wouldn't have factored in being a young widow.

I know she was still grieving when she married the Fuhrer. I could see it in her face. To make it worse, Dad was so good-looking and the Fuhrer was not. That would have been hard to adjust to.

I understand now that moving on is important. It doesn't mean we've forgotten a person or what they meant to us. It just affords us the chance to resume the life we're still living.

But as a distressed child I couldn't fathom what was going on, or why. Adults live in a completely different world to children, but they seem to forget this. Adults often behave as if kids are privy to the same information and knowledge they have about personal situations so they should understand stuff and they're stupid if they don't. It doesn't work that way. Kids have next to no information and no life skills to call upon. And adults rarely explain themselves. How a child's world is affected by the actions of the adults is never even considered. Kids are just expected to fall in with whatever's going on. Which is kind of fair enough because what other choice is there?

However, a lot of love and attention and some basic information during any changes would go a long way to easing anxiety and tantrums and rebelling. A safe child is a happy child and an integrated family functions better than a divided one.

Tuesday 2nd
4.45 pm

At F:D:H last night, we had to pull a name out of a hat and write that person a letter telling them something about them that moved us, or how we were touched by them in some way. We had to hand over the letter at the end of group and they were to be read at home. I got Meredith.

I stared at the blank page before me, then I stared at Meredith. Her head was down and she was busy writing. She looked sad, but she often looks like that.

Meredith's so lonely and she has such a lot of regrets. She regrets marrying a man she didn't love. She regrets not studying and becoming a vet. She regrets not travelling. She regrets not leaving her husband for a man she could have been really happy with. She regrets having only one child. She wishes she'd had at least four. She regrets not maintaining her friendships. She regrets being a follower. She regrets getting to 67 with a shit-load of regrets!

Meredith yearned for things but she didn't know she could actually have them. She was bound by tradition and her parents put all their resources into making sure her brother got the best education and the best chance of a good career. All she was encouraged to do was be pretty and get a husband. The man was the bread-winner. She'd marry and be taken care of.

Her mother lived in a world of pretty frocks and baked dinners. She fixed her appearance before her husband got home. On arrival, she'd hand him a drink and ask about his day. She didn't speak unless spoken to. She was the perfect housewife.

Meredith was endlessly instructed in making sure those around her were attended to first. She was expected to behave like a lady and at no time was she to bring shame on the family. Her behaviour was a reflection on her mother and father and they were fine people and Meredith better continually demonstrate that.

Her family were by no means wealthy but that didn't stop her mother from putting her through all the necessary preparations for being a debutante. That was Meredith's equivalent of University and snaring an eligible young man of means was her degree.

Meredith graduated with flying colours and at 21 married an accountant. He was seven years older. The marriage was arranged and neither of them loved each other. She was a young virgin. He needed a wife. When Meredith told her mother she didn't love him, her mother informed her that people didn't marry for love. They married for security and procreation.

The hubby handled all the money, only handing out a household allowance once a week. Like so many women before her, Meredith was a victim of economic oppression. He made all the big decisions and it was he who only wanted one child. Their sex life pretty much ended after she got pregnant. Not that Meredith cared.

When Meredith was 32, she fell in love with the husband of a friend. There was an electricity between them and they couldn't help themselves. They had an affair and when she thought she was pregnant, she was both excited and afraid. She told the potential father and at first he looked ill but they decided they'd be together. Sadly she wasn't pregnant, but his wife was. Meredith was devastated. They'd never be together now.

The affair got too painful to bear and it ended, along with Meredith's real chance of happiness. Meredith told herself it was for the best because leaving her husband was all too hard and she was conscious of how it would reflect on her family.

Meredith's husband died from a massive stroke four years ago. That's when she discovered they were broke. He had gambled everything, and more. She sold the house, paid his debts and, with the help of her daughter and brother, managed to buy a one-bedroom unit.

Meredith never rebelled. She fell into line and just went along with the wishes of everyone else. There was no use asking for anything because it was denied. And no one listened to her anyway.

Meredith once said that if she had her life to live over, she'd forget that the rest of the world existed and she'd concentrate only on her own existence. I remember at the time that I thought it was a significant thing to say.

She looked up briefly from writing her letter and saw me looking at her. She smiled warmly at me and then I knew how she had touched me. All the freedoms and choices she had been denied, she gave to her daughter. She let her live her own life. She encouraged her to get an education and a career that would take her around the world. She never placed any expectations on her and she didn't try to pigeon-hole her. Her daughter has lived and worked overseas for the past 20 years. Along with her husband and kids, she's still travelling.

Meredith could so easily have clutched her daughter to her, but she didn't. She could have used her daughter to fill her loneliness. She could have burdened her with convention and the fear of what other people think. She could have trapped her in a life she didn't want to live. The fact she did the opposite is a big thing, considering her conditioning.

I wrote all that to Meredith and I told her I was touched by her love for her daughter, her generosity of spirit, and her high level of intelligence and self-awareness. Her daughter was lucky to have such a selfless mother and thanks to her, her daughter would now go on to raise her own children in such an open and loving way. In a very real way, Meredith had quashed several oppressions. If everyone did the same, how different the world would be.

Wednesday 3rd
8.45 am

I've just now read my letter. I treated it like a Christmas gift that I had to wait for. And when I opened it, I was thrilled with the present inside. Di wrote mine.

Sweet, lovely Di is moved by my love for Cool. She, too, has a cat so she understands how a purring ball of fluff can evoke such feelings. She wishes everyone on the planet loved animals as much as we both do. She's touched by my desire to live my life from a place of love and integrity. She's touched that I reached out to my mother when she needed me. She likes how I have emerged from my cocoon over the past months to become a beautiful butterfly who can fly anywhere and do anything. She has enjoyed watching my transition and she often thinks of me if she needs strength. She said I was the type of woman she hopes to be.

How gorgeous is that. Bless her.

I still find myself wondering why Di would want to be a woman. In day to day life, there's not a single advantage to it.

We're commodities, currency, chattel, sex objects, and a form of entertainment. We're often blamed for a man's brutal behaviour towards us. We have to compromise ourselves and modify our behaviour to keep ourselves safe. If we're strong, we're butch ball-breakers. If we're weak, we deserve to be treated badly. If we're a feminist, we're damned. If we're not a feminist, we're damned. If we achieve a high position at work we either slept our way there or we got the job so the company wouldn't appear sexist. And we still don't get paid the same as a man for doing the exact same job. That beggars belief.

We're at the mercy of our hormones. Not once a year or the rare occasion. No, every month, in a continual cycle of fluid retention, bloating, cramps, exhaustion, headaches, and moods. And the actual menstruation – that sucks the big one. It's a hassle and an inconvenience. Not only that, we're conditioned to be embarrassed by it and to refer to it as anything but 'my period'. And please only ever talk in whispers if you must insist on mentioning this highly taboo subject. Women live their lives on a month-to-month basis. How I wish that the day we turned 40, the whole thing would just shut down as quickly as it all began. I pity those poor girls who start their period at 10. It's bad enough at 30 when you're equipped to cope. But 10! Nature is messed up.

Face. Body. Boobs. Boobs. Boobs. Vagina.

Di can't see the lack of advantage to being a woman because she's never faced any of our oppressions. She was raised as a boy with a different set of rules. She'll never know the hassle of the uterus or how it felt to develop, or not develop, breasts and the terrible attention either scenario gets you. I know she's had a life of hell because she was born into the wrong body, but her life wouldn't have been all picnics and rainbows if she had been female straight off the bat. I get the feeling that she thinks it would have been, as if dresses and make-up compensate for all the other shit.

Di told us that before a male can have a sex change, he has to live full-time as a woman for 12 months to make sure he actually wants to be one, because it's so hard. Even psychiatrists agree it's not a bed of roses.

I wonder if the females who want to become male have to do the same thing? I doubt it.

A few weeks ago, Heidi said it best. She brought our attention to Bernadette's art. "Look at these pictures. They show of a time when women were celebrated for their fertility and femininity and sensuality. There were rituals that celebrated our ability to grow life inside our bodies. There were festivals that celebrated all the things that make women unique and special. We were celebrated for our ability to love and nurture; for our emotions; our connection to nature; our Goddess energy. We were respected for our wisdom, perception, and intuition. Today's world has failed women. It makes us feel bad about the things that make us feel good. It's taken away our light and damaged our energy."

Thursday 4th
5.14 pm

At group last night, everyone went to the person who wrote them their letter and hugged them and thanked them.

Meredith had never considered what she'd done for her daughter as being significant or special so she was deeply moved that someone had noticed that, indeed, it was. I told Di that I aspired to be the type of woman she is - warm, wonderful, loving. She cried, naturally!

Heidi wrote to Lou and she'd told her she was touched by her aura of peace and calm. She said she was a pleasure to be around and that her energy brought a sense of serenity and ease to the group. Lou made everything seem possible.

Lou wrote to Eva, and Eva barrelled up to her and grabbed her in a massive bear hug and just held her. Clearly Eva was grateful for what she wrote! Lou had written that she was moved by Eva's story. She couldn't imagine facing the things Eva had, and still be such a loving, deep-feeling person like Eva. She was touched by the fact that Eva never gave up on herself and that she found a way to live her truth. She admired her ability to dust herself off and keep moving forward.

Before she let her go, Eva told Lou she'd been writing in her journal several times a week for the last month. She was mighty proud of herself!

Eva looks really well lately. Her eyes are bright. She's growing her hair. She said she's on a diet and exercising (can't notice any changes yet), and she's taken to wearing the occasional skirt to group! She laughs quite easily. She's not always in a fabulous mood, but 80% of the time she is. She's changed significantly.

We all have.

Friday 5th
2.02 pm

On Wednesday, Bernadette spoke to us about taking a small step in our life towards something we've always wanted. Big change can occur from small actions.

She said, "I've read books that promote the idea of just abandoning your present unhappy life and throwing yourself into a strange and new one. That might be fine for some people but, for the average person, it's not easy to drop everything and run away. We have emotional ties and responsibilities. We have financial limitations. Telling someone to take a leap of faith, and potentially surrendering their sense of security, is a big ask. You don't have to sell the house, sell the kids, sell the car, then join the circus. Just sign up for a class, or take up a hobby. You never know where it may lead. We're so good at talking ourselves out of things that so many dreams and desires go unfulfilled. What I want you to do is pair up, name something simple you'd like to do then notice any resistance to it. Say to the person, 'I want you to just start', then offer a small beginning step."

Gretel and I went to the lounge room. I held her hands and asked her what she'd always wanted to do.

"I want to learn Asian cooking."

"What stops you?"

"I feel so overwhelmed and confused by the complexities of it. It all seems too hard and too fussy. I wonder if it's really worth it."

"Why do you want to do it then? Why not just abandon the idea and choose something else?"

"That's a good question. Because … I have a friend who cooks and I love being in her kitchen when she's working. It smells amazing and I love watching her chop and peel and combine. Then she serves me a plate and as I eat it, I feel nurtured."

"You want to nurture too?"

"I do. But I think I don't know how and that my food would never be as good as hers. It's pointless to start."

"That's your resistance talking. I want you to just start. Tomorrow, I want you to take the small step of going into an Asian grocery and buying an ingredient. Put it in a prominent place in your kitchen so when you see it, it reminds you that you have a desire. Every Thursday, I want you to go back into the grocery and buy another ingredient. Remember - one jigsaw piece at a time will eventually lead you to the completed picture."

"I can do that."

I wrote the 'instruction' on a piece of paper and told her to stick it on her fridge and read it every day. It was her reminder that her life was changing for the better.

My turn. She asked me what I'd like to do.

"Learn Spanish, for when I go to Spain."

"What stops you?"

"I don't believe I'll ever get to Spain, so there's no point. It's hard learning a language and learning one I'll never use is a waste of time."

"Yet you have a desire to do it, so why not do it anyway, just for the pleasure of it?"

"Because it's too hard. Took me weeks to remember, Hola, como estes?"

"You remembered it eventually! But there's your resistance – that it's too hard. I want you to just start. For your small step I want you to buy an English/Spanish dictionary. Carry it with you everywhere and every Thursday, I want you to learn a new word."

"Ok. Write it down for me."

Took that piece of paper with me and bought myself a dictionary today. I have learnt 'cero', which is zero. I'm going to learn how to count first.

Bernadette's right - a start is a start.

Saturday 6th
10.00 am

Dan dad fact: He could play the piano and he did a brilliant Elton John imitation. "In more ways than one, as it turns out!"

My dad fact: He was an impulse buyer. He'd see something, like it, buy it. Drove Mum mad because he was always coming home with stuff he didn't need and stuff that didn't match anything else in the house. She was forever returning things to the shops.

Lou's just stuck her head in to see if I want to go for a walk. Perfect time for a group gossip.

2.45pm

That was a good walk. Lou powers along and I practically have to jog to keep up sometimes. And when she talks, her breathing isn't even laboured.

Highlights the difference in our fitness levels!

Lou worked with Finn on Wednesday night. Finn wants to be a volunteer for all different things all over the world – save this, save that, teach here, hug there. On the inside, she feels like a humanitarian and she wants to help. What stops her is that she already knows the fantasy is better than the reality so by never doing it, she'll be able to live with the idea that she might have made a difference instead of proving conclusively that she never made a scrap of difference to anyone or anything.

Lou told her to take a small step by ringing one volunteer organisation a week. She could either just say 'hello' then hang up, or she could talk to someone about what they do. Either way, it was a start.

Lou's thing is that she wants to save money. She often maxes out her credit card and she's always broke a few days before pay day. She gets annoyed with herself for not being a better money manager and it stresses her out when she's scratching around for pennies. She loves to shop, especially for clothes, shoes and jewellery. The thing that stops her from saving is that she wants stuff straight away and she gets all, 'Why shouldn't I have it? I work hard. I'm allowed to. I don't want to wait'. Instant gratification.

Finn told her to get a jar and put a dollar a week in it.

I asked her if she'd saved her dollar yet and yep, she had. I said to her, "So now you have more than cero dollars."

Ole!

Sunday 7th
2.50 pm

Lou said when she and Finn had finished their 'small step' exercise and they were back in the counselling room waiting for the others to finish up, Finn told her that she and Arrabella were going to house-share and probably Heidi as well. Finn's currently living with her Aunty and Heidi's with her grandparents, so both are pretty keen to move out. They're all young and they're all lovely, so it would be fun and Finn wants to do the F: D:H course with Heidi and Arrabella as well.

Finn also heard that Tina and Marion are going on a cruise together in October because their husbands don't like to do anything or go anywhere. The husbands are a bit put out and unhappy their wives have changed, but the wives don't care! The husbands have had years to do stuff with their wives, and they've done nothing. So the wives are 'doin' it for themselves'. Those wives rock!

Am off to lunch at Mum's. She's invited me and Donna.

9.30 pm

I love when other people feed me. It's always so much better than anything I feed myself. Mum did a roast lunch, and Lou made paella for dinner so I could sample some of what I can expect when I get to Spain!! Delicious. Bet it doesn't come garlic-free in Spain though.

Mum, Donna and I had a really good day, especially because the Fuhrer wasn't home. He was helping a friend build something or fix something or whatever. Didn't know he had any friends.

When Mum rang me on Thursday to ask me to lunch I thought for sure she was going to be full of drama and grief when we got there and that she would consume all the attention. I was wrong! She was actually really good.

We talked about Nan and the funeral straight off. We agreed it went well and that Nan would have liked it. Mum thanked me again for my eulogy and said Uncle J really appreciated his copy!

Over lunch Mum talked about her childhood and how she always felt so shut out by Nan. It felt that no matter what she did, she just couldn't get her attention – good or bad. In fact, the harder she tried, the more Nan closed herself off. It was if she couldn't bear looking at her. (Which is pretty much what Nan had said to me at the hospital.) Mum always felt there was just never enough room for her in Nan's life because all the space was taken up by Nan.

Mum said she realised during the week that she often behaved moody and hurt in front of Nan because she wanted her to notice that she wasn't doing well and then she wanted her to acknowledge that she was responsible for it. She wanted her to say something along the lines of, "I can see that you're very hurt and I take full responsibility for that. If I'd been a better mother, you wouldn't need to be moody, angry, or upset around me just to get my attention. You'd be well-adjusted and happy."

Yep, unfulfilled need. There's a bird that will never fly the coop!

How Mum managed to realise something so major and so significant is amazing to me. That is really good self-awareness. And even more amazing is that she admitted it! Has there been some kind of rare and unusual planetary alignment this week!?

Foolishly, I hoped she'd say those words to me because I do the same, but nope. Another bird to set free. I'll add it to my list.

Then Mum said something that nearly made me cry. "I did love my mum but the agony of it was that I thought she didn't love me. But I think she must have because I love you two and Mick. Love's there, even if it's not always shown."

She then got up and made coffee. Donna and I just looked at each other and mouthed, 'Wow!' In the history of our lives, Mum has never said anything remotely like that.

Mum came back, sat down and the conversation became general chit-chat.

Donna talked about trying for a baby and how they hoped to be parents by this time next year.

Mum said, "You'll be a good mum, Donna. You've got your father's temperament and he was always so patient. He enjoyed being a father. It brought him great joy. I hope it happens soon."

With no pause, she told us about a friend of hers who's getting a divorce at 72. "Who can be bothered?" she said. Then she talked almost non-stop for the next hour about anything and everything. The Fuhrer got home, we wrapped it up quick smart and we were sent on our way.

Mum blew me away today. Her mother dying had a profound effect on her. I don't think she's going to turn all sentimental on us and have some kind of Ebenezer Scrooge transition, but I think she will be kinder to me now. I hope so anyway.

When she said she loved Nan but she didn't think Nan loved her – I could relate. That's how I've always felt. She pisses me off big-time, but I have always loved her. I do want her to be in my life so she must have done enough for me to feel that way. Eva doesn't see her parents and Tina was prepared to give hers up. I've never wanted that.

I'll have to shift my focus and see where she has been a good mother to me. We both deserve that.

Monday 8th
10.45 pm

Di looked like she'd been through the wringer. She visited her parents yesterday to tell them she's a woman.

"I was so nervous, but I knew it was time. I can't live like this anymore. I have a right to be who I am. Nina came with me to say to them that she loved me no matter what. I'm so thankful for her. She never rejected me."

Di could barely get the words out. She was so emotional.

"I didn't know how to dress. Should I go as Mitchell and tell them or should I go as Di? Nina said that I am Diana now. They have to meet her."

Bernadette cradled Di as the tears fell.

"I wore a lilac blouse and a skirt. Nina braided my hair and put tiny flowers through it. I did light make-up. Nina said I looked really beautiful and my parents would be … would be … proud to have me as their daughter."

Tissues were passed down the line. Di wasn't the only one crying.

"I was in knots. I really was. Nina drove and when we got there I couldn't get out of the car. My body was like a lead weight. I told Nina to take me home, but she said no. She said if I can't go to them, they could come to me. And then I knew that I was most afraid of my dad so I told Nina to just get my mum.

"Nina knocked and she spoke to Mum for a minute then she went into the house. My mum approached the car and I was crying so much I could barely see her. She got into the driver's seat and she said nothing. She just looked at me.

"For ages we didn't speak and then I said, 'Mum, I want to be a woman'. And do you know what she did … she took my hand in hers and she said, 'I know'.

"She knew. She'd always known. But she didn't know how to deal with it so she pretended everything was fine and put a lid on it quickly. She said I often tried on my sisters clothes and I used to ask for dresses of my own. At first she thought I was gay, but she realised it was something else; something deeper than that.

"She hoped I'd grow out of it and she encouraged me to do 'boy' things just so our lives could be normal. We both got good at pretending. When I married Nina, she was relieved and thought it had just been a phase.

"We were in the car for about 20 minutes and she said it was time to go into the house. I told her I was worried about Dad and she said, 'We'll deal with whatever happens'. I said that maybe it would be better if I just went home and she could tell Dad, but she wouldn't let me. I had to face him sooner or later. Might as well get it all done in the one day.

"I walked in behind Mum and when Dad saw me he looked so shocked and confused and hurt. Nina had tried to prepare him so he knew it wasn't a joke. I'm his only son ... I was his only son ... and for him, it was really hard. He said, 'How can you be like this? You played sport. You liked trains'.

"How do you explain the inexplicable? How do you convince someone that who you are on the inside is different to who you are on the outside? Unless you experience it, it's hard to comprehend.

"I said, 'I don't have a choice. I don't. It's who I am. Believe me, life would be so much easier if I could just be a boy. But I can't. No one chooses a difficult life just for the hell of it. Why would you?

"People don't choose to be gay or lesbian. It's just who they are. You didn't choose to be heterosexual. It's just who you are. I feel a certain way on the inside and there's no rhyme or reason to it. If you could see me on the inside, instead of just how I look on the outside, you'd understand.

"I didn't just wake up one morning and think to myself that I might have a go at being a woman for a bit of a laugh. It's not a calculated decision. I am a woman inside a man's body. I live it every day, and even for me it's a confusing mix. But I don't want it to be anymore. I want how I feel and how I look, to match'.

"I told them I was going to start hormone treatments and, when I could, I was going to have the sex change operation. My dad said, 'And what do you think about all this, Nina? How can you be ok with this?'

"Nina said, 'Your child is a good person, and that's what matters to me. I loved Mitchell and now I love Di'.

"He said, 'Can't you just stay a man and be a man during the day and then just ... wear a dress or something, at night? Why do you need to be a woman?'

"If I stay a man then I'm doing that for you, and everyone else, not me. It's not a choice Dad, it's who I am."

Di said it was a hard day. She told both her sisters as well and they were shocked, which is to be expected, but they were supportive. Di has to tell extended family and friends and she already knows she'll lose a few friends but she reasoned she can always make better friends. She's a lot more worried about the job situation. She's manager of a call centre but she still goes to work as Mitchell and no one has got a clue. Di is hoping her 10 years of loyal and excellent service will be enough.

Di's dad was a little more understanding by the time they left but he was really struggling with why a man would not want to be a man and why Mitch couldn't just do it on the quiet.

Bernadette said he was in shock. Mothers are often more tuned in to their children's emotional states. Fathers often choose to connect in a different way. Inside herself, Di's mother has been preparing for this moment all her life, so she's not as floored. Berns believed Di's dad would be a great support once he had processed the news. "A huge change has occurred in his life as well. He needs a chance to get his head around it."

Di hadn't thought of it like that. That really helped her to understand his response and his needs.

Di said, "When I first came to group and, to paraphrase Eva, dressed like a drag queen … it's fine Eva, I know you were right … I dressed like that because I thought I had to exaggerate all the features that make a woman, a woman. I believed that the clothes and the make-up would automatically make me female, that there wasn't much else to it. Boy, was I wrong! I have learned so much from all of you about what it truly means to be a woman, and it's got absolutely nothing to do with the way you dress or look. Thank you for giving me an invaluable education."

Di released a lot of shame and guilt and anxiety on the weekend. Telling her parents was the turning point for her. Her journey won't be easy, but it will be easier.

Di is such a beautiful human being, I wish, wish, wish that everyone she tells just hugs her and loves her and says, 'You go girl!'

Tuesday 9th
7.15 pm

Along with Di's awesome news, Eva told us her husband came crawling home saying he'd made a big mistake and that he wanted to try again. He didn't know what he was thinking when he left. Eva was the only one for him and she was looking fantastic.

Eva let him in and gave him a coffee. She was enjoying watching him grovel. The more he rambled, the more he revealed. Seems the big-haired, big-boobed woman he ran off with, ran off with another dude. They'd been living in her townhouse and he was spending up big on her – new car, new wardrobe, etc. They were enjoying a great social life until she met Gary – a younger, more attractive man. She packed her stuff into her car and nicked off.

To add insult to injury, turns out the townhouse wasn't hers. She'd been house-sitting for friends. They returned home, found a strange, lonely man living there and promptly threw him out. Low on cash and homeless, he decided to knock on Eva's door.

Eva listened patiently to his tale of woe. She nodded her sympathy and oohed and aahed in all the right places. The philandering hubby thinks he's got her on side so he starts talking about going to get his stuff out of the car and he'll be moved back in, in a jiffy.

They get up, she follows him to the door, he steps outside and she says, "Fuck you very much for coming by. It was shit seeing you. Never darken my door again. I've filed for divorce. Have a nice day."

Then she slammed the door in his gobsmacked face!

Gretel's doing just as well. She's got a boyfriend – just the one! He was a swinger too but they've decided to be exclusive. He was kinda tired of the whole game and after much emotional release, she arrived at the conclusion that what she really wants is a 'normal' boring relationship where she and her man can wear their pyjamas, snuggle on the couch and watch DVDs.

Love me those girls!

Wednesday 10th
10.25 pm

Seems Bernadette's 'name something simple you'd like to do' was not so 'simple' at all. On the face of it, sure. But it turns out each thing held a deeper meaning. Gretel mentioned it first.

"You're a sneaky one, Bernadette. I went to the grocery to buy some oyster sauce like Jodie told me to and when I'm in there looking at all the stuff, I remembered that I'd said I wanted to cook because I wanted to nurture and then it struck me – 'I want to nurture'. Not necessarily with food, but with my heart. I still have that desire to be a mother. But I'm too old to have my own children so I thought, what am I going to do? Then I got struck again - maybe I could be a foster parent? I got excited by the idea so I made some phone calls and I'm going to see someone next week." She was beaming.

Then Lou gasped. "I want to save money so I can make some changes in my life but I can never save any because if I had the money, I'd actually have to make the changes. I use money as an excuse to hold myself back. I want to do a Yoga teacher course but, conveniently, I can never afford it. See, I've found my comfort zone with my job. I'm good at it. I'm guaranteed to do well. If I tried something new, I might not do so well. If I have money then I've got no excuses for not doing the things I want to do. Bloody hell!"

Tina wants to run a marathon but she fears she's not strong enough – mentally, emotionally, physically - to finish what she starts. She fears failure and disappointing people and letting them down. And there she was thinking she never got started because she was too unfit!

Marion wants to learn the piano but she believes she doesn't have the staying power to go through the long, hard process of learning it. She wants to know how to play instantly and if that can't happen, she's not interested. What she really wants is to entertain people. She wants to be a performer. But she's too insecure to put herself out there as an artist, so she subconsciously overwhelms herself before she even begins.

Finn wants to feel important. Di wants to feel whole. Nicole wants to be respected. Arrabella wants to teach. Heidi wants to feel connected. Meredith wants to be heard. Eva wants to be loved. But we're all so busy making up excuses and sabotaging ourselves, we never allow ourselves to have what we yearn for.

And me – the thing I realise I desire is freedom; to come and go as I please. This is why I long to travel. I could go to Bordeaux for the Doc. Go to Sweden and pretend I'm meeting ABBA. I could walk the road to Santiago. Yet I never book a single holiday. I am trapped in a prison of my own making.

I use the excuse, 'I need to learn Spanish before I get to Spain'. That's rubbish! I would always find an English speaking person if I needed one. My real resistance is: I don't want to travel alone and I don't want to leave Cool.

I said to Lou on the way home tonight, "I can't leave Cool. She'd fret. She wouldn't understand where I'd gone or that I'll be back. She's used to a lot of love and attention and if I'm not around to give it to her, she'd feel distressed. She'd be confused and worried. And what if something happened to me and I didn't come home? Suddenly she'd have no one to love her and what if she went to live somewhere else and someone was mean to her, she'd be so devastated. I need to be around to protect her."

Taking her eyes off the road for longer than she should have, Lou turned to me and said, "Hello. What situation does that sound like?"

Shit, it was me. I was projecting my own life and feelings onto Cool.

Lou said, "I would look after Cool and I promise I would love her as much as you do. And if you never came home, she would live with me forever and I would always protect her and look after her. Dan loves her. Liam loves her. She will never be alone."

And then I burst into tears.

Thursday 11th
9.45 pm

We are rapidly coming to the end of F:D:H and I haven't dealt with my body issues. I will have to bring it up on Monday. I got the albums out and looked at myself when I was 12 and 13. There are a couple of hideous shots of me at the pool about seven or so months after Dad died. Mum took us for the day. I was wearing an ugly orange bikini and Mum took the photos so how she didn't notice I'd chunked out is beyond me. Grief made her oblivious to what was right in front of her.

Rather than skim past the photos because I can't stand looking at them, I had a good, proper look at them, and I do look chubby – but not quite as bad as my head thinks I do. I've got a fat face, a flabby belly and my thighs are thickish and shapeless. I'm boobless, of course! But I'm not enormous. I'm just short and podgy.

I thought about how I managed to put on at least 10kgs in seven months. To be honest, I didn't really notice. My grief had made me oblivious too. I didn't even particularly notice my clothes getting tighter. If I'd said anything, which I don't remember if I did or not, Mum probably just thought I'd grown out of them, as kids do.

I think I know why I developed an emotional bond to lollies and chocolates. Dad loved them. He was mad on lollies and toffees and at least three times a week he'd bring us home a sweet – liquorice, lollipops, mixed lollies - that type of thing. If he took us to the pictures, we always went to the shop first and bought lollies and chocolates to eat during the movie. We did that because it was cheaper than buying them at the cinema and the shop had more choice.

If ever I was really upset about something, Dad would ease the pain with something sweet. All my pocket money went on lollies. I associate some of the happiest moments of my life with confectionary and I especially associate it with Dad.

To keep him close, I ate lollies. Obviously I ate too many and I ate them every day. I was heading for puberty so I was changing anyway so it was just really bad timing that I decided to stuff my face with sweets at the same time as my hormones were kicking in.

I wonder how different my body would have been if I'd been healthier during the transition? I'll never know.

As I looked at my stubby little legs and my round belly and my chubby cheeks, I suddenly started to cry. I felt so sad for that 13 year old girl who was sitting at home one day, reading a book she loved and just minding her own business, when the Fuhrer came along and started telling her she was fat and ugly and unlovable. I'd already been through enough pain and sorrow. Why did he need to add to it? So, what was originally just an emotional bond to sweets became a complete and utter dysfunction around food and my body.

For god's sake, a bit of weight is no reason to hate someone. It's no reason to tell someone they're a sub-standard human. A less than perfect body is not the worst thing in the world to have. I was always kind to animals and I looked out for Mick and Donna. I tried to be a good daughter, a good sister, and a good friend.

I may not have always got it right, but I tried.

Friday 12th
10.20 pm

When Lou got home I asked her if she'd saved her dollar this week?

"Shit. I forgot to put it in the jar. I'll go and do it now."

When she got back she asked if I'd learned my second word?

"Yep. Because you've now got two dollars, you've got more than uno."

"What's two in Spanish?"

"Dos."

"So why didn't you say I've got dos dollars?"

"Because I'm learning one word a week and this week it's one."

"So how do you know what two is then?"

"I cheated and learned how to count to five!"

"You rebel, you!"

Even though we all realised the bigger picture symbolism of our 'small' action, Bernadette encouraged us to keep doing the 'small' thing because it would help us achieve our bigger goals.

I told Lou I'd looked through the albums yesterday and I moaned about my body.

She said, "If you lived on a desert island all by yourself, would you care how your body looked?"

"Probably not. No one could judge me so it wouldn't matter."

"Exactly. So stop giving a shit about what other people think."

If I'd said that to Bernadette, she would have moved in close, looked at me lovingly and asked why I care about other people judging me. Then she would have held me while I cried and raved and released all my feelings. Unfortunately, Lou wasn't thinking like a counsellor and she probably didn't feel like listening to me moan and complain anyway. She was tired after a long week at work. Tough love was all she had. I felt sorry that I'd brought it up.

"You are right," I said. "I'm gonna mention it on Monday though because I want to see how Bernadette deals with it."

Lou softened. "Your body is not as bad as you think it is. Yes, your bum pokes out and your legs are a bit bigger than your upper so you're not in perfect proportion. The hard truth is, you will never be six foot tall and you will never have legs like Elle McPherson. It's never going to happen. You know what I think makes someone attractive - a sense of peace and self-confidence. That does more for someone's looks than any surgery or diet ever could because the way you feel, literally oozes from every pore. Unhappiness and self-loathing can make even the most gorgeous person seem unattractive. It's a cliché but, seriously, it's all about what's on the inside that counts."

"My liver is beautiful."

We laughed.

"You don't mind getting naked and flashing your bod when it comes to sex," she said.

"That's because nature gave us pheromones and hormones to block the embarrassment factor. If it didn't no one would ever have sex. All those noises and fluids and weird faces!"

"I hear ya!"

Yeah, and now I hear you and Liam! Even after all these months they're still frickin' noisy. Sex is not a spectator sport!

Saturday 13th
9.22 am

Dan dad fact: "He loved the ocean, but only to look at. We'd walk along the beach and he'd say, 'People have no business in the sea. It's not our natural habitat. We have no business to feed from it either. We get enough food from the land. It's wrong to take the food that other species rely on for their survival'. He never ate seafood."

"Your dad was a bit of a hippie, I reckon. I know I would have loved him."

"He was a really good guy."

My dad fact: "He was a soft touch. Mick struggled a bit with English at school and if he had to write a story, he would go to Dad, ask for ideas, then somehow get Dad to write the whole thing for him. Mick would get back from footy training to find his homework all done. Mum never knew. If she did, she would have gone mad. To keep up Mick's grade, I took over after Dad died. I didn't mind because I loved writing."

Delicious smells were coming from the kitchen so I went to investigate. Dinner party tonight. We're responsible for the main course this time, so Lou's making two lasagnes – one vegetarian and one meat lovers. I understand what Gretel means about watching someone cook. It's pleasurable. Lou is so good in the kitchen. She says cooking relaxes her. It just irritates me.

"You must teach me how to cook one of these days."

"You hate cooking!"

"I know. But I should learn."

"Why? You've got me."

"For now. It won't be this way forever."

"Maybe not, but it doesn't have to change right now."

Dan stuck his head in to see if he could tag along tonight.

"You're always welcome, Danny boy." Lou said.

"Cool. I'll go and get a couple of bottles of vino."

I'm glad Dan's coming. I won't be the odd one out.

4.30 pm

Popped round to Mick's to see the girls. Sarah's got a cold so I stopped and got a DVD on the way. We snuggled up and watched 'The Incredibles'. And it is incredible! All that brilliant 3D animation. Just stunning. So many clever people on the planet!

It felt odd watching a film and not eating lollies. I was going to buy some, but I remembered that I wasn't going to go against Liz's wishes anymore. She got home just as I was leaving and she was in a good mood. She was very nurturing towards Sarah.

This puzzles me about people – how we can be polar opposites depending on the situation. When they're well, she's tough on them. When they're sick, she's all over them like a cheap suit. Why can't she just be consistently kind?

She could potentially set up a pattern of hypochondria in those girls because they'll soon work out, if they haven't already, that being unwell gets them kindness and good attention.

I'm not sure if I'll ever really confront Liz. What would change? Nothing. All I'd do is set up animosity and discomfort. I'll support the girls. That will be the best thing, in the long run.

Gonna get ready for fun at Lennie and Katrina's. Got my trusty jeans ready to wear. Oh yay, just realised - Lennie won't need to drive so he'll be able to guzzle as much booze as he wants. Can't wait! Better go heavy on the orange oil, just in case.

Sunday 14th

Monthly Dinner Party report coming to you live from Jodie and Cool

Cat's bed at approx. 9.30 am. With a heavy head caused by too many glasses of red, this reporter wonders why she's even awake?

The moment I walked in, I was rushed. Everyone was checking to see if I was doing ok because it's only been three weeks since Nan's funeral. Their concern was really nice. Everyone was glad to see Dan and Liam.

Lennie pointed at me and Dan and said, "Are you two going out now?"

That caught a lot of attention and everyone was waiting to know.

"Should we tell them, Dan?"

"Go ahead," he said.

"Dan and I are fact buddies. Nothing more."

Lennie's eyes popped. "Did you say 'fact' or 'fuck'?"

"Fact." I kinda mumbled it so he still couldn't be sure.

He turned to the others. "Did she say 'fact' or 'fuck'?"

They knew exactly what I'd said because I'd mentioned it to a couple of them previously, but they played along and pretended they weren't sure.

He mumbled to himself. "Has to be 'fuck' because 'fact' doesn't make sense."

That set the tone for the evening. Dan and I were playful and naughty all night and Lennie couldn't take his eyes off us. What I did discover is that Dan and I have a really good rapport and we bounce off each other really well. He's quick. I'm quick.

I drank more than I should have so of course I got even flirtier and friendlier as the night wore on. And when Emma broke the awesome news that she and Brenton are expecting, I touched Dan's arm and said, "Aaaaw, they're having a baby." Then I batted my eyes at him.

"You two are definitely doin' it," Lennie slurred. "I can tell. You just … I've been watching and … Jodes, you're being nice. You're gettin' laid."

That made me and Dan laugh even more. God knows the wine helped.

Katrina put him out of his misery and explained the dad facts.

"Nah. They're doin' it."

And just for a fleeting second I thought, I wish we were!

I'm glad Lou stopped drinking when she noticed I was guzzling more than my usual two, so she was able to drive. If she hadn't stopped we would have had to crash on LenKat's floor, and I didn't fancy that.

Katrina is great when she only has to put up with you in small, prearranged doses. If we'd had to crash, she would have been irritated and put out. She's not that good at going with the flow. I think it's because she's too anal and if her routine is disrupted, she struggles to improvise. Penny said she's been like it all her life. As a kid, she needed structure and organisation and if anyone ever suggested anything spontaneous, she inevitably said no. Apparently family holidays were challenging! I don't know if it's just a pattern or something akin to Asperger's.

It's why Rich left. He couldn't live with it in the end. Drove him mad. They didn't even make their fourth wedding anniversary. Lennie doesn't seem to have a problem with it. He probably likes having someone who does everything. She's efficient. The house is always spotless. The fridge is always full and the kids are organised. Maybe that's why they work - he can handle her neuroses and she can handle his quirks. They're even.

I'll give him his due though. Lennie is a good dad. He's got all the time in the world for Krystal and Harrison. He was super-excited when Kat was pregnant and he was fully hands-on when they were babies. He always says they're good value. You can see he's proud of them.

His ex-wife didn't want kids. So I don't know why he married her when he knew that to begin with! He probably thought he could change her mind, but when it became clear she wasn't giving in, they split. It got a bit nasty though and she managed to take him to the cleaners. That's probably why he can be a sexist sod. He's hurt and, instead of dealing with it, he just leaks his acrimony in caustic little bits. Bernadette would sort him out in no time.

The next dinner party is at Penny and Heath's but we're doing it a week earlier because they're going away for a month. They're taking the kids to Disneyland and Heath is desperate to see the Grand Canyon. He loves geology.

Now, am I going to get up or am I going to go back to sleep? Hmmmm?

Sleep it is.

Monday 15th
11.15 pm

Bernadette rubbed her hands in glee when I said, "I hate my body."

"Yes! Every time I run a new group, this always comes up and it's one of my favourite things. I was just beginning to think it wasn't going to come up this time around so thank you, Jodie. Ok, who here hates their body or parts of it?"

Every hand went up. "What do you hate?"

We had: stretch marks, baby scars, saggy boobs, no boobs, fat, flab, cellulite, bunions, big knuckles, big feet, spider veins, varicose veins, cankles, wrinkles, grey hair, body hair, freckles, jowls, big hips, no hips, a penis, too short, too wide, barge arse, pancake arse, bat-wing arms, fat guts, stubby toes, thunder thighs, no proportion, big nipples, muffin tops, double chins, weird labias, rolls of back fat, saggy skin, Adam's apple, fluid, large pores, age spots.

"Excellent. Stand up and form a circle." We all stood. "Now strip down to your underwear." With that, Bernadette started to undress.

The panic and stress that went around that circle was phenomenal and I swear the temperature shot up about 20 degrees! You'd think she'd asked us to get naked and star in a porno. We all stood with our arms folded across our chests, wide-eyed and slack-jawed. We protested, defended our right not to have to, questioned the merits of it, held it up as pointless and ridiculous, said it was exploitative and highly inappropriate. Anything and everything we could think of so as not to have to do it. Eva threatened to walk.

Bernadette stood there, proud as you please, in large undies and a sensible bra. She's got a big belly, no bum and thin legs.

"Come on, take it off. Trust me. It won't be as bad as you imagine it is. You know I would never do anything that would hurt or embarrass any of you. Think about all the weeks you've been coming here and all the techniques we've used. If you believe that any of those things haven't helped you, painful as they may have felt at the time, then you can sit this one out."

No one moved. She grabbed her belly and started to jiggle it. "Look how soft and round my belly is," she said.

Heidi and Arrabella nodded to each other and they both stripped to their underwear. They're young and slim so for them it would be like being at the beach. Eva was sweating bullets. "I can't," she said. She looked stressed.

Di swapped spots in the circle, took her hand and said, "I will, if you will." Eva gave a small sob. Bernadette moved next to her and held her other hand.

Finn, Gretel and Marion went for it, followed by Tina. Lou joined the party – but Lou does have a good body, and then more of us were undressed than not. Meredith and Nicole stripped so that left me, Eva and Di. A few eyes were on us but mostly people were trying to look as if they weren't there. No one was loving this.

"I'm wearing big knickers," Di offered, by way of explanation for not stripping. "I need to, to keep my penis tucked in." Then she laughed nervously at what she'd just admitted. "I wore a lacy G-string once but it was a disaster. It just kept falling out."

It was said in jest so we all laughed. Eva gave a light chuckle.

I said to Di and Eva, "We could all undress together."

I looked around the circle and there were all shapes and sizes. There was young and there was old. There was firm and there was flabby. There was scarred and there was flawless. And yet I had no real thought about any of it.

"I'm going for it," I said. "Are you with me?"

I took my jumper and t-shirt off first because my top half is my best half. I pointed at my moulded cup bra and said, "My boobs are so small they don't fill the cup properly."

Di let go of Eva's hand and said, "We'll take our shirts off together."

When they were done, Eva glanced at Di's shirtless chest and she looked sad for a second because the first and most obvious thing were the fake breasts inside her lacy bra. Eva looked self-consciously down at her own ample breasts inside her rather plain bra.

We were halfway there.

We slipped off our shoes. Di unbuttoned her skirt, removed it and threw it onto her chair. I'd kill for Di's legs – long, lean, toned. Eva and I pulled down our tracky pants, and kicked them away. We were both wearing socks and I laughed at how we looked. We took our socks off then we both burst into tears.

Di gripped Eva's hand and she said to me. "Come by me Jodie, hold my other hand." I swapped spots and Di clutched my hand in hers.

And that was it. 13 women stood in a circle in only their underwear, desperately self-conscious; desperately embarrassed; desperately wishing they'd worn better underwear; desperately wishing they'd shaved their legs and underarms; desperately wishing they'd done a bit of exercise; desperately hoping no one was looking at them.

Bernadette clapped. "Now I want you to grab a flabby bit or a bit you don't like, and shake it, jiggle it, wiggle it. Make noises if you want."

Bernadette grabbed her belly again and made blub, blub, blub sounds. It was funny. I grabbed my saddlebags and jiggled them. Lou grabbed her bum and wooshed it up and down. When everyone had a handful of something and the strange noises filled the room, we started laughing and we started to look at each other.

"Swap where you're grabbing and get yourself a handful of something else," Bernadette said. She grabbed her boobs and jigged them side to side.

I ended up laying my hands all over and I noticed I had a different noise for each part. Eva pummelled and kneaded and shook and jiggled. She looked a bit shell-shocked during the whole thing, but she got into it the same as the rest of us.

And really, it was bloody hilarious. The more we did it, the funnier it became. We were cackling and snorting and whooping. When we were done, Bernadette said, "Now just take a quiet moment and look at each other. Really look and see. Notice everything about each woman's body."

We took it in turns to turn sideways and backwards so everyone got the full 360 perspective. I reckon we did that for about 10 minutes. There was the occasional giggle, but mostly we were quiet. As I looked at those women, I took in their size and shape and their 'flaws' but instead of reeling in horror or thinking they needed to hide themselves away, I just saw beauty and diversity and good people.

Bernadette looked at me. "Jodie, I want you to choose a woman and tell her you hate her because she's got an imperfect body."

I actually balked. "I'm not doing that!"

"Why not?"

"Because that's just not on and it's just not true."

"Yet you'll happily hate yourself for your perceived imperfections. What's the difference?"

She knew I'd have no answer. Then she said, "Ok, hands up anyone who is offended by Jodie's body."

Nothing.

"I don't know who set the current standard of what constitutes the perfect female body but it will pass, the same as every other 'ideal' before it. If you go to an art gallery, you will see how standards of perfection have changed throughout history. There are statues of full-bodied women, paintings showing fleshy, soft bellies and small breasts. Hips that are wider than shoulders. Full, milky thighs. Women of all shapes and sizes have been celebrated in art for centuries. And all of them are beautiful.

"The size and shape of your body is not the only thing you are. To live your life as if it is, is really selling yourself short. There is so, so much to appreciate about yourselves yet most of you discount all your goodness because you've got a big bum or your toes are gnarly. I hope you can see how ludicrous it really is. Don't let the oppression dictate the quality of your life. Treat yourself with kindness. Not only do you deserve it, you've earned it.

"However, accepting your body does not give you permission to endlessly shove junk and crap into it. Take care of your body. Nurture it with good food and drink. Enjoy everything in moderation. Move it every day.

"Now I want this half of the circle to walk to the woman directly opposite. Hold hands and say to each other, 'I love you because you're a wonderful human being'."

Now that we could all do.

Tuesday 16th
1.18 pm

Bernadette has got powerful magic. She just gets to the heart of your shit in seconds. I still don't love my thighs but after seeing all those different bodies, up close and personal like that, I realise that the average body is not that bad. None of us looked like dancers or athletes, but we were still ok. When you take a person as a whole package, you see them in a very different way. Cellulite and chunky bits really don't register.

We have spent the last few months together revealing our deepest secrets and insecurities, yet we were still so shy and reluctant to stand together in our underwear. It was as if we'd just met for the very first time. Really, people wear less at the beach with no problem! It proves we can still feel so isolated so quickly. Staying connected takes work. Thank goodness for laughter. It fixes everything.

Bernadette stayed undressed the rest of the class but we all quickly got re-dressed the moment the exercise was over. I started to feel more self-conscious about my hairy legs than my blob thighs! Another oppression! Di was the most impeccably groomed of all of us and both Finn and Heidi had hairy pits, which they seemed perfectly fine with.

And in news that thrilled me, Meredith told us her daughter is coming home for Christmas. Meredith was so excited but she was even more excited because she's decided to go back with her daughter and spend six months overseas. She'll be based in England but she's going to travel to Europe and Ireland. She's always wanted to go to a proper Irish pub and have a proper Guinness. I told her to have one for me as well.

Wednesday 17th
11.17 pm

Monday's underwear exercise was designed to break down some of the negative patterns and beliefs we have about our bodies but because Eva and I struggled the most, and because I brought it up in the first place, Bernadette wanted to work on helping us release some of the deeper feelings. I went first.

I talked about Dad and lollies and my weight gain and how the Fuhrer berated and belittled me and how his words took root and grew into their own living entity because, when I looked around, I saw that society agreed with him. I cried that I was just so disappointed in my body and I couldn't understand why I couldn't have been blessed with something nicer, something that I would have been happy with. Why did life have to be so hard and unfair?

And Bernadette did exactly what I needed – she moved in close, held me, nurtured me, and said she was so sorry that life felt unfair. She was sorry I couldn't see the beauty in my body and that I broke myself down into shapes and sizes instead of seeing myself as a whole person – mind, body, spirit. She was sorry someone had made me feel like crap and had set out to purposely undermine me. Then she pretended the Fuhrer was next to her and she did what should have been done at the time – she stood up for me.

"How dare you speak to Jodie like that. Shut the fuck up, right now.

How dare you be so spiteful and hateful towards a young girl, you powerless, weak, frightened little man. Leave her alone. Leave her alone now and don't you ever dare say anything like that to her again. Do you hear me. If you so much as say boo, I will kick your sorry arse."

With each sentence, I cried harder. It felt so overwhelming to be defended. It felt so foreign. And when she said, 'I'll kick your arse', a laugh broke through the tears.

"I will karate chop your spleen. I will Chinese burn your scrotum. I will yank out your hair. I will flick your eyeballs. I will kick your shins. I will stamp on your toes. And you know what – you've got ugly knees. Jodie is a warm, wonderful, beautiful girl. Never, ever come near her again. Loser."

Eva got pretty much the same deal and she responded in pretty much the same way.

I would like to think my attitude towards my body will change. It's been such a focus in my life for so long, I can't imagine it becoming a secondary force. The first step is admitting the issue out loud and the next step is working to smash the beliefs and patterns and dysfunction and releasing those long trapped, unexpressed feelings. I've done that now but I have a feeling it will take a little time for this one to fade away.

Bernadette said my brain has to rewire itself now that we've shattered the perpetual loop my 'body recording' played on. By releasing the feelings, that information no longer 'exists' so as my brain rewires, it can't get laid down anywhere. What I'll put up with for a while is just an echo, but the echo will fade and one day I'll notice my thinking and my attitude has changed. That day can't come soon enough!

Bernadette also said that when we're kinder about our bodies, we're kinder to them. That sounds promising.

Thursday 18th
2.10 pm

I can't believe it - next week is our last week of F:D:H. We've got two classes left. Bernadette said on our last night she'd like us to present something that shows the group something of ourselves, such as sing, dance, write a poem, tell a story. Anything at all. We'll be given centre stage for a few minutes.

She also asked us to write a letter to ourselves. We're to seal it in an envelope, address it to ourselves and bring it on Monday. Bernadette will post it to us in 12 months time.

I wrote my letter this morning and I was going to record it in you, dear Journal, but I decided not to. I want to get it in 12 months and be surprised by what I wrote.

Di told us that her mum rang to see how she was and to tell her that her dad is feeling a lot better about Di's news. She and Nina are going for lunch on Saturday. Di hasn't told work yet but she's planning to do it sometime in the next few weeks. Around the time she starts hormone treatments, I think.

Bernadette practised half a dozen scenarios with Di for what she could say. Some were funny, some were serious. In all of them, Di released a lot of feelings. That poor woman is a nervous wreck! And timid with it!

In a few of them, Bernadette was making Di be all empowered and demanding. It was funny to watch. In a couple of them, Bernadette got Di to tell her news and Bernadette yawned and was all 'whatever', and acted completely bored as if the news was no big deal.

Di didn't know whether to laugh or cry so she did both, usually together. And there was a lot of cold sweat as well, which is a sure sign of fear.

Bernadette worked really hard to take away the fear, shame, and anxiety. She worked to make the issue so ordinary that it was equivalent to Di telling upper management she was having a ham sandwich for lunch. Di will need to do a bit more release work before she can confidently make her announcement. She wants to keep her job so she wants to make sure she doesn't get steamrolled or bamboozled and find herself being made redundant at her own behest. Bernadette reminded her that if she releases the feelings, the confidence and expectation of getting what she wants will naturally follow. She trusts that Di can do it.

And … it's official. Heidi and Raven are an item. She told him about her mum and he was completely understanding. He was so happy Heidi sorted out her issues because he really likes her a lot. He believes they've spent many lifetimes together and he said to Heidi that he was thankful her mum had her so they could spend this lifetime together as well! Who could not love a man like that? He will treat her so well. She's very lucky. I hope so much that they are happy, happy, happy.

While they all continue to study and work towards their new career goals, Arrabella, Finn, and Heidi are going to share a house ... with Raven as well! They'll sort Raven out in minutes flat if he's got any unexpressed stuff, or if he tries to oppress them! If they're half as happy as me, Lou, and Dan, they may never end up going their separate ways. Especially if one of them is an amazing cook!

Friday 19th
10.00 am

Lou and Liam have just left for a long weekend getaway. They'll be back Sunday night. Dan's having some mates over for a poker night so I'm going to Alice's.

I'm going shopping today and I am going to buy some new jeans and maybe a dress. I will not have a mental breakdown in the change room and I will remember that my body deserves nice fabrics and nice styles.

Lou told me to buy a little black dress, some fake boobs like Di's, stockings, and high shoes. She told me to truss myself up like a Christmas turkey. The boobs would give me better proportion and the shoes would give me longer legs.

"Fake it," she said. "Everyone else does."

I feel like getting a cut and colour too. I'm lucky. I managed to get an appointment for uno o'clock.

5.30 pm

Shopping sucked less than usual. I forced myself to buy jeans and I got a little black dress too. It's so sweet. It's off the shoulder with a fuller skirt that comes just below the knee so it fits properly and it gives the illusion of balance. The lady in the shop was sympathetic to my uneven dilemma and she chose perfectly. For the first time in my life, I asked for help from a salesperson and she was fantastic. Usually I walk in, scan the racks from a safe distance, then leave. Spurred on by the dress, I did what Lou said and got stockings and shoes as well. I gave the boobs a miss because the style of the dress doesn't need them.

Don't know when I'll ever wear the outfit, but I like having it.

My hair looks amazing. Julia was beside herself when I said I wanted a new cut and colour. She gave it golden highlights and layered it. Of course it looks good because she knows how to style it. It suits me when it's layered because it goes shaggy. A bit messy is better for me. I can't do perfectly coiffed. I look like I'm pretending to be an adult or something.

Am off to Alice's to show off my fabulous do and eat her delicious home-made pizza. I chose my friends well!

Saturday 20th
2.30 pm

Last night, I got home about 11 and the poker game was in full swing. John, Nick and George were still here but Matty had done his dough so he'd gone home. He had to be up early for work anyway. Cool was fast asleep on Matt's empty chair. The cigar smoke, noise, and smell of stale beer and microwaved nachos obviously didn't bother her.

I was going to brush my teeth and head to bed but the guys told me to come and sit with them. They were in fine form and we were having a good laugh and then I had a beer and a cigar, followed by another beer. Next thing, Dan staked me $20, I was wearing a visor, and I was in the game.

I'm crap at cards and I'm even crapper at gambling, but I managed to win a few hands – purely out of luck. My little cash pile grew and I had another beer to celebrate. I don't even particularly like beer, but when in Rome.

The guys were trying to figure out my 'tell', which I don't even have but they reckon I was a shark because I won four hands in a row. The ante was 50 cents and John tried to throw in 20 so he was forced to do a nudie run around the room. Let me tell ya, that ain't a pretty sight sober but at 3am and five beers down, it's Nureyev. High-fives all round.

John was the first to crash. He went to the loo and never returned. We went on a hunt and found him asleep on the bathroom floor with a hand towel on his head.

Nick was next. He got up to stretch his back. He lay on the floor to do a twist, farted, and just fell asleep. We were poking him, but he was gone.

Dan was 'have you heard my Sean Connery' drunk and I was half a beer away from doing a nudie run of my own. George kept nodding off mid-hand so we swapped his cards for losing ones. We did that for three rounds until he woke up mid-swap. We let him win that hand. At 4.30 we were well and truly done. George crashed on the couch. I got him a blanket and pillow so at least he'd have a decent sleep.

I stepped over John, brushed my teeth and headed for bed. Cool was still fast asleep on the chair.

I was just in my room when Dan reeled in.

"Hey fact buddy. It's Saturday. Wanna hear my dad fact?"

"Now?"

"Yeah. I just thought of it. Hold on a sec."

He disappeared for a minute then returned with a photo album. He lay on my bed and opened it.

"I got this from my mum yesterday. Check this out. That's my dad. He wore platform shoes and flares. He dressed like Greg Brady."

Before I had a chance to have a look, Dan fell face first into his dad's paisley shirt. He was fast asleep.

I wrestled the album from under him, he rolled onto his side and slept on.

I pushed Dan over, got under the covers and fell blissfully asleep.

I woke up about nine. Dan was still there and Cool was curled up in the nook of his body. I was so thirsty that I couldn't go back to sleep and the combo of last night's pizza, beer, nachos, and cigars wasn't doing my breath any favours. I'd brushed my teeth before bed but there wasn't a hint of mint to be found in the dumpster that was my mouth.

I staggered up, weaved my way to the bathroom, stepped over the still sleeping John, and brushed my teeth and tongue. It could tell it was going to take a tongue transplant before my mouth felt normal again.

I needed a coffee. When I put the kettle on, John and Nick appeared. Nick had a big crease across his face. God knows how he got it. Grunts were used in place of words as water was guzzled, toast was scoffed and we had two coffees each. I brushed my teeth and tongue again.

George got in on the second round of coffee. We were a seedy, sorry lot.

The guys helped me clean up the mess and the empties, then they left.

It was 10.30 by then and Dan still hadn't appeared.

I was ready for sleep number two so I went back to bed. Dan and Cool were still there. I just hopped in and fell straight back to sleep.

I woke up just over an hour ago and Dan and his album were gone. I had a shower, more coffee, toast, tongue brushing, and now I feel a little more human.

11.25 pm

When Dan got home, I was in my pyjamas, snuggling under a blanket reading a book. I don't know how he does it, but he looked good. No bloat. No sallow skin. No glassy eyes. Shiny sapphire peepers sparkling in a shiny, bright face. He asked if I wanted a coffee but I opted for a herbal tea instead. My coffee quota had already been over-filled.

"Are you staying home tonight?"

"Yep. Just me, my pyjamas and my cat."

"Good. Me too. I went shopping for food. I'll cook us my famous mushroom risotto to say thanks for cleaning up."

"What time did you get up?"

"Not sure. Sorry I fell asleep on your bed."

"It's alright. I just shoved you over. I don't think you moved all night."

"Those guys are a bad influence."

"Tell me about it!"

He brought me my tea.

"You know what. I'm gonna have a shower and put my PJs on too."

"Yay. Pyjama party."

"That's if I still have them. My mum got them for me. I've never worn them."

After his shower, Dan found his PJs, still in the packet. Cotton. White with blue stripes. He said they were comfy. "I feel like Hugh Hefner, wearing pyjamas at five in the afternoon."

He cooked us up a delicious storm and we even managed to get a glass of wine down us. He's good in the kitchen too. Relaxed and happy to cook. Maybe I've just got an attitude about it because of my food issues.

Full and happy, we were on the couch. Cool was asleep on the rug.

"Shit, I forgot to ask. What's your dad fact?"

"I'm gonna go same as yours this week," I said. "My dad also wore platform shoes and flares."

"When did I tell you that?"

"About 4.30 this morning. You brought your photo album into my room, told me your fact then fell asleep."

"I don't remember. I did wonder why the album was there. And I did wonder how I ended up on your bed."

"Mystery solved."

"I'll go and grab it."

It was like looking at my own albums, but with slightly better shots. Page after page of the same ugly shirts and facial hair. The same distant shots. There were shots of Dan as a kid. He was so cute.

We started at the start again and Dan lingered on the shots of his dad. He ran his fingers across some of the photos. "He was really kind. He helped out once a week at a homeless shelter, making sandwiches and soup."

"When's the last time you saw him."

"It was just before he went back to America. I was 20 so … 1984. He went there in 1980 to work. He worked in France as well. He came home for six months, then went back to the US. He didn't look good when I saw him but we didn't know he had AIDS."

Dan went quiet.

"I didn't even get to say goodbye."

Dan's face fell and his eyes went shiny. It's hard for a man to cry and it's even harder to do it in front of someone. Shame and embarrassment will shut them down before they have a chance to begin. I figured if I could get him to kind of forget I was there, he might allow himself to feel.

I put my arm around his shoulders and guided him towards me. "Lie your head in my lap."

And he did. And he cried. I stroked his hair and said nothing.

He sobbed as quietly as he could. Tears ran across his nose and fell into my lap. This whole 'dad fact' thing has really stirred up some deep grief in him.

As I stroked him gently, I made a wish for men – that they would allow themselves to express their pain and sorrow. Feelings are perceived as a weakness but it's just not true. It takes great strength to express feelings.

He must have been exhausted because he fell asleep. I just kept on touching him and loving him.

Sunday 21st
8.30 pm

Dan slept for about two hours. When he woke up, he sat up and looked a little disoriented. He found it hard to look at me. I offered to make him a cup of tea but he decided to go to bed.

I stayed up and did the dishes then I wrote the last entry.

This morning, I could hear him in the kitchen. A few minutes later he knocked gently on my door.

"Come in."

He opened the door. "I've made breakfast if you'd like some."

I followed him to the kitchen. He'd done bacon, eggs, mushrooms, tomatoes, toast. There was enough to feed four.

As we ate, he talked about a guy from work who's restoring an old car. I pretended as if what we were doing was perfectly normal and it was business as usual.

After my shower, he asked if I wanted to go to lunch at the pub.

"I cannot eat another thing. How about a walk on the beach instead."

"It'll be cold."

"Rug up."

There were a few lone souls on the beach. We ambled along not really talking about much, but you could literally feel the unspoken words in the air. I was relieved when he finally mentioned his dad.

"I miss my dad. A lot. We had a really good relationship. He was always so interesting and I liked the way he thought about things."

"You must have been devastated when he died."

"I was. But I think what hurt most was that I didn't even get to go to his funeral. He died in California and his boyfriend had him cremated. Mum got a phone call after the event, and that was it. It was a bit shitty."

I reached out and took his hand.

"He contracted PCP and that's what killed him."

"What's that?"

"Some kind of pneumonia. It was a common thing with people who had AIDS."

We stopped and looked at the ocean. "I was with Miranda since I was 16. I got married a year after he died and I never told Miranda he had AIDS. You probably remember how it was in the '80s. Everyone was afraid. I thought she wouldn't marry me if she knew."

I folded my arms around Dan and held him. "I'm sorry you never got to say goodbye to your dad and I'm sorry you had to hide the truth. That was a big secret to carry."

He squeezed me tight. Then the hug went longer than it should have. The air between us changed. It was so charged that neither of us could pretend we hadn't felt it.

We parted. He smiled his gorgeous smile and he touched my cheek.

"Thank you."

My insides were doing flip-flops. I grabbed his hand and we resumed walking.

I knew I fancied him after that lunch at the pub. It was just easier to deny it. Now I can't. What am I going to do?

Dan and I went our separate ways when we got home. I don't think Lou and Liam noticed anything different when they got home. Actually, I think it's just me who feels strange and everything else actually feels as it always has.

Why is he so gorgeous? Why? And how am I going to get past this?

Monday 22nd
7.30 am

It's the crack of dawn and I'm wide awake! Daniel. Daniel. Daniel.
I'm going for a walk.

10.00 am

It was freezing out there! And there were so many joggers and walkers. Who does that at that hour! Insane people, that's who.

Nearly every song my iPod selected was a love song and it chose two Silverchair songs and who's the lead singer of Silverchair – Daniel Johns.

It's a conspiracy.

6.00 pm

Dan's just got home. He was so normal and so ... normal. I have got to stop thinking about him.

How can so much change in just one day?

10.20 pm

I said to Bernadette, "I'm sad for men. I'm sad they struggle to express anything and get deeply embarrassed should a feeling accidentally come out."

She said, "It's a form of oppression to deny a human being the right to have a feeling. There's no logical reason for doing it. Feelings are real. We all have them. It cannot be denied they exist.

"It's a very strange 'rule' that boys don't cry because anyone who has ever raised a son or been around a young boy knows they do cry. They cry as readily and as easily as a girl, and for the same reasons. All human beings have a similar set of triggers that start a feeling going but for some unfathomable reason, boys are conditioned early to deny it, suck it up, swallow it down.

"Boys are often cuddled less and left alone more. Apparently because hugs and connection will make them 'soft', and we can't have that! This sets them up to be unfamiliar and uncomfortable with closeness. Anger seems to be about the only emotion they're not shamed for expressing because it's a 'tough' emotion, not a sissy one. From very early on, they're prepped to 'be a man' – strong, fearless, stoic.

"They're often burdened by over-responsibility if someone 'strong' is required. They're told they're the gender who 'do' stuff like protect, hunt, fix. They're sent to war and expected to kill as if it means nothing. And if they have a feeling about it later, they're encouraged to repress it. 'Suck it up Soldier. This is war'.

"Males get treated as if they don't feel pain – emotional or physical. A man is told to harden up if he hurts himself. He's expected to shrug it off and carry on. The same applies if his feelings are hurt.

"They are flesh and blood and heart and soul like you and me. If you feel it, they feel it. The best thing we can do for boys and men is welcome their feelings, never judge their feelings, never shame them for their feelings, hold them, love them, encourage them to express, never shut them down, don't try to 'fix' them and, again, welcome their feelings.

"If boys are treated like this from the start then men won't have a problem. But that's in a perfect world. Because the oppression already exists, the best we can do is stop perpetuating it and, starting from now, welcome their feelings. Eventually they'll get comfortable with expressing and even admitting that they do feel and they do hurt and they do love and they do want closeness.

"The feelings spectrum is huge and that men have to choose from one half of it and women the other is restrictive and limiting. All the emotions are available to all of us. Choose from the full range."

"I love you, Bernadette. You know everything. Thank you for doing what you do."

Bernadette gave me the best hug. "It's a pleasure."

Tuesday 23rd
12.22 pm

On my walk this morning, what was the third song my iPod threw at me – Elton John's, 'Daniel'! I cannot believe this! When we start to focus on something, we suddenly notice it everywhere. It's like if you buy a red car, you suddenly notice how many red cars there are on the road.

I have really got to figure out what's going on with me. Do I have feelings for him or do I just feel protective and nurturing towards him because of Saturday night? Am I so lonely that, because we've had a bit of fun and we've been sharing our dad stuff, I've gone and made it into something it's not?

I don't know????

I do think about him. A lot! I think about his gorgeous face and his gorgeous hair and his perfect smile and his hot bod and the easy-going way he has about him.

See … look at that. That's lust right there!

Maybe that's it – I haven't had sex for a long time, I'm just bloody frisky!

Stop thinking about his hands. Stop it! Think of something else …

Nicole said she was going to do something … what was it? Oh, I remember – Nicole is quitting her high-stress job and she is going to Alaska!

She's tired of feeling tired and she works, works, works. She is so busy doing everything for everyone else at work and at home, she's taking some time for herself.

Her husband did not like it one little bit but Nicole calmly explained that if he wanted her to stay sane and if he wanted to keep their marriage and their family together, he had no choice in this. Deny me my freedom and get a divorce. Send me off with your support and save me and our marriage.

She's renting a cabin and taking eight weeks to renew and refresh. Then she'll return, find another, less demanding, job and their life can continue.

Man, that is huge!

Huge like Dan's ... stop it!!!!

Wednesday 24th
12.30 pm

It's our last class tonight and I feel so sad about it. 20 weeks have flown by and I still cannot believe how much has happened to me in that short amount of time.

I'm not sure what to do tonight? I could read that picture book I wrote? Nah, needs pictures to make it work.

We have to show something of ourselves so, who am I?

I am Jodie Winters – daughter, sister, sister-in-law, aunty, friend, animal and nature lover, writer, walker, journal keeper, big thinker, feminist, avid reader, movie lover, left-winger, wanna-be traveller, selectively spiritual, dreamer, freedom seeker.

I am Jodie Winters - hopeful.

11.45 pm

It was an emotional class tonight. Everyone was sad we'd come to an end but everyone was looking forward to the future.

Bernadette started the proceedings. She sang a beautiful old Scottish song her mother used to sing to her when she was a child. Her voice had a beautiful lilt and her eyes filled with tears when she sang. It came straight from her heart.

Heidi spoke about the Aura. She described its layers and colours and she said that our auras had expanded and grown so much over the past months. Our expanded energy would touch more people and we'll find that people are drawn to us because we'll feel so nice to be near. Then she read a gorgeous quote from Rumi – 'You are not a drop in the ocean. You are the ocean in a drop'. She said it reminded her how alike we all are, and how connected.

Nicole showed us a picture of the cabin she's rented in Alaska. She's leaving next Thursday. She's going to read and hike and meditate and get massages and facials and just do nothing. She's going to use the time to figure out who she is because when she was trying to work out what she could do tonight, she struggled to think of something that defined her in some way.

Marion did a stand-up comedy routine! It was hilarious. She is very funny and she's so good at the delivery. Along with some original material, she threw in a few of her favourite jokes and the one I remember that tickled my funny bone was:

Doctor, doctor, do you think I need glasses?

You certainly do – this is the post office!

Di loves shoes so she brought in half a dozen pairs and told us where she got them from, why she chose them, what they mean to her and how she felt the first time she wore them. She had this silky-looking red pair she'd ordered on-line from some exclusive shop in Paris that cost her $2,000! Apparently, from that shop, they're a cheap pair!

Finn played the guitar and sang a song she wrote. It was amazing. Her voice is like listening to Angels sing. She could make millions out of it. In all the weeks we've been coming here, she never once mentioned she could play music and sing. That would be the first thing I'd tell everyone!

Arrabella wrote a poem called 'The Transformation'. It was about an oyster who lived all alone on the bottom of the sea. One day a fish swam by and saw how sad and lonely the oyster was. The fish wanted the oyster to know happiness so it brought the oyster a grain of sand and laid it gently on her heart. Slowly and lovingly, the oyster created a pearl. It was really beautiful

Meredith can paint! These women are so talented, I can't believe they weren't shouting this stuff from the rafters. She showed us two of her works – a beachscape and a portrait of her daughter. Absolutely and unequivocally mind-blowingly awesome!

Gretel tap-danced. Yes, tap-danced! Many years ago she took a class and she learned one routine. She gave it up after that but she never forgot the steps. She dusted off her shoes, practised for a few days and dazzled us with her lightning feet!

Tina's a dark horse. Turns out she's Wiccan. She made each of us an herb sachet containing lavender and fennel for healing. She blessed each sachet and told us to carry it with us so we could benefit from its energy.

Eva did coin and card tricks. That girl has got sleight of hand Copperfield would envy. She moved the coin along her fingers and she made it appear, disappear, re-appear in random spots. And the cards! I wouldn't want to play poker with her. My brain couldn't keep up.

You really just don't know what skills and talents and spiritual leanings people are hiding.

Louise handed out her most delicious orange and secret ingredient cup cakes. I have no idea what's in them but they are by far the most delicious thing I have ever tasted. As each woman took their cake, Louise told them how they were like the cake – sweet, light, airy, etc. When she gave me mine she said I was the perfect finish to every day. Gorgeous.

And me. I told them that I love the simple things – the sound of rain on the roof, watching a lightning storm, being snuggly and warm inside when it's cold out, reading a book in bed, hearing the birds in the morning, Spring with all its new life, holding a child's hand and putting my face next to theirs, making up songs and dances with my nieces, laughing with my friends, being with my family, looking at photos, smelling flowers, Cool - because she's relaxed, content, in the moment, unaffected, genuine, non-judgemental, loving, and funny. And that a hug, a kiss, and a warm, genuine smile are more valuable to me than a mine full of diamonds.

Thursday 25th
11.25 am

Before we left last night, Bernadette said, "It can become a habit to be a victim. Some people move from one self-help group to another so they can continue to receive attention for their hurts. I would encourage you not to do this. If ever you feel the need to milk your stuff for all it's worth – ask yourself why it suits you to be a victim and work on releasing the feelings around that.

"You will still have hurts and things you need to work on, but you know enough now to be able to do that. You have each others contact details, use them. Ring each other, ring me, and have a rant over the phone - you know you've always got someone who will listen to you without judgement and without trying to fix you.

"You have all transformed in the most amazing ways and I am always so sad, but so excited, to let you go. You can come back anytime, of course, and do this all over again. I am always here for you. If you need me, just ask.

"Life can be so beautiful. Look out your window at the vastness of everything and realise that the fears, dramas and sorrows we put upon ourselves are not worth the time or the trouble or the energy we give them. Smiles and laughs make us feel good for a reason. Aim for happiness."

When I was hugging Bernadette goodbye, I said, "I'm going to miss you. It's ironic - I didn't want to come and now I don't want to leave."

"I have that effect on people."

"Thank you so much for all you have done for me. I can't even begin to explain the impact you've had."

"Then show me instead. Be happy and live a good life."

7.35 pm

OMG. OMG. OMG. Dan just asked me if I wanted to go to dinner with him tomorrow night. On a date. A DATE!!!!!!!!!

He came out of his room just as I was heading to mine. He stopped me, touched my arm and said, "Jodie, would you like to go out with me tomorrow night ..." He took a breath. "On a date?"

I don't know how my face looked because I just stared at him for a second and he must have thought I was trying to think how to say no because he said, "You don't ..."

"Yes. Yes. I'd love to."

And then, like a giddy school girl, I ran off. I've lived with that man for just over three years. We've been out by ourselves plenty of times yet I behaved as if the best looking boy in school had just asked me to the dance!

All I wanted to do was rush to Louise and tell her the news. But Dan headed in her direction, so I went opposite.

He wants to go on a date. That means he must like me in that way. It's not just two friends getting a bite to eat. It's two people taking the time to see if they connect in a meaningful way so they can, hopefully, develop their relationship further and then, god willing, shag like rabbits!

Ok, I'm going to casually stroll out of here and see if Louise is alone. Back shortly.

8.00 pm

Lou was by herself. I got her, dragged her into her bedroom and told her. I was virtually jumping out of my skin but she looked a little confused. Then I thought, of course, she doesn't know what's been going on between us this last few days. I filled her in. Then she got excited.

"Liam said you two were good together."

"Did he?"

"Yeah. He wondered why you weren't a couple."

"Interesting."

"You are good together. You're a good match."

"Do you think so?"

Lou nodded. "Tell ya what, I'll stay at Liam's this weekend so you won't feel weird or inhibited if you end up in the same bed."

Bless you Louise Kathryn Peterson, because we will end up in the same bed if I've got any say in it.

On my way out I noticed her jar with dos dollars in it. "It's Thursday. Put your dollar in the jar."

Friday 26th
7.30 am

All I can think about is my pubes. I'm obsessing about them. I think it's a safe bet Dan and I will be having sex later so I want my bits to look, I don't know, good. It's not like they're feral. I do keep them trimmed. Should I bite the bullet and get the lot waxed off or shave them into a love heart shape or something like that?

Aaaagh!!!! What am I doing?

I hate that women remove all their pubes. It's not natural. We're women. We're supposed to be hairy. Children are hairless. Having sex with a pubeless woman would be like having sex with a child. Yuk. The whole thing is so morally and socially wrong.

Stuff it. My pubes are staying. Betchya Dan isn't worrying about his pubes!

Now that's sorted – what am I going to wear?

Of course! My dress. My little black dress. You perfect, wonderful, beautifully timed purchase.

I seriously do not ever remember feeling like this before.

Breathe. Relax. Do not make this a bigger deal than it has to be. Just treat Dan as you always have and behave as you always have. After all, that's the girl he likes.

I'm going for a walk.

5.30 pm

We're leaving at seven and I'm trying to be casual. I'm not dressed but I'm made-up. My hair looks really nice, thanks to Julia's miracle scissors. I'm wandering the house in my dressing gown. Dan's been home half an hour and he's acting a little different as well. There's an energy between us that feels so … heightened. I swear it would be easier if we just forgot about dinner and headed straight for the bedroom.

Dan's in the shower. I'm thinking about my thighs.

Saturday 27th
10.00 pm

Dear Diary,

♥ I'm in love with a boy named Daniel ♥

This is the first chance I've had since we got home last night to pick you up, Journal. Dan's asleep. I'm too hyped.

At 7 o'clock I emerged from my room in my dress and shoes. Dan looked me up and down. He had such a smile on his face.

"Wow. You look beautiful."

And you know what – I felt beautiful. He looked gorgeous too, so I told him. We were both kind of nervous, but both trying to act as if we weren't.

We were quiet in the car and I suddenly laughed.

"What?"

"Look at us. So formal. A couple of weeks ago I was burp-talking and you were armpit farting."

We laughed and laughed. We laughed because it was funny and we laughed to release the nervous energy. After that, we were ok.

We managed to relax enough to be who we are. But we talked about different things; deeper things. We talked about the shift in our relationship and I told him that I started to fancy him after we'd been to the Willow and Ash. He said he started to feel a bit different that day as well. Must have been something in the air.

He didn't think I'd be interested in him though so he tried to move on. But he struggled. He looked for every opportunity to hang with me and the fact we always had so much fun was making it harder. After Saturday night and the hug at the beach, he knew he had to do something.

I told him that I never thought in a million years he'd be into me.

"Why not?" he asked.

"You're gorgeous!"

"So are you."

I think I actually blushed.

I wasn't very hungry because my stomach was full of butterflies. I vaguely remember eating some chicken thing. I had a couple of wines to mellow me out. Dan had one glass because he was driving.

After dinner we went for a drive to the hills. We got out the car and looked out over the city. It was cold so Dan pulled me into him. It felt so nice and so cosy and so … right.

Then he kissed me. He leaned in and his face was so warm and his skin smelt so nice and his lips were so soft and so gentle.

Is there anything sweeter than a first kiss?

It is a perfect moment.

I breathed a contented sigh. "Nice."

When we got home, the sexual tension between us was fit to explode. We headed for his room because Cool was asleep on my bed.

We stood by the bed and we kissed and kissed. I ran my hands up his body. He held my face.

Then we undressed each other. I think we could have easily ripped our clothes off, thrown ourselves down onto the bed and just gone for it. But there was another feeling mixed in with our passion and our lust, so we savoured the moment instead.

My dress fell to the floor and I was left in my underwear, stockings, and shoes. I felt self-conscious at first but I remembered it was Dan. He has seen me in every state and those blessed pheromones were so thick as to create a haze cloud.

He was naked and we were pressed against each other. He guided me to the bed and lay me down. He took off my left shoe and he suddenly looked cheeky. He put the shoe to his ear and said, "Hello Chief, it's Max."

I burst out laughing. My eyes followed his every move as he peeled off my stockings and kissed and nibbled my legs.

He hooked his thumbs into my lacy knickers and slid them off. He twirled them around his finger then flung them away. He kissed his way up my belly, and nuzzled my neck. He lifted my body, unhooked my bra and tossed it away.

We were naked. And it felt good.

He lay on top of me, looked into my eyes and smiled. Right then I felt something I have never felt before – actual love. It was the most beautiful moment I have ever experienced. He literally took my breath away.

And the sex. The sex was delicious and desperate and greedy and hot and so very beautiful. Dan has got skills and moves I have never had the privilege of enjoying before. And we were in sync. We just knew what to do, how to move, how to please, how to be.

I have always loved sex but Dan took it to a whole new level. It wasn't just passionate and sensual. It was intimate.

And we were so very, very hungry. We couldn't get enough of each other. He made my skin tingle. I have never felt that before. And his mouth …

God, just writing this down has got me all fiery again.

And he was glad of my pubes! He ran his fingers through them, enjoying the tactile experience. I love that he did that.

In the last 24 hours we've left the bed only when we've had to. We can't stop touching each other. We can't stop being close.

And somewhere in all the wonderfulness we managed to fit in a dad fact.

Dan said, "I know for a fact, my dad would have loved you."

"And I know for a fact, my dad would have loved you."

Afterword

I did Re-evaluation Counselling (RC) for ten years, beginning around 2001. My group leader was a passionate, brilliant, insightful woman by the name of Sheila. The character of Bernadette is loosely based on Sheila, but Bernadette's words, ideas, and methods are entirely my own interpretations of the techniques and information Sheila presented to the group.

There are also teachings and situations in this book that were not part of RC. I created them for the purposes of the story.

The characters in the Feel:Deal:Heal group are not based on any individuals. They are amalgamations of people in general. Archetypes, feelings, and the issues we face are universal. For example, grief is grief no matter how it is caused. Personal scenarios vary but, generally, our feelings and responses are much the same.

RC is an **active** form of therapy in that anyone who does it is fully involved in the process. You're educated in the whys and wherefores of it and understand from the outset what each method aims to do and why. There is no mystery to it. You are not passive in your healing journey nor kept separate from it. There is no professional/patient dynamic. You counsel and are counselled. It aims to teach you, empower you, and treat you like an equal.

I would like to thank Sheila for her warmth, her nurturing, her wisdom, and her never-ending desire to heal and produce fellow healers. The world needs more people like you. You are the proof in the pudding.

I would also like to acknowledge the many women and men (yes, men are a big part of the RC community too) who counselled me and allowed me to counsel them. We shared many powerful moments and a lot of healing.

www.ingramcontent.com/pod-product-compliance
Lightning Source LLC
Chambersburg PA
CBHW020952180626
46814CB00003B/1053